THE IMMORTAL CIRCUS

THE IMMORTAL CIRCUS

A.R. KAHLER

47NORTH

Text copyright © 2013 A.R. Kahler
Originally released as a Kindle Serial, November 2012.

Published by 47North
PO Box 400818
Las Vegas, NV 89140

ISBN-13: 9781611099447
ISBN-10: 1611099447
Library of Congress Control Number: 2012953329

DEDICATION

To my family—circus and nuclear—
for supporting me the world over.

CHAPTER ONE: CIRCUS

W ho the hell did this?" Kingston whispers, staring at the corpse.

Sabina's body is on the pedestal she uses in the show, and she almost looks like she's performing. Almost. Her legs are tucked behind her ears in a perfect backbend, her fingers laced under her chin. She's even smiling, her brown eyes fixed on a point far away.

I'm right beside Kingston, doing everything I can not to vomit on his black Chucks, run from the tent, or do an embarrassing mixture of both. Right then, I'd give my left kidney for him to wrap an arm around me to shield me from the atrocity before us. But he's not mine, and probably never will be. And even if he were, he's not the comforting type. I can feel his heat against my arm. I don't know why that sticks out at the moment, but maybe that's just the way shock works.

We're both standing in the dust of the center ring. The rest of the troupe quickly filters in with gasps and screams. Sabina looks perfect—poised like she's holding a pose for the audience's applause. Except her sparkling unitard is usually white, not stained a wicked crimson. The long gash across her throat is a second smile leaking its secrets into the ring.

Someone is crying behind me. I don't look back. I don't look at anyone. I just look at Sabina and wonder what sort of shit-show I've gotten myself into.

I hear a shout and look up to see Mab storming into the tent. Her wild black hair is in disarray and the sequins of her midnight-blue dressing gown sparkle in the lights. Not for the first time, I can't help but think that she looks like an early incarnation of Cher. Her porcelain face is flushed, and when she catches sight of her star contortionist, she stops dead. Mab's perfectly manicured hands clench and unclench at her sides. After a deep breath, she stalks forward, stepping over the ring curb and into the spectacle. She goes right up to Sabina and lightly puts a hand on the girl's knee. I see something flash across Mab's face—the tightening of her eyes, the barest strain of her lips. Then she withdraws her hand and faces us, her company.

Her minions.

"Which of you found her like this?" she asks. Her voice is deep and smoky, like an ex-jazz singer's. Even though it's a whisper, it carries to every wall of the big top.

A woman to my right steps forward. I've never asked her age but she looks like she's in her forties, maybe younger, with aquamarine eyes and fiery red hair that falls to her waist. Her skin is as pale as pearls, and even though she wears a rumpled blue bathrobe, she looks ready to take the stage. I can't help but glance down at my own wrinkled pj's, and hate her for it.

"Penelope?" Mab asks.

"Yes, my Lady." Penelope's voice is crystal clear. Everything about her screams vintage pinup model, even the way she's holding her robe closed with one hand. It's like she practiced how to be perfectly disarrayed. "Not five minutes ago, I was making coffee when I noticed the tent lights on. I thought...I thought someone was practicing."

"And she was...like this?"

"Yes. Exactly so."

Mab stares at the body, the corners of her mouth barely tilting into a frown. She's not staring at Sabina like she's sad over the death of one of her troupe. No, Mab's expression is purely calculating, like she's facing a particularly frustrating Sudoku puzzle. One that might, at any moment, piss her off.

"I assume no one knows who did this?" she asks.

No one speaks. No one even breathes.

I mentally prepare myself, waiting for her to fly into a rage. Not that I've ever seen Mab in a rage. But it doesn't take a genius to know there's a storm brewing under that well-maintained facade. I can only imagine that "Hell hath no fury" refers to her. But instead of ripping us a new one, she strokes the corpse's short brown hair. Things are clicking behind Mab's green eyes, things that subdue everybody—even her. A crowded tent has never been this quiet.

"Well then, my loves," she finally whispers, almost to herself. "It appears we have a murderer in our midst."

She lifts her hand. Like ash scattering to the wind, Sabina's body dissolves, collapsing in on itself in a hush of glitter and smoke.

There is still a great deal of congestion near the grey-and-blue main tent, but it's pretty quiet at the pie cart, next to the forgotten bacon and boxes of cereal. Kingston stands by the serving table, grabbing a coffee before the rest of the troupe shakes itself from their post-murder stupor. He looks like a rock star at the peak of his glory days, all pale and angular and assured. His black hair is sticking up in the back from sleeping on it funny, and there's a line of stubble on his jaw. His white T-shirt hangs loose over lithe muscles; through it, I can see his lats. They curve under the fabric like wings, highlighted by the faintest shadow of a large serpentine tattoo. I shouldn't be staring. Melody would kill me if she knew.

Damn circus performers and their perfect bodies. Damn them to hell.

"I guess this doesn't happen very often," I say, trying to focus on the fact that someone has just been killed, and not on the way Kingston's triceps cord when he starts pouring coffee into a second cup.

"Never," he says, still facing away.

"Do you think Mab will cancel tonight's shows?"

Kingston chuckles humorlessly. He turns around and stares at me over his mug, one eyebrow tilting up like I'm a complete idiot. His eyes are dark brown, almost black—the same color as the coffee steaming in his hands. I look away.

"Don't count on it, Vivienne," he says. "Mab doesn't cancel a show for anything. Ever."

"Even if someone here is a killer?"

"Especially if."

He looks toward the tent and sighs. He's only a couple years older than me—Mel told me in secret that he was twenty-four—but sometimes, when he gets all quiet like this, he seems much older. "The show must go on."

If this was one of those perfect movies, this would be the moment for him to shake himself from his reverie and come over, say something comforting to the new girl or at least give her a hug. But like I said, Kingston doesn't act like that with me. If he has that soft side, he hasn't really shown it. He's funny, yeah. Dependable, definitely. But comforting? I'd have better luck trying to warm up to Mab.

I stuff my hands into my pockets and look back to the chapiteau in time to see a huddle of men carrying out the contortion pedestal. Sparkly purple dust wafts off it as they move it to the backstage tent. The sight brings Sabina's dripping body back to mind. For the second time today, I'm glad I didn't eat breakfast.

"Why do you think Mab suspects one of us?" I ask.

"That's the thing," answers another voice. "It can't be one of us."

I look back to see Melody walking over. She's twenty-two, the same age as me, though we look nothing alike. We share the same slight build and hazel eyes, but that's where the resemblance ends. She has angular features and is an inch or two taller than me, not that I'm short. My ash-blonde hair reaches my back, while her brown hair is styled in a pixie cut.

She looks like the type of girl you'd expect to find in some Bohemian cafe, reading poetry and chain smoking hand-rolled cigarettes. Less Hepburn, more hippie James Dean. Whereas I'd probably be the girl serving the coffee, the one you smile at but forget the moment you have your triple espresso—pretty, normal, but utterly pass-over-able. She's Kingston's assistant onstage. And offstage, wherever one goes, the other is sure to follow. I hate to admit it, but they're the perfect couple—always teasing, always thinking of the other person, and never dipping into the PDA.

Mel gives me a nod before taking the coffee cup Kingston hands her, as if he'd been waiting for her arrival. I guess it was too much to hope the spare was for me. Her eyes are shadowed. She shrugs deeper into her loose knit cardigan, in spite of the early summer heat. She looks like she hasn't slept in weeks.

"Why not?" I ask. It's not like many people wander around the fields our show usually haunts. Besides, I can't imagine there being a killer that…artistic in rural Iowa.

The two of them exchange a quick glance, and Kingston answers.

"Because it's in the contract. We aren't allowed to harm other troupe members."

"Right," I say. "Because people always do what their contracts say they will." If that was the case, *going postal* wouldn't exactly be a phrase, now would it?

"Maybe not where you're from," Melody says, taking a long sip of her coffee. "But in this company, yes."

I bite back my witty retort and wonder if I'm the only sane person working here.

❖

"Is this what you really want?" Mab asked.

Her voice sounded sincere, but it was impossible to know; an hour wasn't nearly enough time to figure out her tells. If I were judging books by their covers, she'd be one of those smutty romances you keep hidden in your sock drawer. All I'd gauged of Mab was that she was powerful, mysterious, and probably a ball-breaker. That said, I felt a hell of a lot safer with her there.

We sat in her trailer, candles flickering from skull-and-crystal sconces along the wall. It seemed larger inside, as though stepping through the rickety aluminum door had led to somewhere…else. I could have sworn I heard wolves howling in the distance, even though this was the middle of the day.

In Detroit.

"Yes, I'm sure," I said, though my wavering voice was anything but.

Running away, joining the circus—that was what I really wanted. I needed to get the fuck out of Dodge, and this seemed like the most reliable way. My nerves had me shaking like I was in a caffeine crash. It felt like I'd been running a thousand miles and hadn't stopped to breathe. I couldn't keep my fingers from rattling the pen she handed me, its nib tap tap tapping on the ornate ebony desk. I could see the ghost of myself reflected in the glass, the rings of shadow under my eyes from too little sleep and too much fleeing. A smudge of something dark on my pale cheek. The half-reflection made me look even more pallid, more worn-through than I felt. And that was saying something.

Mab grinned like one of her skull sconces and raised one hand. With a snap of her burgundy-manicured fingers, a book floated down from a shelf behind her. I couldn't hold back the gasp. I knew from the moment I saw her on the street that she wasn't like everyone else; somehow, the rain seemed to bend around her, leaving her red silk dress and bone stilettos perfectly dry. As the book settled in front of her and opened to a page covered with names, I knew without doubt I was stepping into something big. I didn't care; I just wanted as far away from…whatever I was leaving…as possible. At the bottom of the list, my name was inking itself into being, scrawled by some ghostly hand in ink as dark as blood.

"Well then," she said. "Let us examine the terms, shall we?" Her finger paused beside my now-completed name.

Vivienne Warfield.

My name had never looked so menacing, so concrete. Everything else blurred as she began reading through the contract, line by line. Only two things stuck out.

One was my name. Her words eddied around it like it was a stone in a stream. The other was the growing calm that came with knowing that the crazy I was stepping into was far less dangerous than what I was leaving behind.

Or so I thought at the time.

At noon the troupe starts to warm up in preparation for tonight's shows. Kingston was right; Mab wasn't canceling anything. You'd think that after a murder there would be a whole hell of a lot more crying and a bit more fear. But everyone looks calm. Maya walks back and forth on her practice tightwire in suede boots, earbuds firmly in place. The three jugglers—I still haven't caught their names—are doing cartwheels and catching whirling clubs. The remaining two contortionists are stretching out on a panel mat in the shade. Even from here, I can tell they're trying to come up with a new routine. I can't help it; I'm impressed by everyone's resolve. And a little weirded out by the ease at which they gloss over not only a murder, but a concealed killer. Just the thought makes goose bumps prickle over my freshly sunburned skin. I try not to keep looking over my shoulder every time I hear a noise.

"I still don't get it," I say.

"I'm shocked," Kingston replies.

He and Melody are facing each other, going over a new magic act for the show—something lighthearted. Something that doesn't involve their usual daggers-through-the-heart bit because, as Kingston said, there's been enough death for one day. Melody has a handful of roses in one hand, and on each of Kingston's shoulders perches a white dove.

"Seriously, though," I say. I lean forward on the wooden crate I'm calling my front-row seat. The boards are digging into my ass, but there's only so much shifting I can do without it being obvious. "Why isn't anyone, I dunno, searching for the killer?"

Melody flourishes the roses in front of Kingston, who studiously ignores the romantic gesture. One of the doves ruffles its wings.

"Because," she explains. "Mab's on it."

"But you said it couldn't be one of us. Why isn't she calling the cops to hunt whoever it is down? He could be hiding anywhere, maybe even in one of those barns out there. You know, just waiting for a moment of weakness. Like when one of us goes to a Porta-Potty." I'm trying to keep my voice light and witty, but I can't lie to myself. The questions are honest, and so is wondering if someone is lying in wait to strike again.

Kingston raises his plastic magic wand and raps Melody's knuckles. The flowers explode in a flurry of red petals and sparks. Judging by the eyebrow Melody raises, I'm not the only one who's reminded of Sabina's unnatural end.

"We're called The Immortal Circus for a reason," Kingston says. He sighs and waves his fingers in a lazy circular gesture, as though he's more annoyed by having to explain this to me again than the fact that there's reason to bring it up. The petals on the ground swirl in a gust of wind and then, with a small burst of fire, become a dove that flies up and lands on his finger. Most magicians spend years trying to make their tricks look like real magic. Kingston, I quickly learned, has precisely the opposite problem. He answers in his bored-yet-amused voice, "So long as we're under contract, no one and no thing can hurt us."

"So how was Sabina killed?" I ask. Because if that's the case, murder is a pretty huge breach of contract.

"That," he says, lifting the bird to the top of his head, "would be the million-dollar question. Someone found a loophole in Mab's magic. You're welcome to bring that to her attention, if you like." He flashes me a grin, and even Melody looks amused at the notion of pissing off our ringleader.

"Aren't you worried, though? That you'll be next?"

"If anything, I'd be more worried about you."

Something clenches around my heart, that old feeling of fight or flight. I adjust my position on the crate in hopes of stifling it. It doesn't work. "You think they'll go after me?" My voice squeaks. I'm grateful neither of them looks to see the blush rising on my cheeks.

"Doubtful," he says, looking at Melody. "I just think you're the only new thing in this troupe for the past, what would you say, Mel? Three years?" Melody shrugs, and Kingston turns his gaze back to me. "Awfully suspicious, don't you think? Barely a month after the new girl starts and someone winds up dead?"

"What? You think *I'm* the killer? You know I'm not that type."

And I'm not. I'm too scrawny, too quiet. I'm a vegetarian, for Christ's sake. I never got into fights or did competitive sports. I've never even done gymnastics or cheerleading. Or band. At least, not that I can remember. Which is probably why the only job Mab could find for me was as a cotton-candy seller.

Kingston laughs. The doves ignite in that instant, flaring up like strobes and disintegrating into ash. My breath catches at the way his brown eyes flash in the flame.

"Viv, this is show business. Nothing here is what it seems."

Not, I'm sure, even him.

"This isn't like any other circus," Mab said, her fingers idly caressing the handle of a whip coiled on her desk. The book of names and contracts had flown back to the shelf behind her, and now she was staring at me with green eyes as intent as a jaguar's. "All of our performers have…eccentricities."

A haze surrounded the exact terms of our agreement, but I didn't really care. I no longer felt like the world was crashing down around me. Still, her gaze made me wonder if I was stepping from the frying pan into the inferno.

"What do you mean?" I asked, though I already knew. My mind wrapped around the idea of this place much more easily than it should have. Magic, circus

freaks...it seemed more natural than it rationally should. I knew in the corner of my mind that these should all be warning signs, signals that something was terribly wrong, that I should be getting out now. I shouldn't be letting myself believe in magic or flying books or any of this. That voice was tiny. The stronger voice told me it was okay, it was all normal, and my tired mind was all too happy not to fight it. Luckily, Mab didn't give me any time to fret.

"I only hire exceptional performers. And, like you, they were often in a bind. And I," she said, flourishing her hands, "am a humanitarian at best. I help. In return, they work for me, using their talents to capture the imaginations of our audience."

"But I don't have any talents," I said, thinking we should have had this conversation before I signed the contract.

"Oh, love, everyone has a talent. Yours will blossom in time. Trust me." She smiled at me, and something in her eyes told me that I didn't have a choice.

"Circle up, lovelies," Mab says, striding into the huddle of performers. Inside the main tent, the muted rumble of another full house is masked by the creepy tones of live organ music. It's just before the 8 p.m. show and somehow the sky is already turning dark. Mab is wearing her ring-leader outfit—a hideously sparkling getup made of a bedazzled tailcoat and top hat, nude leggings, and high-heeled black boots. Her whip is coiled at her side, and her long black hair falls down her back like the River Styx. Despite having disposed of a body earlier that day, she seems remarkably nonchalant.

Everyone does.

"As you know," she says, once we're all in a huddle, "this morning we lost a dear member of our troupe. Sabina will always live on in our hearts, and she will be greatly missed. Tonight, let our show be in honor of her work. A moment of silence, please."

Everyone bows their heads.

I'm standing just outside of the huddle. I'm not one of the performers, so I don't get the sparkly leotards and elaborate headpieces. I just get a black T-shirt that reads *Cirque des Immortels* on the front and *Crew* on the back. But at least they let me stay back here for opening, unlike most of the concessionaires, who are just hired locals.

After a few moments, Mab takes a deep breath that even I can hear, and everyone looks up again.

"For Sabina," she says.

The members of the troupe put their hands in the center and shout.

After that, the twenty-something performers run to their places. Everyone goes out for the opening act, the charivari. They don't need me to sell cotton candy until intermission, so I sneak to one of the side entrances to catch a glance. I lean against the cool metal supports of the bleachers and stare out into the center ring, trying to ignore the kid banging his feet against the seat to my right. In the aisle around me, keeping out of sight, are a handful of the performers, their faces set in concentration. Kingston and Melody are on the other side. I can barely make them out in this light, but Melody's giant wig is a dead giveaway.

The music changes. Organ music shifts to heavy downbeats, bass floods the tent, and then the five-piece band kicks in with swinging violins and saxophones. On cue, the troupe floods into the ring in a swarm of beautiful chaos. Twin aerialists drop from the air, wrapped in sheets of burgundy fabric, as the acrobats burst from the back curtain, tumbling and leaping over each other in an intricate dance. Jugglers flip over the ring curb and toss their flaming knives across the full space of the ring, creating an arc of fire and steel that illuminates the contortionists twisting themselves on arms and elbows. I look over just in time to see Kingston and Melody whirl onstage like salsa dancers, their feet stepping a quick rhythm perfectly synced to the throb of techno. The moment they spin apart, Kingston raises his wand and shoots a shower of vivid purple sparks. Melody does a perfect aerial through it, landing in a split that makes the crowd roar with applause. More performers crowd into the ring. A pair of women do a one-arm balance on the heads of their burly bases. Men and women in leather and velvet wield flaming staffs and poi, swirling the fire in arcs that sear ghostly traces in my vision. More aerialists drop from the ceiling, this time dangling and stretching from hoops and a spinning trapeze. My hands already hurt from clapping so hard. In these fantastic moments, it's easy to forget that just this morning, one of our members was murdered right where the hand-balancers are standing now.

Almost as soon as the manic party has begun, the troupe assembles near the back of the ring. With one quick call out, half the performers leap onto the thighs of their bases, creating a human wall of color and smiles. The fliers clap and wave, then spread their hands wide as the music changes once more. Then they freeze.

The lights in the ring dim, and colors fade to black and blue and silver-white. Fog appears from the thick black curtain in the back, filling the round stage with a pool of writhing mist. The music becomes haunting again as a pipe-organ chord rises above the drum's downbeats and the cello's churnings. A strobe goes off, and Mab is there, revealed in a whirl of fog like Venus emerging from the sea. Only this Venus glitters with a thousand tiny Swarovski crystals and sports a top hat. And a whip.

The crowd, of course, goes wild.

"Ladies and gentlemen," she calls, her voice as thick and dusty as the smoke that curls at her feet, just as soft and just as overpowering. She strides forward and raises her top hat, sweeping it down in a bow that seems to encompass everyone in the crowd. When she stands, her green eyes are sparkling as bright as her outfit. "Welcome to Cirque des Immortels! Tonight, we have a show to ensnare and entwine, filled with acts to allure you, hellish and divine. Tonight—tonight only—we offer you this, a night of ecstasy, a night of bliss. For once our shows are over and through, for the very select—the most special of you—to our backstage, we cordially invite, to wine, to dine, relax and…delight. Curious?

You should be. Just ask, and you'll know. But for now, sit back, relax, and enjoy our show."

With that, she unfurls the whip from her side and raises it high into the air, snapping the tail with a perfectly timed crack. The lights flash. And then she's gone. The audience applauds as the music resumes and the troupe runs offstage to make room for the first act—the jugglers.

Melody whirls past me, and I follow her and the line of performers out into the night. The moment I'm out of the tent, the air seems to drop ten degrees, sending lines of goose bumps over my arms. Melody and the others are already gathered near the backstage tent. It's a small, pavilion-style thing that looks like it should be holding a barbeque rather than a bunch of props and costumes. I wander back toward her. I've seen the juggling act enough to have it memorized. And besides, my cotton candy won't miss me.

As I'm walking around the side of the tent, I catch the faintest hint of movement under the bleachers. The bottom of the tent sidewall has been pulled up to allow for more ventilation, and clambering among the wires and discarded popcorn boxes is a girl dressed all in black. The kid is watching the show from between the audience's feet, completely hidden from the crowd. I'm about to duck under and drag her out—she probably thought she could just get a free show—when she turns her head and I see the familiar green eyes that never fail to give me the chills. Lilith, Mab's right-hand man. Well, girl. She doesn't look older than twelve. She's short, with curly black hair, green eyes, and a roundness to her face that makes her look cherubic and somewhat lost. I've never seen her doing anything in the show, either in the ring or behind the scenes. Hell, I practically never see her period. But wherever she is, Mab isn't too far away. The one time I saw them together, Mab practically petted Lilith's head like a kitten.

She glances back at me and smiles a grin of pure childlike delight, then goes back to watching the show. That's when I notice another small movement as her cat, Poe, slinks around his master's feet. The tabby curls up around Lilith's ankles and watches me with calm yellow eyes. I shiver and turn away, quickly making my way toward the backstage tent. When I reach Melody, she's already halfway into her next costume. Her blushing makeup and enormous Marie Antoinette pink wig make her look like some fetishistic baby doll. The pinstripe suit isn't helping much, either. I wonder how long it will take me to get used to seeing her in costume—the contrast between pink Lolita and refined hippie is still jarring.

"Hey, Viv," she says as I approach. "Gonna watch the new act?"

"Of course," I say. "Got nothing else to do."

I pause as Kingston walks over. He's got his cape in one hand, magic wand in the other. He's in sequined trousers and shiny shoes...and nothing else. My eyes catch on the single drip of sweat slowly edging down his chest toward his aggravatingly perfect abs. The head of his feathered-serpent tattoo is angled down one pec. The rest of its body curls over his shoulder and behind his back, its tail twisting over one hip and disappearing into his trousers. *My face is up here,* I can nearly hear him say, and I tear my eyes back toward Melody, praying neither of them caught it. He's a magician, and magicians aren't supposed to look like heavily inked Calvin Klein models. They're supposed to be, like, old and wrinkled and wear funny clothing. It's not fair.

"How's it going?" he asks, tossing the cape down on a crate beside him before helping Melody get her other arm into her tux. I'm still refusing to stare at him, but my eyes keep lingering on places they shouldn't. He has those lines at his hips, the *come fuck me* lines, I seem to remember someone calling them. Yeah, Mel would have my head.

"I'm all right," I say, trying to keep my voice detached.

The two of them move like they came out of the same womb. Melody said she's only been here for five years, but they move in such sync that I'd have expected longer. Just watching them makes the guilt squirm in my gut. Kingston is with her; I shouldn't be staring at him like a fangirl. But it's not like he's making it any easier. God made shirts for a reason.

"Speaking of new acts," I say, trying to keep myself from thinking in third-wheel terms. "What was with Mab's new introduction?"

If I hadn't been looking at them so intently, I would have missed the brief flick of understanding that passes between them. Then Kingston is looking at me, his eyes carefully guarded. He still hasn't shaved his stubble.

"*Tapis Noir*," he whispers. "The Black Carpet event."

I raise an eyebrow. There's something in the way he says it that makes butterflies hatch in my stomach.

"The what?"

He looks around to make sure no one's listening in. No one is; they're all practicing and psyching themselves up for their acts. Even so, he leans in a little bit, and Melody tilts her head closer.

"The Black Carpet event. It only happens once every couple of stops, on the new moon. It's...for VIPs. A sort of after-party."

"Cool," I say, because that's really all my brain can come up with. Thinking smart when he's leaning this close is difficult. "Do we get in?"

"You don't want in," he says quickly. "It's not for people like... like you."

"Concessionaires?"

"No, Viv. Mortals."

The word hangs in the air like a concrete veil, separating me from him and Melody and the rest of the troupe. It's not something that I thought would ever be used against me. Not until I came here. I'm just a mortal, a normal, while the rest...they're something else entirely. I'm still not entirely certain *what*.

"I see," I say. Though, of course, I don't. All I can see is that it's one more reason Kingston and Mel are more suited for each other. And another reason I'll always be an outsider with the two of them.

"Just stay away from it," Melody says. "Trust me. I've only been once and that was more than enough."

"What about you?" I ask Kingston. Is it my imagination, or does that actually make him blush?

"A gentleman never tells," he says. Then he stands up straight and grabs the cloak from the crate. "Come on, Melody. We're next." I hadn't even noticed the music inside the tent change or the roar of applause. Before I can wonder if I managed to piss him off, he's dragging Melody across the grass and toward the back curtain. They disappear under the flap, but not before Melody throws me a quick apologetic glance.

I look around the backstage area at the performers completely lost in the routine of the show. The jugglers are changing into new costumes, the fire eaters are organizing their torches. Everything is so smooth, so refined. So absolutely unaware of my existence. Mab hired me with the promise of greatness, but this? So far, the only people who seem to notice me are Melody and Kingston. And even that's not saying much. Especially not when he'll never notice me the way I want him to.

Suddenly, the memory of Sabina's corpse flashes across my vision. The broken smile and the blood. It makes my skin grow cold. It reminds me that not being noticed right now may be a good thing.

Chapter Two: Sweet Dreams (Are Made of This)

The night air is cold as the crowd leaves the main tent. They file toward the parking lot on the other side of the road, their chatter loud and excited. Only a few of them linger back by the chapiteau, fingering their tickets with nervous anticipation. A new, smaller tent has been constructed on one side of the dirt promenade, though I never saw it go up. It glows in the darkness like a black lotus. The interior flickers in shades of violet and crimson, and music filters out. It's a heavy downbeat that has a pulse, an urgency that tugs at my hips, but no one moves toward it. I can't help but stare like the rest of the loitering guests.

"Fancy a go?" says a voice at my side.

I nearly jump.

"Mel," I say. She's changed out of her costume and is now in pink pajama bottoms and a long, tattered knit cardigan, her thumbs poking out from the sleeves. She's also grinning like a fool.

"Well?" she asks, nodding to the new tent.

"Are you?" I ask, my heart suddenly thumping in my chest in time to the music. There's a ring of men and women in black suits surrounding the tent. They're all wearing sunglasses. Did Mab hire bodyguards? What sort of after-party requires bodyguards?

"Hell no," she says, "but that doesn't mean I wasn't invited."

She holds up a small purple ticket. *Cirque des Immortels* is scrawled across the front in heavy black ink.

"Won't they notice?" I say, gesturing toward the guard. Rebelling isn't in my nature—I'm always the one who gets caught. But something about the tent is calling to me. It's promising me things I can't imagine, but would surely regret missing. Somehow I know that rebelling is precisely what the Tapis Noir is all about.

Melody eyes the guards before laughing.

"The Shifters? Please. So long as you've got a ticket, they don't give a fuck who goes in."

I glance back to the bodyguards and try to imagine the Shifters dressing up in suits, which is nearly impossible. The Shifters are the tent crew and part-time freak show. Most of them looked like they were part of a biker gang. I wonder what Mab had to do to get them into Armani suits.

Mel holds the ticket out. I hesitate. Then, because that small tugging voice inside of me is really digging the edge of danger thing, I take it. On the back, there's a small block of handwritten script.

You are cordially invited to the Tapis Noir,
our premier, no bounds after-party.
Indulge and enjoy irresponsibly.
xx Mab

Performer is stamped down the left-hand side.

"Just make sure you get the right mask," she says as I study the card.

"What do you mean?"

She leans in close and whispers in my ear, as though she doesn't want any of the punters—the more endearing name we used for the public—to hear. "The black mask. If you get a white one, turn around and leave. Immediately."

I slip the ticket in my pocket.

"Why do I have a feeling this is more than just a party?" I whisper as she steps back. Why do I have the feeling I *want* it to be more than a party? And why do I want Kingston to be there?

She just grins and shrugs. "Hey, we already warned you, not that that means anything. The rest, well...you'll just have to find that out for yourself. You won't forget it, that's for sure."

As if on cue, fire leaps up around us. I wince at the instant heat, then realize it's one of the fire-breathers standing on a pedestal. More fire-dancers appear in the crowd—women with claws of fire or flaming hula hoops, men with torches and poi and flaming rope darts. None of them are wearing more than a few scraps of leather and rings of steel. If that. One of the fire-clawed women is only adorned in swirls of black body paint. Melody's grin widens.

"That's you," she says, patting me on the shoulder. She begins to walk away and calls back, "Have fun."

I don't have time to second-guess. The crowd of punters huddles closer together, their faces glowing red in the flame. The air smells of kerosene and dust and heat and something that makes my stomach churn with excitement and an inexplicable feeling. I huddle in between a man in a tweed suit and a woman in jeans and a shawl. I'm staring with as much awe as the rest of them as the fire dancers whirl and manipulate the flames they twine about their bodies. One of the men blows a huge cloud of flame over the promenade in front of us. When the fire billows out, Mab is standing on the walkway.

It's not a Mab I'm comfortable calling my boss.

She's wearing what looks like a cross between a corset and some Victoria's Secret nightgown—a tube of white silk with black lace over the bust and black stripes down the seams. The dress barely reaches her thighs, and from there down she's in sheer black stockings and diamond-encrusted black stilettos. The worst part is, she pulls it off flawlessly. She has the perfect model physique, the curves to kill, the agelessness and allure. Her fingers are covered in rings that look like talons and skulls, and it's only after a second look that I realize the heels of her shoes are black spinal columns. In one hand is a black half-mask, also covered in diamonds. She gives us all a smile I'd prefer she reserved for the bedroom.

"Follow me, my lovelies. The Black Carpet awaits," she says. Then she turns and heads across the grass. She doesn't look back to see if we follow. But we do. We follow her like she's a provocative pied piper. The fire-dancers continue to twirl around us in a pyrotechnic escort.

She leads us around the tent to an entry hidden in the back. There are guards on each side of the velvet flap. Beside the entry is a table covered in purple satin and a variety of masks. Mab walks straight through the entry, then sticks out a hand to gesture us in with one ring-encrusted finger. The music pulses in my gut even from here. I feel like I'm waiting outside some L.A. nightclub, not standing in a field in the middle of nowhere. Not that I knew what being outside an L.A. nightclub felt like.

The crowd files in one-by-one, handing the guards their ticket in exchange for a mask. So far, everyone ahead of me is given a white mask, which makes the panic start to slide through my veins. Melody's warning rings in my ear. She wouldn't put me into a dangerous situation, though, right?

It's not for people like you...for mortals.

I grip the ticket tighter. The music from inside the tent vibrates through my bones, growing louder every time someone pushes aside the flap and enters the dimly lit interior. I can't make out anything inside. Minutes scrape by and then I'm standing up front. My heart's in my chest as I hand over my ticket. For a brief moment, I wonder if being caught and turned away would be worse than being let in.

The guard examines it and pushes up her sunglasses.

"Vivienne?" she asks.

I gulp. I don't really recognize her—she's got pink hair and brown eyes and a slight figure. A single silver ring is in her nose. I know I've seen her, but the Shifters tend to keep to themselves. A couple hellos were all I got when I signed on, and after the first day, our paths never really crossed.

"Yeah."

She chuckles and looks to the guard on the other side, a tall dark man with vibrant red dreads pulled back in a ponytail.

"Kids grow up fast, don't they?" the guy says.

The woman slips the card into her pocket and hands me a mask. Black.

"Have fun," is all she says. I look down at the mask in my hands, then step forward through the curtain.

It's like stepping into another world.

The tent is enormous on the inside. The draping walls and roof are beautiful strips of purple and black. Sconces and chandeliers of glass and iron hang from the ceiling, flickering with firelight. Aerialists dangle and pose from hoops and slings, each wearing less than the last. Everywhere I turn there are half-naked bodies, men in suits without shirts, women in corsets and torn evening gowns, all of them in black masks. The masks have curving noses or devil horns, all of them looking like demons in some sort of erotic masquerade. The floor of the tent is covered in black rugs and plush chaise longues, leather armchairs, and glass tables. In one corner, a girl is inverting herself on a tall pole; in another, a contortionist wearing little more than string and mesh is twisting her body on a table covered in wineglasses. Underneath it all, underneath the moving and sweating and grinding, the music pulses like another frantic heart.

There's a hand on my arm and I look over to see Mab staring down at me—there's no mistaking her, even with her mask.

"*Tsk tsk*, Vivienne," she says, and I know she's about to tell me off for entering uninvited. Like I said, I always get caught. But all she says is, "This is no place for nudity." She grins. "Mask on at all times. Please." She winks and turns away. I reach up and tie the mask to my face.

For a while I just stand there, completely at a loss. This isn't anything I'm used to. I seem to be the only one, though. The white-masked punters are completely enthralled by the music and scandal, drawn into a world I couldn't have prepared myself to be a part of. I watch as one man laughs amid a group of black-masked men and women, completely oblivious to the fact that the performers are pulling his clothes off one article at a time. A woman across from me reaches up and is pulled onto one of the steel hoops, smiling as her heels fall into a punch bowl with a clatter. And on the sofas…there's much less clothing and much more giggling and grinding. Even behind the mask, I can feel myself blushing.

It's not until someone bumps into me from behind that I realize I'm still standing by the tent's entrance. Every time someone in a white mask comes in, someone in black comes forward to pull them deeper. No one does that to me, probably because I'm already in the black. I walk to one side of the tent and grab a glass of red wine, watching the sin unfold and kind of wishing I'd taken Kingston's advice and stayed far, far away. I take a drink and hope the wine will help me accomplish just that.

A topless woman with a white mask comes up to the wine table and reaches out, grabs the front of my shirt, and pulls me closer.

"Are you on the menu too?" she whispers, her words slurred. How are these people already so drunk?

"Not tonight," I say.

She exaggerates a pout, but lets go and turns away. I take another drink of the wine and try to sink back into the shadows. But everything in the tent is shadow and candlelight and bass. There's no getting away from it. After a few more minutes of feeling like a horrible voyeur, I decide this really isn't my scene, that Kingston was right. This *wasn't* for people like me, though I have no idea how being mortal plays into it. I set the glass down and turn away, head to the exit. Only there is no exit. I spin around and try to find the black curtain, but it's not there. Just purple and black walls.

"Going somewhere?" a man beside me asks, snagging my sleeve with a finger. He's wearing a black mask, but I've never seen him before. He's tall, very tall, and lithe. His eyes are shining blue behind his mask, and there's a blue feather boa around his bare shoulders. His muscular chest and stomach are covered in intricate tattoos.

A woman slides up next to him, also in a black mask. She's wearing a V-necked red dress that dips dangerously below her navel. I focus on her eyes, which are warm amber. If those tits are real, I'll eat my wineglass.

"She must be new," the Playboy model says. She reaches out and slides one sharp finger under my chin. The man's hand reaches up to my shoulder, though it doesn't stay there long. For some reason, I don't have the will to push it away when his touch slides toward my chest. They're both so close I want to back away, but there's nowhere to go, and I have a feeling it would be worse than bad manners if I did. I don't move and try not to flinch as their touches grow bolder.

"Mab told me about you," the woman continues, "her latest *acquisition* to this menagerie. I'm quite surprised she let you in, considering..." but she doesn't say why, just smirks and steps back, scratching my skin in the process.

I don't rub the spot, just keep focused on her eyes. The man's hand has found its way to my hip. His touch is colder than ice.

"Come on, Fritz. Let's enjoy the party." She puts an arm over his shoulder and he wraps an arm around her waist, and then they're sliding back into the crowd. The tingle of his fingertips still clings to my skin like frostbite.

I look around. It hadn't hit me how many people there were in the tent; the people in black masks far outnumber the white. Mab's been inviting people in, and it's clear from their garb that they know the occasion well. I watch as two men in black masks and torn suits tilt a white-masked guy's head back, pouring wine down his throat. Oh yes, they know the occasion well. The music pulses, the heat grows. Something deep down inside of me is growling. It doesn't want to be sitting in a corner. It feels the music. It wants out. It wants to play.

On a chaise longue in front of me, a man is stripped naked, except for his porcelain mask. Black-masked men and women caress his arms and thighs and neck with fingers and tongues. The man groans as one of the men bites into his hip. The sight of it makes my heart thud faster, and my fingers grip tighter at my side. A small trail of blood drips down his pale skin but he doesn't seem to notice. In fact, he reaches down and runs his fingers through the man's hair as he laps up the blood, slowly, slowly licking.

"Trust me, dear, he isn't to your taste."

It's Mab. She stands beside me with a grin on her lips and a drink in her hand, watching as her black-masked patrons bite and lick and bleed her guest.

"What…what is this?"

"If you're interested," she says, ignoring the question, "there's a delightful young man next to the birdcage. Twenty-one, wishes to be a dentist…"

"I don't…" The man being drained is writhing in ecstasy or agony. More and more black-masked patrons come in to bow at his side, and bring their lips to his bleeding flesh like some lustful Communion. No one comes to his aid; no one seems to notice anything is even wrong. Around him, couples and groups are locked in limbs and lips as they sway to the hypnotic music. No one in a white mask is clothed or alone, not that I can see.

"In that case, what about the young woman being entertained on the hoop over there? I don't judge. Besides, she's much too young for Stephanie."

"I'm not…" I glance over to where she's pointing, to the girl hanging naked on one of the hoops, her arms bound above her head and a woman running her hands over her chest and back. Red lines trace themselves into her skin, but she doesn't seem to be in pain. If she is, she likes it.

"You see, Vivienne," Mab says. She takes a sip from her glass. "We are the peddlers of dreams. Some people come to see a show, but for many, that isn't enough. Their dreams are darker, less…publicly recognized. And as I said, I am a humanitarian. This is my way of giving them what they truly, deeply desire. This is how we get the strongest dreams of all."

"You're killing them," I say. I can barely see the man on the chaise longue through the crowd of hungry patrons.

Mab shrugs.

"Not everyone wishes to live forever." She sets her glass down on the table and takes a half step forward. Then she stops and looks back. "Although we cater to all wants here—even voyeurism—I might recommend leaving. The party's just beginning, and I doubt you'd want to be here when the Night Terrors arrive." She winks like it's our little joke and slips into the crowd, disappearing in the sea of black masks and ball gowns.

A cool breeze blows at the back of my neck. I turn. There, like a deeper shadow on the wall, is the entrance. I move toward it and then close my eyes. The music behind me is a hook, an anchor. The fire in me burns, wants to lose itself in the throng. But all I can picture is the bleeding man. I try to block out how his blood would taste, how his skin would feel beneath my fingertips. I bite my lip until I taste my own blood and force myself to leave the tent. When the flap closes behind me, the cool air hits me like a snap to my senses. I drop my mask on the table and head to my trailer.

I don't look back.

By the time I'm a few steps away, I'm running.

"How'd it go?" Melody asks.

She's sitting on a lawn chair in front of the trailer, right outside the door to my bunk. She's got a shit-eating grin on her face and a book in her hands.

"I hate you," I say. I put a hand on my door.

"I warned you," she says. "It's for your own good."

"What do you mean?" I ask. "I just watched…" I pause, trying to find the right words. "Actually, I have no fucking clue what I just watched."

"Probably exactly what you think you did."

"What *was* that?"

She gives me a small smile.

"You know those stories you heard growing up? All those fairy tales about shadows in the woods and monsters under your bed?"

I nod slowly.

"Yeah, well, that's the Winter Court. They're the creatures you're taught to fear. Once every couple of sites, Mab throws a party for her most beloved subjects."

"Now you're just being a bitch."

"What?"

"You seriously expect me to believe that Mab—*Mab*, who is currently wearing a teddy as an evening gown—is the queen of the faeries? Like Shakespeare's Queen of the Faeries?"

"She's older than Shakespeare," she says as though it's obvious. "She just liked him well enough to let him write about her."

I sigh and lean against the trailer, which makes the whole thing rock a little. Hopefully it didn't wake anyone up.

"This place is fucked up," I say.

"What was your first clue? Signing your name in blood?"

I close my eyes. The memory is vivid, the sear of pain as my name inked itself on the final line on a blurry page of contractual obligations. I hear the creak of Mel's chair as she stands and steps over to me. She puts her hand on my shoulder.

"I know how it feels. Most of these performers, they've been here thirty or forty years. They forget what it feels like to be the new girl. I've only been here for five. Some days the first day feels like yesterday."

I force away the images of the tent and try to focus instead on this moment, on the kindness in her words. This is the first time we've really gotten the chance to talk, at least without Kingston around. I want to hate her for giving me the ticket, but it's hard to be mad at someone who's actually seriously *seeing* you when no one else does. Would she still look at me that way if she knew what I thought of her boyfriend? I try to shove my guilt and the question down to a place neither of us can see it.

I open my eyes.

"I've got your back," she says.

"Thanks," I say. *Would you still, if you knew how I feel about Kingston?*

"Of course."

She smiles and steps back, walks over and picks up the book from where she dropped it on the ground. Then she turns to me.

"That's why I'm going to tell you to be careful."

"What do you mean? You're the one who gave me the ticket."

She shakes her head.

"You had the black mask. At worst, you'd have seen a couple mortals get eaten in some sexually frustrating way. I'm not talking about that. I'm talking about earlier."

"You think people will suspect me?"

"I think you're liable to make them suspect you. I know that look," she says. "Today, when we were practicing. It's the *I think I can be a heroine* look. But shit's going down and people are getting hurt, and the last thing you should be doing is getting involved. Got it?"

"Yeah."

She sighs. "I wish I was fey."

"Why?"

"Because then, you telling me you'll stay out of trouble would be binding. Like, contractually so."

"I won't get involved. You're right. Mab's got it covered."

Melody just laughs and walks over to the trailer facing mine.

"My second piece of advice is to work on your lying. Otherwise you won't make it another month."

She looks over to where the VIP tent is. I follow her gaze. There are shadows moving in the field, dark, lumbering shapes that I can tell without doubt are far from human.

"Mab told you about the Night Terrors?" Mel asks.

I nod.

"Yeah, that's them now. I wouldn't recommend lingering if you're hoping for some decent sleep." She winks. "'Night, doll."

Then she steps into her bunk without looking back.

Once she's safely inside her trailer, I look down the row at the door I know is Kingston's. The light's off. It's late, yeah, and he could be fast asleep. But for a moment, I can't help but wonder if the reason he didn't want me to go to Noir was because he didn't want me to see him behaving like...like the others. The question is: Am I glad I didn't see him, or just disappointed?

I can still feel the music in my veins as I undress and get under the covers. For the first time since I signed on, my bunk door is locked. There's also a pocketknife hiding under my pillow, though I have a sinking suspicion that it wouldn't do much good if Kingston was wrong and I was the next target. In spite of all that—in spite of all the fear I know I should be feeling—I'm not scared. The music from the tent pulses, drowning out everything except the most primal instincts. As always, the circus still feels safe. Like how home should be, not that I really have anything to compare it to. I close my eyes and try to sleep. When that doesn't work, I stare at the thin light splashed across my ceiling, and try to ignore the muffled snores coming from the bunk next to mine. I want sleep to come, want to forget everything about the Tapis Noir, everything from the shit-show that was today. But I can't. Every time I close my eyes, I see the man being eaten alive. Every time I close my eyes, his face becomes Kingston's.

I can't tell if the image repulses or arouses me.

That alone scares me more than Sabina's murder or whatever creatures Mab invited over for dinner.

CHAPTER THREE: MER GIRL

The sun is just rising above the woods to the east, but the pie cart is already bustling as the cast and crew ready for the next jump. Off to one side, mulling over cups of coffee and cigarettes, are the Shifters, no longer decked out in suits and sleek sunglasses. Instead, everyone is covered in ink and piercings and ragged denim. The men have mohawks or no hair at all, and the girls have multicolored dreads. On jump days, they play tent crew. Odd to think that seeing them like this seems more normal than when they're dressed up. One of them nods when he sees me glance over, and I nod before looking back to my friends. Melody is wrapped in a gray knit shawl, and Kingston wears his university hoodie. Each is nursing a coffee and cinnamon roll.

When I woke up this morning, the VIP tent and all its inhabitants were gone. The parking lot on the other side of the road, however, still has a few cars waiting like tombstones. I don't mention it. To her credit, Melody says nothing about our encounter or the ticket. Kingston doesn't give her the chance.

"I still say you should tell her," he whispers.

"They're just nightmares," Melody says, giving her head a shake. "Everyone gets those."

"Really?" he asks, then looks at me. It's enough to make my heart do a double-step. It doesn't help that when I see him, I can only picture him in place of the man on the chaise longue. "Been dreaming much lately, Vivienne?"

I take a drink of my coffee and try not to wince at the bitterness. These carnies like it *strong*.

"Not that I recall." Thankfully. I can only imagine what my mind would have come up with after yesterday.

"Precisely," Kingston says.

I sigh. "Let me guess, that's in the contract, too?"

"For most of us," he replies.

Maybe I should retract my previous cold-heart-warm-six-pack assumptions about him. He's looking at Mel with real concern in his eyes, that brotherly type affection that makes my insides melt. He really does care about her. I can tell from that one exchange that he would do pretty much anything to keep her safe. I try to tell myself that's a good thing, that I can be attracted to him for something more important than his body and charm. But it only drives one deafening point home: all that love and affection is directed toward someone else. So far, I'm still thinking I'll be lucky if I reach good friend status.

Before he can say anything else, the Shifter guy who nodded to me is tapping Melody on the shoulder.

"You ready for tear-down?" he asks. He's got at least a dozen piercings in his left ear alone, and his mohawk is tipped with light blue. I think his name is Roman. Melody glances to the Shifter leader and then back to her untouched breakfast.

"Yeah," she says. She yawns again and hands Kingston the roll. "Ladies," she says with a small curtsy, then turns and follows Roman to the rest of the group.

"Why are we leaving so early?" I ask.

Kingston takes a quick glance around. Then, without so much as a twitch of his nose, the spare roll goes up in a puff of fire and smoke. He flicks the ashes to the ground and looks back at me.

"Mab's always itchy the day after Noir. Doesn't like lingering."

"So I see."

I look over his shoulder to where the Shifters are already disassembling. A few of them have begun pulling down the sidewalls from the tent, while the rest have gone inside to start tearing down the bleachers. I still don't see why Mab doesn't just have Kingston magic the tent into the giant semis that carry our load. Apparently, she's against using magic in broad daylight. That said, as I watch Roman jump into one of the semi cabs, I can see he's already bulked up to twice his normal weight. Shapeshifters: the perfect grunts.

The very mention of Tapis Noir brings back memories I don't want. It's not just the thought of what I saw in the tent, but what my mind brought up in the darkness after. Scenarios I'm too ashamed to admit even to myself: Kingston in a black mask and torn pants, me in white, and I don't care if he's biting or if the roles are reversed. Kingston on a hoop, on the sofa, his skin soft and hard and glowing in the candlelight. I feel the heat rise to my face and turn away, pretending to study the table of fruit beside me.

So much for focusing on his caring personality.

"You feeling okay?" he asks.

"Fine," I say, grateful my voice doesn't give a pubescent crack.

"You better not be getting sick, too."

"I'm fine," I say. When I think my cheeks aren't as red anymore, I look back at him, trying to push aside the image of him completely naked. My love life prior to joining the circus is a blur like everything else, but I know without a doubt that Kingston isn't the type of guy I'd go for. Or, if I'm being honest, he isn't the type that would go for me. He's in control. He's powerful. And, without a doubt, he's out of my league. And very much in love with someone else. I try not to be that much of a masochist. This time it doesn't appear to be working.

"Really?" he asks. "Because you look like Melody does every time she sees someone she wants to fuck." He's grinning as he says it, which just makes the fading blush brighten anew. Then his smirk fades, and I worry for a brief moment things have clicked and he's read my thoughts.

"Shit," Kingston says, glancing over my shoulder and then studiously regarding his mug. "Penelope," he mutters.

I sigh. "No rest for the wicked."

"There you are, my darlings," Penelope says from behind me. I turn around, a smile already plastered on my face.

Even in faded jeans and a hoodie, she looks like she's onstage, a feat I've never understood. I can't help but wonder how long she stared in her mirror this morning, making sure she looked just disheveled enough. I don't want to believe it comes naturally; it would make people like me hopeless. She smiles and reaches out to wrap an arm over my shoulders. I can't make out her perfume, but I'd be willing to bet *Ocean* is somewhere in the title.

"Which of you lovelies would like to help me with the front of house?" she asks as soon as she lets me go.

"I'm on costumes this site, I'm afraid," Kingston says. Though he's so quick about it, I can tell not one bit of him is sorry. "Vivienne should be free."

"Yeah," I say. Technically speaking, I should be helping load up the concession stands. The first time I tried, however, it became wildly clear that the Shifters not only had it under control, but saw me as a hindrance rather than a help. I was now the proverbial floater, which meant a morning talking business and sideshow fashion with Penelope. "I'd love to help."

I can't help but notice Kingston's smirk as Penelope guides me away. In truth, it's probably for the best. I have a feeling that being around Kingston when he's in one of his flirtatious moods would be dangerous. Especially after what my mind was dreaming up last night.

Melody was right; I need to get much, much better at lying. Otherwise I'll never be able to look Kingston in the eye again.

It's not until we're halfway to Penelope's trailer that something Kingston said strikes a funny chord. *"You look like Melody when she sees someone she wants to fuck."* Those aren't the words I'd expect him to say, not about his own girlfriend. Not while smiling. I take a deep breath and try to calm the sudden quickening in my pulse. Now's not the time to start thinking I had it all wrong. That hope is far too dangerous right now.

Front of house is mostly administrative work. While the rest of the crew is loading the trucks, Penelope and I sit in the shade inside her trailer, the hum of the air conditioner almost drowning out the thuds and clangs of the demolition outside. The performers' trailers are just that—double-wide trailers divided into even smaller cubicles. Mine has a bed that wouldn't pass for a twin, a desk, and enough shelf space for a few pairs of clothes and the huge rubber boots Kingston recommended I buy at our first site, in case of a mud show. Penelope's space is twice the size. It's nearly half a trailer, with a queen bed in one corner and a large vanity with a fish tank against the other wall. In the middle, bolted to the floor, is a table covered in receipts and ticket stubs and a small laptop playing some sort of classical shit.

"So," she says as I sort the ticket stubs into piles based on show time and seating area. She's typing something into the laptop, and even though I can't see the screen, I don't doubt for one second that she's just checking her email. How long has it been since I've checked mine? Once the thought passes, it fades like mist in the sun, replaced by Penelope's voice. "How are you enjoying our troupe so far?"

"It's great," I say. "The people are really nice." I hope it doesn't sound as fake as it feels.

"Mmm," she says. "I'm glad to hear that. You're making friends, yes?"

I nod, then realize she isn't looking. "Yeah. Mostly Kingston and Melody."

She smiles and I look at her for a moment, trying to pinpoint her age. There are tiny crows'-feet at the edge of her eyes, almost perfectly hidden beneath her foundation.

"They're a lovely pair," she says, giving one of the keys a sharp tap and then looking up at me. Our eyes meet, and her smile becomes inquisitive. "I have to wonder...do you miss your family? Your old friends?"

I look back at the ticket stubs and try to focus on reorganizing them. My mind goes as blank as my face.

"I don't really have a family," I say.

A beat passes, and I know without looking up that she's staring at me even more intently, and the thought makes my face go red.

"Everyone has a family, Vivienne."

I close my eyes.

The words I want to say aren't forming in my head. All I can visualize is an empty apartment and grey concrete and feeling cold...and hunted. I try to imagine my mother, but she's just a blur of brown hair and reprimands. My dad isn't even an impression. It never really bothered me before, the fact that I couldn't recall much about my past. I just didn't think about it. After all, what you can't remember can't haunt you. I was always one of those *focus on the present* types.

"I'm sorry," she says, and then she's standing behind me, her arms wrapped around my chest in a tight hug. It takes a lot of self-control to not push her away. "I didn't mean...I didn't know you were an orphan." She hesitates. "Like me."

I take the bait, if only to shift the attention. "Like you?" Up close, her perfume is positively suffocating. *Cloying*, I think is the right word.

She lets go of me and sits on the side of her bed, staring at the bubbling fish tank.

"I was Mab's first act," she says. Her blue eyes have gone hazy, like a fog swept over the sea. "She found me when I was but a babe. My parents...well, I don't remember my parents. They left me there in the sand, waiting for the tide to come in and wash me away. Mab saved me and raised me in the Winter Court as her own."

"Why would your parents do that?" I ask. I can imagine her, a swaddled baby on the side of the sea, crying at a grey sky as the rain pelts down and the foam of the tide pulls farther in. And then there's Mab, dressed in black and gossamer purple, sweeping down just in time to rescue the struggling thing from drowning.

Penelope smiles, and it's easily the saddest smile I've ever seen. She doesn't say anything, just raises one hand and flexes her fingers. Scales ripple from her flesh, glimmering pale-blue and soft. A shake of the wrist, and they're gone.

"We Shifters, we can't always control our forms, especially not as children." She looks at me. "I was lucky. In my day, children like me were considered changelings—faeries switched with mortal babies. They believed that the only way to get their true child back was to burn the impostor. Or worse."

I swallow and stare at her and can't help but wonder just how many other Shifters were killed by their own parents by mistake.

"What was it like in Mab's Court?" I ask. I want to steer the subject as far away from murder as possible. After last night, the idea of Mab's nightmarish home is both intriguing and terrifying. I can't imagine someone like Penelope, someone clearly more comfortable in posh digs, growing up surrounded by such lecherous monsters. Maybe that's why she pretty much keeps to herself. Ignorance is bliss.

I should know.

"It was so long ago," Penelope begins, and I expect her to wave the question away. She doesn't. "But Mab's Court isn't something one can simply forget. She made sure of it."

"What do you mean?"

Penelope rustles around in the nightstand beside her bed and pulls out a necklace. It's a simple silver chain, and on it hangs a diamond that glints as black as night. She loops the chain in one palm and holds it out to me.

"This," she says.

It's the second time in twenty-four hours that someone's handed me something without explanation. *Fool me twice...* I eye it, not moving to take it from her.

"It won't hurt you," she says with a small smile. "One of Mab's jewelers made it for me. It's hewn from the very walls of her castle."

I still don't move.

"What's it do?" I ask.

"So suspicious," she says, though the smile doesn't fade. "It's a memory stone. It allows me to record and recollect my history. Otherwise, I'd have trailers and trailers of diaries."

"You sure you want me to know all that?"

She laughs.

"It will only show you what I want it to."

She motions her hand once more. I take a deep breath. Hopefully she's never been to the Tapis Noir...

The stone drops into my palm. It's warm and tingling and as the heat spreads up my arm, the world grows black.

❖

A few blinks and my vision clears. The light is dim and pale blue, like all the light is diffusing through blocks of snow. Penelope is standing beside me, but she's barely there, just a flicker of a figure. When I glance down, my hands are just as ghostlike. We're in a hall made of arching black stone. Blue flames flicker along the wall, the fires contained within giant crystals. Plush white carpet lines the hallway, and although the air is as warm as the trailer, everything looks frozen, from the glossy walls to the way the carpet piles like freshly fallen snow.

"This was the main hall," Penelope says. Her voice is clear, but seems to be coming from far away. I look at her apparition as she talks. Her lips don't move.

I blink, and now she's standing a few feet away. Another blink, and she's even farther. I move to catch up. The motion is jerky, like I'm a character in a broken film reel. I only see the hall blink past in flashes.

Moments later we stand before a large set of doors. They spread from wall to ceiling to floor, made of dark black wood inlaid with silver in curling thorned filigree. She pauses, one hand pressed to the door. She looks at me.

"Would you like to see the birth of the circus?"

I can't imagine any other reason to be here, so I respond with a muted, "Yeah."

She looks back to the door, a staccato flicker of her head.

Then she's gone.

I look at the door that stands easily three times my height. I put a hand to the wood. I push.

I'm inside.

If the hall was large, this room is beyond comprehension. To say it's a cavern is an understatement, but that's the only thing my mind can connect it to. The ceiling domes up, way up, hundreds of feet above. The entire thing is illuminated by crystals and flickering lights that zip around like fireflies. The light falls like snow, dusting down to the floor and fading into the white carpet. Stalactites and stalagmites reach down and up like teeth on all sides, their surfaces carved and inset with silver like the doors. More tiny lights flicker around the formations. And there, sitting right in the center amid a wall of silver stalagmites, is a throne the height of a house. The actual seat rests a good twenty feet from the ground, sitting atop a disturbingly thin spire of stone. The chair back is silver and crystal, the arms ebony and ice. Mab sits there in a dress of white silk and fur. A crown of black ice sits atop her head.

"Your Majesty?" a young girl asks. She stands at the foot of Mab's throne. A few steps closer and I can see her clearly. It's a younger Penelope, with the same blazing red hair and porcelain features. There's a doll in her hand, one with wings and glittering green eyes. Then the doll twists its head toward me, and I jump back.

"We have traveled the world together, yes? And you've enjoyed it?" Mab asks. I can't help but stare in awe at this incarnation of Mab. She looks every inch a regal queen, from the crown on her head to the hem of her dress that dangles ten feet below the edge of her throne. She is nothing like the debaucherous Mab I know, but there's a power they both share, a presence that tells me they are without question one and the same.

"I have, my Lady," Penelope says. Her voice is perfectly composed—not a hint of fear or doubt.

"But you've grown lonely," Mab purrs. "You desire friends." She seems to regard the doll in Penelope's hand. "Real friends."

The young Penelope pauses. Apparently, even at an early age, she knew Mab's offers usually had a hook. Or twenty.

"Yes, my Lady."

"Then perhaps I have a solution."

Mab waves a hand and the carpet at the young Penelope's feet ripples, as though the floor is trying to push its way through. Peaks form and colors melt across the fabric as the carpet becomes a series of tents in blue and black. Tiny shadows move about the tents, and I can hear the sound of applause.

"What is it?" the young Penelope asks.

"Your new home," Mab replies. "I have decided our show is too informal. My scouts in the mortal realm have confirmed that Philip Astley's show is a great success, and I feel it is in our best interest to follow suit. We are creating a circus."

The young Penelope leans in to examine the tents.

"Imagine it," Mab says. She floats down from her throne and kneels down opposite Penelope. "An entire show filled with people like yourself—fey and mortals and divinities. Every act a sensation, every performer a new friend."

As I listen, I can't help but wonder if this softer side of Mab still exists, or if it's been hardened over the years. Could she really have created an entire show for Penelope? Or was that only a ruse to make Penelope feel better about being forced to join?

A voice calls out from the corner of the room.

"I hate it."

I jerk up and see her striding toward us. She's in a lacy purple dress and her black hair is tied with ribbons, but there's no mistaking her face. It hasn't changed a single bit. And there, prowling from the shadows, is her familiar.

Lilith and Poe.

She walks straight to the circus and stomps on one of the tents. The tents fade instantly. So, too, does the vision.

❖

I blink and we're back in the trailer. "What was…what was *she* doing there?" I ask.

Penelope reaches over and plucks the necklace from my hand, returning it to her nightstand before replying.

"Lilith has been with Mab for many, many years. I was the first to tour the world with her, but Lilith existed within Mab's court long before I did."

I shake my head.

"But she looks exactly the same. Why did you grow up?"

She shrugs and smiles, though there's no happiness there.

"I've never asked," she replies.

"Why did she—"

A loud crash sounds outside, one that makes the glass makeup jars on her vanity tremble. We both jump to our feet in the same instant. She glances out the window.

"The king pole," she says. "It's fallen."

Then she rushes past me and out the door. I'm not far behind.

❖

The tent is a tangle of steel and cables. The canvas walls and roof are gone, but one of the four king poles—the central poles that hold up the highest points of the tent—is on its side. People are shouting and Penelope and I are running full out. The Shifters are already trying to lift the thing, which is easily two stories long, from where it's toppled onto the bleachers. That's when I see her, hiding under the tangled mess: Lilith. The king pole is barely two feet above her. Poe is mewling, just clear of the wreckage.

There are other crew members yelling at her to get out, but no one's willing to take the chance to go after her. The pylons are slowly crushing down on the bleachers, shifting inch by precarious inch. If she doesn't get out of there fast, she'll be jelly. Trouble is, anyone trying to get in might just disturb the whole thing and make it crush sooner.

Something in me takes over. I duck into the maze of aluminum and steel and make my way toward her. She's curled in a fetal position, I can tell that much. But with all the yelling and groaning of steel, I can't tell if she's making any noise. She sure as hell isn't moving. I swing through the mess until I'm just a foot away. Lilith's shaking, her black dress covered in dust and rubble. One arm is bleeding. Above us, the massive king pole hovers precariously, pitched between a crunching pile of bleacher bits. The thing shudders and eases an inch closer to my head. I hunch down even further and try to reach for her.

"Lilith," I say. She doesn't move, so I call her name again, a little more harshly this time. She looks up. "Lilith, we have to go now."

"Scared," she says. Her green eyes are wide and her face is completely ashen. "Scared scared scaredy cat."

"Come on," I say as the king pole shifts again. "Please."

"Can't." She curls tighter. "Scaredy cat scaredy cat scaredy cat."

And that's when something clicks.

"Poe misses you," I say. "He wants you to come out."

Her head tilts up again. "Poe? Kitty kitty?"

"Yes," I say, extending my hand further. "Poe misses you, but he's too scared to come in here. He wants you to come out and play with him. He wants you to take my hand."

A screech rends through the air and I flinch as cold metal touches the back of my neck. Lilith doesn't seem to notice. She's looking at me, her expression still dazed.

"Please," I say. "Poe misses you. Now."

"Okay," she says. And she takes my hand. My vision explodes.

Fire fire roaring fire
fire burning fire killing fire
laughing fire fire blood and red and
fire blood and fire fire fey and faerie blood—

I scream aloud as the hallucination tears me apart, and then I'm stumbling and falling and letting go and it's gone. It's gone and the world is white white white as color slowly seeps back around the edges and my head splits apart like a cleaver is carving it in two. Faces first, then voices. Faces looking down. Kingston and Penelope and Melody and someone's got a hand on my forehead. Ice water trickles down my skin and down my neck and under my skin into my bones, and I close my eyes and wait for the water to drown me, dreaming of scaled skin and burning blood.

CHAPTER FOUR: SPOTLIGHT

I s she awake yet?"

"Not yet. Wait…yep, there she is."

I peel my eyes open, which feels like rubbing burning sandpaper inside my temples. It takes a moment, but after a few blinks the dim light solidifies into something I can make out. Kingston hovers overs me, Melody at his side. We're in my tiny trailer room, and I'm lying on the bed. They're both looking down like they're expecting me to grow horns or die. Or both.

"Morning, sunshine," Kingston says. He touches my shoulder, and once more that cool ice-water sensation slides across my skin and seeps into my head. It feels like bliss.

I shift under his touch and stare up at those brown eyes. For once, I have his attention. All it took was nearly getting crushed to death and an act of stupid heroics. I smile, and he smiles back.

"What happened?" I ask, because I'm afraid if we keep smiling at each other I'll forget that Mel is still in the room.

"We were going to ask you the same thing, doll," Melody says. Her eyes are even more shadowed than before, especially in this light. Is it just my near-death experience, or are her fingers shaking?

"What do you mean?" I ask. I try thinking back, but it's all a blur. Something deep down feels fire, feels burning, but I can't put my finger on it. Like steam, it just floats around in my subconscious, smoldering invisibly.

"Well," Kingston says, removing his healing touch. "We all saw you jump into the wreck and pull Lilith out. But we don't understand why you were screaming when you got her out of there. Then you passed out." He traces a finger down my arm. I shiver, but not from any magic he might possess.

"No injuries," he says, almost to himself. "No trauma. So why did you faint?"

"I don't…I don't remember."

Still, the memory nags at me. I've got Lilith's huddled form in my mind. I remember taking her hand, and then…that's it.

"Maybe she's just got a weak stomach," Melody says. She chuckles, which turns into a cough. Kingston glances at her; his eyebrow cocks in a strange mix of concern and curiosity. She holds up a hand until the coughing fit stops. "Sorry," she says. "Must be coming down with something."

"Must be," Kingston says. "You better not die before our act tonight." He turns back to me.

And that's when I notice that they're both in costume. Melody's not wearing her tuxedo coat or wig, but she's in her tight pinstripe trousers and a clean button-down. Kingston is in a white shirt and black sequined slacks. The tip of his tattoo is curled around his bicep. I blink because I'm pretty certain that's not where the tail was last time. I push myself up to sit, which just makes my head swim even more.

"What time is it? How long have I been out?"

"A full day," Kingston says softly. "We're already at the next site."

"No way," I say, sinking back down onto the bed. "Shit."

"The show's in an hour," Melody says. She slips something into my hand. "But Mab's giving you the night off."

I look at the ticket stub in my hand. *Cirque des Immortels* is in swirling black ink on the front of the dusty purple card stock, my seat number and row are on the back. VIP seating, nice.

"She doesn't ever give people the night off," Melody says, nodding to the ticket in my hand. "Let alone reward them for it. She must be impressed."

She and Kingston share a look.

"You're *sure* you can't remember anything?" he asks.

"I wish," I say. The absence of memory sears.

Melody leaves a few minutes later, when a particularly strong coughing fit sends her out the door in search of tea and honey. Kingston stares after her with a look on his face that tells me he feels he should follow. He doesn't, though. And after a moment of looking at the door, he turns back to me.

"That was brave," he says. He's leaning against my desk, almost in arm's reach. The scent of his musky cologne fills the trailer. I realize that, for the first time, we're alone in a room together. The thought makes my heart beat faster. He smiles, and it's not the usual sarcastic grin. "I'm glad you're safe."

I don't know what to say to that, so I let out a half-chuckle and look down at the admissions ticket.

I hear him shift, and then he's standing next to the bed. Next to me. I don't look up. I know if I do I'll be tempted to say or do something I'd regret later.

He puts his hand on my shoulder. The ticket stops spinning in my hands but my pulse speeds up. What would Mel say if she knew we were alone like this? I can't hurt her, not after all the kindness she's shown me. But after what he said yesterday, a large part of me is holding on to the hope that they aren't a thing.

"You surprise me," he says. I look up at him.

"Is that a good thing?" I counter. I'd probably fuck things up if I said anything remotely serious or tried to be smooth. But there's something in his eyes, something in our closeness that makes me want to reach out and touch him, even if every part of me knows it's a horrible idea. I can't stop telling myself that he's looking at me differently than the way he's looked at Mel. I try to convince myself it's just from fainting.

"I'm not sure yet," he says. He studies me like he's actually trying to figure me out. No one's looked at me that intensely since I started here. The silence between us grows, and I don't want to do anything to make it end. He looks at me and I look at him and his hand is still on my shoulder. His touch makes my skin tingle. He bites his lower lip.

If this were a movie, I think this must be the part where tragedy and heroism bring us together and we make a really stupid decision. One of us has a moment of weakness, forgets the relationship-thing due to overwhelming passion, and then it's nothing but lips and discarded clothes and murmurs of love—

Kingston shakes his head and steps back.

"I better get going," he says. "Wouldn't want any rumors about us, you know." He winks and heads to the door. Before stepping through, he turns back and gives me the grin I'm starting to love. "And, Viv, I know my act is good, but try not to faint before intermission." He chuckles and leaves me sitting there.

He's just toying with you, I try to convince myself. But my body's not listening. I stare at the door for a while and feel the after-trace of his hand on my shoulder. I tell myself that there are more important things to think about, like finding the killer and keeping Kingston and Mel safe, and figuring out why I fainted in the first place. More important things. I stand up and search my shelves for a clean shirt. There are much more important things than a guy I barely know. A guy who's gorgeous and strong and could set my ass on fire if he wanted. A guy who I'm now only ninety percent certain is dating my best friend. *Right.* I can still smell his cologne.

❖

An hour later, I'm milling about in the promenade with the rest of the punters. Stalls and booths of every kind flank each side of the makeshift road that leads up to the blue-and-black tent. *Cirque des Immortels* blazes in acid-purple neon above the gaping maw of an entrance. I'm in my everyday jeans and T-shirt, nothing to set me apart from the rest—no *Crew* splashed across my back, no tower of cotton candy in one hand. Tonight, I'm just like everyone else. I hadn't realized how appealing that thought would be.

I grab a box of popcorn from the concessionaire booth and am saved from making small talk; today it's run by a new girl from the nearby town, someone I haven't met and maybe never will. All she sees is a girl with a VIP pass that entitles her to free food and drink. Even that small act of anonymity makes me feel a little more at home. Being surrounded by people who know you 24/7 isn't something I'm used to. Small memories of another life flutter through my head like moths—all grey images and tearstains—and then I'm leaping out of the way to make room for a stilt walker.

It's dressed like a giant black rabbit trundling around on eight-foot-tall legs, except the rabbit head is actually a raven's. And when the beast walks past me, I distinctly see the eye blink. A whole line of walkers moves through the crowd. All the creatures are like some tame sort of nightmare, their legs nimbly stepping around and over the people below. Kids are calling and screaming and laughing, and even the adults stare up in wonder as the creatures roam and pirouette and leap. They're all headed in the same direction. To one side of the promenade there's a wooden archway set up between concession booths. The stilt walkers narrowly duck under a sign as they vanish down the side alley. *Freakshow*, the sign reads.

I grin in spite of myself. Although they are technically hired as tent crew, sometimes, when they're really bored or want to shake things up, the Shifters set up their small carnival-styled area to put on their own show. It's like a two-for-one deal. For once, my luck seems to be swinging toward the positive.

I take a step toward it, but then the music inside the tent changes, and the jugglers come out into the promenade twirling clubs of fire. They shout at the top of their lungs, "Show begins in five minutes!"

I'd kill to see what the Shifters are putting on at this site. Last time, Roman made himself rotund and covered every inch of his torso in tattoos, so he resembled an old-school globe. But the ticket in my hand burns at the thought of some kid stealing my seat. I follow the throng toward the black entrance curtains. I'll catch the freaks at intermission.

"You've never seen anything like this before," Kingston said. Two days in, and he and Melody were still the only ones who talked to me, but it was better than nothing. We stood at the back of the tent. He was in his costume and I wore a new pair of jeans and T-shirt that had miraculously appeared in my bunk the night I settled in. The performers were running in and out of the tent to catch their cues. To me, it all looked like well-orchestrated chaos. Kingston motioned for me to sneak closer, so I did, standing beside him and peering out through a crack in the curtain. Even then I was horribly aware of his proximity. I could see the contortionists doing their dance onstage, their white costumes sparkling in the magenta lights above as they folded themselves on top of each other, balancing on elbows and chins, tips of toes curling under shoulders. I looked over to Kingston, who had a smile on his face even though he'd already admitted to seeing the show a thousand times. He looked over at me and caught my stare. "You're a part of this, now. It's your home."

I looked out again and watched the contortionists stand and take their bows, bathing in the applause. I closed my eyes and imagined myself out there; I could feel the pulse of fear and adrenaline and ecstasy, the mix of fight-or-flight that somehow pushes performers to entertain. The roar of the audience filled me. Home.

The first few acts go off without a hitch. The jugglers begin strong and don't drop a single club or dagger. The contortionists follow, dancing their beautiful duet of entwining limbs and arching backs. I can practically feel the crowd's excitement as each act gives way to the next, the anticipation growing with every performer. Three violet lengths of fabric lower from the ceiling, rippling like water as the aerialists ascend and begin twisting and dancing high above, their white costumes flickering in the spotlights. I can remember only one of their names—Arietta Skye, a girl no older than me with brown hair and eyes the color of the ocean. She seems to lead the other two in their dance. She is the first to roll in a dizzying drop toward the ground, and she is the one who smiles the widest.

I applaud louder than usual as Kingston and Melody take the stage. When they take their bow, I distinctly catch Kingston winking at me. Then he's waving and running offstage. It's not until the next act—Spanish Web—that I realize I'm still blushing.

It's during the flying trapeze act that I notice her. At first, I thought it was just a shadow moving high up in the cupola. But then I squint and make out a figure moving up among the narrow catwalks strung between the lights. Lilith. I shake my head, trying not to wonder how she can stomach being up there when just yesterday she was nearly killed by the very poles she's dangling from. I'm surprised no one else is pointing up at her, but then again, she's wearing all black. I have a feeling that she's done this so many times before, she knows no one else is going to see her.

That one glance makes my head ring. The scent of smoke fills my nostrils like an afterthought. Nothing's burning, though, and the moment I look away from her, it's gone.

The trapeze artists climb their two tiny rope ladders that attach to the foot-wide platforms high up above. They are dressed in dark, shimmering outfits that remind me of dragonfly wings, and the dim blue lights onstage make them look otherworldly. Mist seethes along the ground as the music changes to something deeper, slower, more ambient and foreboding. It's all strings and drumbeats now. The singer, Gretchen, hums into her microphone as the first performers grab on to the trapeze and swing out above the crowd's heads. There's no net below them. *No one dies in this circus,* Kingston had said. Every act is a testament to that promise.

The fliers swing out, then back to their platforms. A simple swing. Then as one of the fliers lands and poses on one platform for the mild applause, the other is inverting himself and latching his legs on the bar. He swings toward the other platform with his hands free. The man who just took a swing changes places with a girl, who launches herself over the space, swinging toward the inverted man who arcs toward her with open hands. The girl releases her grip at the swing's apex, flips twice in midair, and latches on to the man's wrists. They glide gracefully over to the platform, where she dismounts and waves. He grabs hold of a tether to keep from swinging out again, one arm raised in salute. The applause is deafening.

But this is just the intro. Another man swings out from the other platform, flying through the air. He inverts as well, while a young man is readying himself on the free trapeze. With perfect timing, he launches himself off, arcs up and over the crowd, flips not twice, but three times in midair, right before his partner expertly catches his wrists and swings him back to safety. The crowd goes wild.

I feel a huge grin on my face as the energy of it all catches me up in its thrall. When I glance down, practically beaming at the crowd as though it was *me* up there, risking life and limb for their entertainment, I see that not everyone is enjoying the show as much as I am. Across the ring from me, sitting almost precisely in the middle of the bleachers, is a man in his thirties with sharp blond hair and angular features. I can't tell much about him, except that he's staring straight up at the performers with a frown on his face. I look up, wondering if maybe one of the aerialists is giving the crowd the finger—apparently it's happened before—but everything's as it should be. I look down again.

That when I realize he's not looking at the performers. He's looking past them, into the cupola.

At Lilith.

The man's gaze flickers to me, and it feels like vertigo slaps me in the face, twists around my stomach. I look away, look up to the fliers that are readying for another trick, and try to force the sickness back down.

Each trapeze has a man swinging out toward the other, then back to their platforms. As they swing back, they invert, grab the hands of the waiting girls, and swing out again. Both girls release at the same time, one flying high over the other; the lower girl curls tight into a ball, the one above spreads in a wide *X*. They both reach the awaiting partner at the same time. Grips catch in a snap of chalk dust. But the lower girl only locks one hand. The other hand slips. In that horrifying moment, I know she's fucked. The crowd gasps.

It's only a second. Only one terrible second as gravity connects and her swing pulls her back down to the earth. That one tentative grip slips, and then she's plummeting to the ground.

Someone in the audience screams, or maybe it's many people, I don't know. All I know is that the girl only falls for a moment, then she gives a jerk, like something's snagged her, and her descent immediately slows. She lands lightly within the mist, clearly shaken but doing her best to smile and pose. Something flashes as she turns to face all sides of the crowd, which is now applauding as fervently as though she'd landed the trick. I see her safety lines. Two long black cables stretch from her waist up into the cupola. They caught her and kept her from landing in the dirt in an explosion of blood and bone. She unclips the cables and they slink back up into the heavens.

Except I know without a doubt that we don't use safety lines because no one in this circus messes up. Ever. Either Kingston or Mab is covering an accident that shouldn't have happened.

For some reason, I look away from the girl on the ground—Jillian is her name, I think—and catch sight of the blond man across from me. He's still not clapping, but at least he's looking down now, still scowling. He looks disappointed that the girl is alive.

Although intermission follows immediately after the flying trap, I don't wait until the end of the act. I awkwardly make my way toward the aisles and bolt out the exit, heading around the tent toward the backstage. Despite the fact that someone almost died, no one seems to notice something went wrong. People are changing or stretching or relaxing. That's when I notice Kingston standing beside the backstage curtain. He's peering out through the crack like when we watched the contortionists together. His fingers are clenched into fists.

"What was that?" I ask when I reach him. He jumps slightly but doesn't make a sound. When he sees it's me, his fingers relax just a little. He really should wear a shirt backstage. His abs are distracting, even at the worst of times.

"Wait," he whispers. "Just in case." He turns back and continues to watch through the curtain. A few moments pass while I watch the performers mingling backstage, and then the audience breaks into loud applause. He steps aside just before the trapeze artists run through the back curtain. The girl who fell spots Kingston and wraps him in a hug.

"Thank you," Jillian says. There are tears in her eyes and her makeup is smudged.

Kingston just returns the hug and whispers something in the girl's ear that I can't hear. Then the rest of the trapeze artists are circling us, asking what happened. I can't tell if they're asking Kingston or Jillian, but it's Jillian who answers.

"I don't know," she says.

The guy who caught her—Peter—chimes in.

"Everything felt good from my end," he says. "That was a perfect toss."

"I know," Jillian says. She shakes her head. "It felt perfect. But then... I don't know. Right when I was about to catch, something just...just took my breath away."

"What did you smell?" Kingston asks. I stare at him. The question seems ridiculously out of place.

Jillian rubs her arms. Peter steps up behind her and wraps his own muscular arms around her. She leans back into him, but she's still shaking. It takes her a while to answer.

"Lightning," she finally says. "It smelled like lightning and cut grass."

Kingston's face darkens.

"They wouldn't dare," he whispers. "I have to find Mab."

"What is it?" Peter asks.

"Summer," Kingston says.

The small crowd gasps. I have no idea what he's talking about.

"Take her to her trailer," Kingston says to Peter. "Watch her. If anything changes, find me immediately."

"Am I in danger?" Jillian asks. Her voice trembles.

"Keep her out of sight," Kingston replies, looking only at Peter. Then he's off, heading toward the trailers.

The trapeze artists disperse the moment Kingston leaves. Jillian's practically carried off by Peter and the rest follow in a half-circle behind. I don't wait around. I jog over to Kingston's side.

"What's going on?" I ask him again. He doesn't slow.

"This doesn't concern you, Vivienne," he says.

I reach out and grab his arm, force him to stop. He turns. His eyes burn and I nearly let go. But I don't. I'm not going to just stand around and wait for someone to include me. I don't know where this inner fire came from, but I'm not going to fight it. After all, it already saved Lilith's life. Maybe it'll save someone else's, like a heroic sixth sense.

"I'm part of this troupe," I say. "What's going on?"

I can see the frustration in his eyes, the immediate desire to push me away. I steel myself for the outburst, but it doesn't come.

"Summer," he finally says. "They're here."

If this wasn't clearly a serious situation, I'd make some witty comment about it being obvious it was summer, seeing as how it's eighty degrees even after dark. He must notice I'm clueless because he doesn't wait for me to say anything.

"The Summer Court. Mab's rivals. They're here. They're interfering."

"You think they tried to kill Jillian," I say. Pieces are clicking together in my head.

"I think they're trying to make a point. Which means we need Mab. Now. Before they make any more."

He turns to go but I grab him again. Touching him is addictive and, in this instance, allowed.

"How do you know?" I ask. "What if she just fell?"

"That doesn't happen," Kingston says, not even turning around. "Besides, even *I* could smell Summer magic at work. I just needed Jillian's confirmation."

We're nearly to Mab's trailer when he turns around.

"Please, Vivienne. Stay out of this. You don't need any more attention. Just go back to the show." His eyes are pleading, and he doesn't give me time to refuse. He turns and heads around the corner of a trailer. I don't follow.

Instead, I turn around and head back toward the front of house. I don't stop until I catch sight of the blond-haired guy who was sitting across from me. He didn't make it hard; he's standing at the concessions booth right in front of the tent, looking over our DVDs with the mildest amount of interest. He's tall and thin—taller than me—in a grey pin-stripe suit that makes him even more angular. I stand on the other side of the promenade and watch from the popcorn queue. The man keeps glancing around, but he doesn't seem to notice me noticing him.

Mab comes out from the crowd before I reach the cashier. The man in the suit puts down the brochure he was pretending to read and smiles, but it's not even close to friendly—it's the grin of a man looking forward to a conflict. Mab doesn't even return the forced affection. She strides right over to the blond guy with a grim look on her perfectly painted face. A few people stop and stare and make like they're about to approach her for an autograph, but there's a darkness to her presence, something that radiates *don't fuck with me*. And the whip at her waist only pushes that point home.

The two share a look, but I don't see their lips move. Instead, she turns and escorts him away from the booth, behind the picket fence separating backstage from the front. I know that following her would be suicide, but something in me can't resist the temptation. I don't know why the hero thing has taken over, but the very thought that this guy might be the one trying to hurt someone in my troupe—my *home*—makes my blood boil. *No one messes with my family.* In that moment, I realize it doesn't matter that I've felt like I'm still on the edge of this place. These people took me in. If nothing else, I'm indebted.

I watch her take him away from the chapiteau—not toward the backstage tent and not toward the trailers. I grin in spite of myself. She's taking him to the freak show.

Without hesitating, I head toward the makeshift wooden sign and enter the tunnel of freaks.

CHAPTER FIVE: FREAK SHOW

On my second night in the troupe, I was gathered around a bonfire with Kingston and Melody and a few others, listening to stories of past shows and the wild adventures people had experienced off-site. Some had gone skinny-dipping in the Arctic. Others reminisced about buying out an entire town's stock of glazed donuts. Kingston sat next to me, our arms brushing as he laughed. He kept waving his hand over the thermos being passed around, magically refilling it with unknown booze. I hadn't really grasped that at the time. There were mostly Shifters with us, and they could hold their drink. Most of them, anyway.

That's when they started playing Outfreak the Freak.

It was Melody's idea, probably because I'd just asked her why members of the tent crew were called Shifters.

It started by her daring Stephanie to turn into Mab, which made the girl crow with laughter and ask *which incarnation?* Mel just smiled, said, "Present."

Stephanie stood up, brushed herself off, and cleared her throat.

"Presenting," she said, "the most feared faerie in history. The one, the only, Mab!" With that, her features melted and stretched, melding into a perfect likeness of Mab. If not for the fact that Stephanie was wearing shorts and a hoodie—something I doubt Mab would ever get caught dead wearing—she pulled it off spectacularly.

"Fail!" Melody yelled.

Mab/Stephanie glared at her.

"Mab's eyes are more hunter green. I'd call yours mint."

Stephanie kicked sand in Mel's face and sat down, promptly shifting back into her normal pink-haired Goth self.

"Let me try," said Heath, a heavily tattooed man with thick round glasses. He stood up and gave himself a shake as his blond hair turned black and wild, his features angling up into a vision of Mab that was frighteningly realistic. Minus two things.

"Boobs are way, way too big," Roman said.

"Not big enough," countered another guy.

Moments later, every Shifter around the fire was doing their best impersonation of Mab—some aiming for exactness, others just going wild. There were snake-headed medusae and Mabs with red skin and devil horns. Others had two heads or five breasts. It just got worse from there, as they deviated from impersonating Mab into creating the weirdest creatures they could think of. Soon, the campfire was surrounded by bleeding harpies and twelve-foot-tall stick men and—strangest of all—a round blob of human flesh with no eyes or appendages, just a giant mouth filled with broken-syringe teeth.

"That, my friend," Melody laughed, "is why they're called Shifters. Shapeshifters, if you want to be precise."

"How the hell do they do that?" I asked, watching the blob slurp itself back into the form of a tiny girl with a green buzz cut.

"Lineage," Kingston said. "You know all those stories about gods mating with mortals?" I nodded, thinking of Zeus and all his bastardized offspring. "Yeah, well, replace 'gods' with 'faeries' and that's what you get."

I watched as Heath—at least, I thought it was Heath—mutated into one giant blue breast.

"Not as refined as the stories, eh?" Melody laughed.

"Never is," Kingston said.

❖

Roman is the first guy I recognize in the throng, though it takes me a moment to connect the guy I'm looking at with the heavily pierced, blue-mohawked guy I'm used to. This new, changed Roman is wearing a three-piece suit that looks like it was in at least a dozen pieces before he resurrected it. Patches are fraying off the elbows and I can't tell if it's mostly brown or tweed or black pinstripe. He's also at least seven feet tall, with thick black tattoos curling around his bare wrists and tunnel plugs in his ear that are big enough to pass a tennis ball through. His general face shape is still roughly the same, albeit pointier, a bit more elfish. But he still has the blue mohawk.

"Vivienne," he says. His voice is much deeper than usual, rumbling in the depths of his chest. "Enjoying the show?"

"Yeah," I say, looking around, trying to find my quarry. Everything here seems dusty and antiquated, from the hand-painted signs proclaiming the bearded lady (classic), bat boy, and serpent fingers, to the make-shift tents and pavilions set up for the shows. I don't see Mab or the blond guy anywhere.

"Looking for something in particular?" he asks, the hint of a joke on his lips. "I hear the fire eater's quite hot this time around."

"Mab," I say, ignoring the horrible pun. His face becomes serious in an instant.

Roman clears his throat. He doesn't ask me why I want to know, doesn't ask if I'm getting into trouble. We stare at each other for a moment; it's clear he already knows something's up, and he's not interested in getting involved. Mab doesn't come into the freak show; whatever's going on is serious.

"She went that way," he says, pointing to the side.

I glance around. The tents back here are chaotic, all jammed together with no real rhyme or reason. Small alleys appear between a few tents, leading off in more directions and more shows. Hiding somewhere behind them is Mab and the man, and my time to find them is running out fast.

"Any idea which one?"

He shakes his head. "Went down Alligator Alley. You'll have to look."

Across the circular pitch from Roman stands a tank as wide as I am tall, and twice my height. In its depths, waving slowly with a grin on her face, is Penelope. Her red hair floats around her in a halo, her pale skin looking even paler in the clear water. She's wearing a bra made of sequined seashells, and from the navel down, her body is that of a fish, with opalescent blue scales and a beautiful fin as diaphanous as a betta's. She smiles at me, a tiny trail of bubbles escaping her lips, and I wave back, trying not to look as rushed as I feel. To the right of her giant aquarium is a space between a couple tents. A wooden sign strung above it reads *Alligator Alley* with a bitten-off chunk missing from the side. There are a few people walking in and out of the narrow space, heading for or returning from the other tents nestled in the back.

"Thanks," I say.

"Be careful," he says in return, not looking at me. I nod and head into the crowd.

The air back here is stifling. It smells of sawdust and horses, kerosene and sweat. I cram down the tight passage next to a couple others and squeeze my way forward. I can't see Mab or the blond guy over the heads of everyone, and I've got a sneaking suspicion they wouldn't just be standing out in the open. They're hiding.

I come to an opening in the tent on my left. I glance up. *Tarantina the Tarantuless— "spiderphobes beware"* is written in black ink on the wooden sign. A rubber spider hangs off the edge. Deciding to start at the beginning, I duck inside.

The moment I enter the tent, I feel like I've stepped into the Amazon. Stunted trees arch under the tent's canopy, and long strands of moss droop down like broken wings. All I can see is the winding path in front of me. The floor is dirt and the air is thick and moisture immediately starts dripping down my forehead. There isn't much of a crowd in here, and it doesn't take long to figure out why; every surface is covered in spiders. Brown fuzzy creatures the size of my thumbnail or larger than a plate roam freely over the tent. They dangle from webs in the ceiling, crawl over the moss. A few scurry across the path in front of me.

I shiver in spite of myself. I've never been afraid of spiders, but that doesn't mean I enjoy the idea of a large one dropping down the back of my neck.

I creep through the undergrowth, careful not to step on any of the spiders making their oblivious way underfoot. The only sound in the tent is the hum of cicadas and the occasional disturbing crunching noise; I can't hear the music from outside or the voices of the audience. I feel completely alone. I walk a few steps deeper and turn a corner. The trees close in, reaching out with their leg-like branches. Cobwebs stretch from floor to ceiling.

Something slides across my neck and I jump, my hand immediately swatting at it.

A woman stands behind me. Her hair is long and braided, her skin deep brown. She's wearing leopard skin and leather. Her feet are bare. There's a tarantula the size of my fist on her shoulder and another creeping through her hair. Tiny spiders crawl up and down her legs.

"Vivienne," she says, flashing a razor-toothed smile. Her eyes glint gold and black.

I take a deep, steadying breath and thank the gods I didn't scream.

"Taran...tina?" I say.

She laughs, though her voice deepens. Her face changes.

"*Heath?*"

He chuckles. It's just Heath's face—stubble and all—that's similar. The rest is definitely feminine. He gestures to his body with the hand not holding the spider.

"Convincing, eh?" he says. "Janet usually does this gig, but she's on security instead."

"Security?"

Heath's smile slips. He doesn't answer.

"Oh, right." I pause. "Has Mab come through here?"

"Hell no," he says. "You're my only visitor so far. Well, a couple kids came through but they ran off when they met Honey." He holds up the tarantula.

"Okay, thanks," I say, turning around.

"You're not looking for trouble, are you?" he asks, his voice sliding back into cool feminine tones.

"Never," I say, and head toward the exit.

"Good," he/she says. "Because I've got a feeling trouble won't have any problem finding you."

❖

The alley is a little less crowded now. I can hear the music from the big top and know they've probably already called out that the second half is about to start. Everyone is heading toward the chapiteau. I stand on tiptoes, trying to peer over the crowd, and see a shock of pale white hair near the end of the path. I don't wait. I push into the crowd and make my way toward the end of the lane.

When I get there, the man is nowhere to be seen. The crowd has thinned out and I'm standing alone in a small cul-de-sac. I turn around. I would have seen him leave, and Mab wouldn't have allowed magic with punters around. That's when I notice the small space hiding between the tents. A backstage exit.

I step toward it and then stop. If Mab catches me sneaking out through there, she'll know I was following her. I might as well sign my own death warrant. I need to be crafty. Inconspicuous. I glance at the tent next to the alley. *Human Pincushion—adultz only* is written on the sign in curling ink. I have to be sneaky.

I duck under the tent flap and enter a room filled with dim light and the scent of hay and oil smoke. The sounds of a viola are coming from a man in the corner, and it's like I've been transported back a few dozen years to the heyday of sideshows. The inner tent walls glow orange in the lantern light and there, on a wooden platform, is a Shifter girl. Her hair is pink and done up in six-inch spikes, and the only thing she's wearing is a black dog collar around her neck. Every square inch of her naked flesh—from neck to nipples to heels—is pierced. Rings, studs, even what look like nails and acupuncture needles, all sparkle in the lamplight as she weaves a small, slow dance on the platform. The tent contains mostly speechless men, all watching her undulate like a slow-motion belly dancer. She catches my eye as I walk in and winks, then goes back to entrancing the crowd. The black cauldron at her feet is already brimming with bills and coins.

I take advantage of the crowd's fixation and sneak to the edge of the tent, where the canvas overlaps, and crouch down. I peer out through the tiniest of cracks. Hidden from the crowds, Mab and the blond guy stand beside a few crates. They're talking, but I can't make anything out over the music. I don't want Mab to see me, but I've already come this far. And besides, I now feel like if someone's fucking with the circus, they're fucking with me. I take my chances and give the occupants of the tent one more glance to make sure no one's looking, then slip out into the night.

I stay low, crouching behind boxes and sticking to the shadows. Mab and the man are talking near one of the parked company semis. I crawl closer, praying that she's too fixated on the man to notice me slinking around. I weave behind the semi and crawl underneath, until I'm only a few feet away from their legs. I nearly yelp as something brushes past me, but a quick glance shows it's only Lilith's cat, Poe. Which means…I look to my other side and sure enough, there she is, hiding next to one of the wheels like a solid shadow. If she sees me, she doesn't make any motion to show it. I try not to sneeze as the scent of brimstone fills my nostrils.

"…direct violation for you to be here, you know this," Mab says. I inch closer and peer up, trying to see her face, but all I can see are her stockings.

"And you are in direct violation of the Blood Autumn treaty," says the man. His voice is smooth and deep, almost musical, with the lilt of an accent I can't place.

Mab pauses.

"I have no idea what you're talking about," she says.

"Don't play stupid. Your time among the mortals is making you soft. I know what I've seen."

"This is a circus," Mab says, her voice pitched dangerously low. "Eyes are meant to be deceived here. What you speak is nonsense. And what you've done is unforgivable. You dare stand in the Winter Court's own land and challenge its queen?"

The man doesn't answer. He shifts his feet, though, which is answer enough.

"I could have you killed," Mab says, "and not even your Summer King would bat an eyelash. You know you are not welcome here, and you know your life is forfeit the moment you step foot on my land. Now, unless you wish to pay for tonight's near-disaster with your life, you will leave. And you will not return."

I expect the man to run. There's blood in Mab's words, a fury begging to be unleashed. Instead, he stands his ground. I have to give him credit; he has balls.

"As you say, Queen Mab," he says. "But we are on to you. The dream trade will stop unless you meet our demands." He steps back and turns, begins walking away. "Even queens must pay for their actions. Even queens must die."

Then, without any signal I can see, the man vanishes from the night.

Mab sighs and stands there a moment longer.

Then, reaching down to the tabby cat now purring at her feet, she says, "You can come out now, Lilith dear. It's safe once more. The bad man is gone."

Lilith comes out of her hiding place, her frilly black dress smeared with mud.

"What does he want?" Lilith asks. Something about her voice makes me shiver. It's not as vapid as usual.

"Nothing important," she says, stroking Lilith's hair like a pet. "Nothing to worry yourself over. Come, let's get you some cotton candy."

She guides Lilith away, Poe following close at their heels. I stay there a moment longer, waiting for the blond man to show up, waiting for someone to come under and yell, "Hah! Found you!" But there's only the rumble of the crowd behind me. The music in the tent changes, but I don't head back to my seat. I don't wend my way back through the sideshow. I just lie there in the cold mud, too distracted to shiver, watching the woods on the far end of the field.

I know without a doubt that there's more to Sabina's murder than a random act. Mab is hiding something. And I have a terrible feeling that her secret will get us all killed.

Chapter Six: Thief of Hearts

The next morning, before the sun is even up, someone bangs on my trailer door. My heart sinks the moment I gain consciousness. Experience has proven that waking up like this is never a good sign. I pull on a shirt and shorts and open the door. Sure enough, it's Kingston, looking like the whole world's on fire and he's just too tired to give a damn.

"We're leaving," he says, handing me a travel mug of what smells like coffee. "In twenty minutes. They're disconnecting the water in ten, so you might want to hurry if you want to shower."

"Wait, what? What time is it?" My head still feels like it's swimming and I've got that sharp taste in my sinuses that I'm positive is God's punishment for waking up at the ass-crack of dawn.

"Five," he says without checking a watch. "And I already told you the important part: we're leaving."

"But, we aren't scheduled to jump 'til tomorrow." I take a deep drink from the coffee, hoping that maybe it will help me remember the day of shows I've apparently missed.

"And Mab changed her mind last night. Look," he says, and I really do look at him. He looks about as bad as Mel did yesterday, with dark circles under his eyes. His black hair is tangled and I'm pretty certain that's the shirt he was wearing yesterday, but I don't mention it. "Don't ask questions, okay? For your own sake. Just go take a quick shower or brush your teeth or whatever you do in the morning, grab something to eat, and get in the truck. You're riding with Lilith and Penelope."

"But the tent," I say, and then I realize why something about the view seemed off. My door opens out to the chapiteau. And yet right now, it's all empty field. It clicks. "Wait, so Mab...she used *magic* to take the tent down? I thought she refused to do that."

"Don't assume," Kingston snaps. He takes a deep breath, grabs the coffee from my hands, and takes a drink. "To be more precise, she used *my* magic last night to take the tent down. And now, I either want to sleep for the week or die. I'm not fussy. But I'm also not asking questions, and I suggest you do the same." He takes another drink, grimaces, and swirls his fingers over the lid. I don't see anything happen, but the next swig he takes brings a relieved smile to his face. "Much better," he says.

He takes another big gulp and hands it back to me, then turns away and starts back to his own trailer. "Ten minutes," he calls back. "And be careful with that. It's strong."

I take a drink and nearly burn my throat. He's spiked it with something that tastes like Kahlua and nail varnish. I dump it out in the grass and go find my toothbrush. When I go back outside, I'm not at all surprised to see that spot of grass is already turning brown.

No one knows where the next site is.

Apparently, Mab's completely changed the tour schedule overnight, refunding everyone who bought in advance and donating a dollar to Clowns Without Borders for every refunded ticket, just to soften the blow. At least, this is what Penelope tells me in the truck as we make our way to some unknown destination, following the semi in front of us. I'm hoping no one needs to stop for a piss on the way—myself included. I've got a feeling Mab hasn't scheduled any stops for the drive. Penelope's driving, with me riding passenger and Lilith riding bitch. Poe is curled up in Lilith's lap, fast asleep. The kid hasn't said anything, and Penelope—usually full of conversation—isn't doing her part to mend the silence. NPR is playing in the background, but all I'm really paying attention to is the landscape sliding by and my deep, deep desire to pass out with my face pressed to the window. I am not a morning person, and the clock on the dashboard is telling me it's only 7:13.

"What you did the other day," Penelope says, breaking me from my stupor. "It was quite brave." She reaches over and rustles Lilith's hair. "If you hadn't jumped in there, our little girl might have been crushed." She smiles over at Lilith like calling her "our little girl" is some sort of compliment or like the kid is completely mentally vacant. It's probably a bit of both.

"Just seemed like the right thing to do," I mutter. Clearly it was the right thing to do; the surprise came from the fact that no one else had done it.

For her part, Lilith just stares at the road ahead, not really responding except by stroking the contented Poe.

"What did you get up to last night?" Penelope asks, seemingly out of nowhere.

I glance at her.

"What do you mean?"

"Well," she says, not taking her eyes off the road. "I saw you come into the sideshow, but I never saw you leave. And I was in that tank for quite a long time. I find it to be relaxing." She says the last bit like it's some secret, as though swimming in a tank for a crowd of gawking people is her idea of a spa day.

A beat passes. My brain is too tired to try and come up with a suitable answer. I hadn't gone back to my trailer until the second act was nearly over, and although I'd gone to bed right away, I couldn't sleep at all. She's got me cornered, but she doesn't seem to realize it.

Apparently my lack of an answer is enough for her.

"It was a curious night, was it not?" she continues.

"I guess so." I wish she'd just let me sleep. There's no way I'm going to make it out of this conversation without sticking my foot in something.

"Did you run into Mab last night?"

I can't help but jerk my head to look at her. She's still not looking at me, though, and her voice is light.

"I only ask because I saw her enter Alligator Alley a few moments before you. It's quite rare that she makes an appearance backstage. Especially with company. That man she was with…perhaps she found another plaything."

Of course Penelope would have seen Mab and the man go backstage. I do my best to look completely unfazed. Disinterested.

"Didn't see her," I lie, and pray I'm getting better at it.

For a horrifying moment, I envision Lilith saying that she and I were hiding out under one of the trailers, spying on Mab, but she doesn't seem to be paying us any attention.

"Hmm, well, they didn't come out the same way either. They must have found something worth exploring." She giggles to herself, and I lean back against the seat. I close my eyes. *Just let me sleep.* I really couldn't care less if Penelope thinks Mab was screwing dangerous-looking Scandinavians.

"I've been wondering," she says, after I've had just enough time to drift. "The terms of your contract, what are they?"

I sigh. Force myself awake. There's no point trying anymore; Penelope wants company. And she certainly won't get any juicy stories out of Lilith.

"I don't know," I say as I watch the road signs fly past.

"You don't know?" she asks. There's an incredulous note in her voice I don't like.

"I don't remember," I say. "All I remember is signing the contract."

"Interesting," she says, almost a purr. "*Remembering* one's contract is often a part of the contract itself, lest people forget why they joined on in the first place. I wonder if she had Kingston—" Then she catches herself, though the slip seems far from unintentional, and switches the subject. "No matter. The past is the past, after all."

Lilith stirs beside me, making it impossible for me to concentrate on this new piece of information.

"Kingston. Kingston is pretty. King, king, king of hearts." Her words are quiet, barely a whisper to her cat.

"He is pretty," I say. Lilith is nearly a teenager, but I feel like I'm talking to a baby. "But I think he and Mel are a thing."

Penelope laughs, then, which sounds horribly loud in the cab. When she finally gets herself under control, she throws me a glance and a devious smile.

"Oh, my dear," she says, "I think not. Melody is, well. Melody plays for the other team, if you know what I mean."

I arch an eyebrow. "Melody's gay?"

"You didn't realize?" she says. "Your brain must be more addled than I expected. Haven't you noticed how she looks at you? No, Kingston and Melody are not a *thing*. He hasn't been in a serious relationship for at least a dozen years. Trust me, I know everything in this company."

If it wasn't 7 a.m., and if I didn't feel like my head was stuffed with cotton candy, I would have laughed. Melody's gay. And Kingston is single. Which means I'm in the clear. I have been all along. I don't know if it's relief flooding through me, but I definitely feel better than I have since falling for him. Then the other half of Penelope's statement tries to crash through my sleep-deprived mind. A dozen years? Is that some sort of joke? I don't say anything, though. My feelings for Kingston are something I refuse to let her know about. Lilith is still humming Kingston's name under her breath, singing it like some nursery song to Poe.

"Don't tell me you have a thing for him?" Penelope says, looking over at me with an eyebrow raised.

"I don't—"

Lilith pipes up then, "Kingston is pretty. I like Kingston. He understands. He burns, too."

Penelope continues on like Lilith's not even there.

"Well?" she asks. "Don't lie. I'm ever so good at picking out lies."

And I'm ever so shit at lying.

"I guess…yeah," I say. So much for keeping my cards hidden. Lilith looks at me. One eye twitches, and her expression doesn't look so blank. "I think he's nice," I continue, though under Lilith's gaze it comes out more as a question.

"Kingston *is* nice," Lilith says, and her voice is a dangerous whisper, a frighteningly sane contrast. "Kingston is nice to me, and Kingston is mine."

I stare at her a moment and then her face glazes over again, and she's stroking Poe and humming under her breath once more.

Penelope casts me a glance. "Looks like *someone's* got a crush."

I can tell she's not just talking about Lilith. I lean back against the window and close my eyes, wishing I'd shut up ten minutes ago.

"Well then," Mab said, standing in one feline-smooth motion. It was only then that I realized she had changed clothes completely without me noticing, sometime between meeting me outside and coming in here. She was now in an elegant black lace dress, a burgundy bra and panties showing through the sheer fabric. I felt the heat in my cheeks rise at this—she's probably old enough to be my mother, which she made an easy fact to forget—and looked at the walls. She continued speaking as if she weren't wearing something almost too scandalous for Victoria's Secret.

"Now that your terms are settled, I'll show you around the company. You'll find that we are a very warm, open community here." She swept around the desk and put a hand on my shoulder. "Are you ready?"

She helped me to my feet and opened the door to the trailer. It was still pouring outside, but the moment she stepped out there was a large lacy umbrella in her hand, the type you'd expect to see Morticia holding in The Addams Family.

She held it out for me, and when I stepped out into the rain, the door shut behind us on its own accord.

She led me around the trailers, pointing out who lived where and what the daily schedule was like, when to wake up for breakfast, and when my turn for washing pots would be. The exact memory was hazy; sometimes, when I thought back, I remembered blood on the knees of my jeans. Other times, I just remember them being ragged.

"And this," she said, leading me to a small tent pitched up next to what she called the pie cart, "is Kingston. Consider him your tutor, if you will."

"Vivienne," Kingston said, and I was too entranced by everything to realize he already knew my name. His eyes were deep brown, the color of coffee, and there was something about the way his lip curved in the corner that made it look like he was on the verge of a joke. He was stunning. "It's nice to meet you. Mab said you'd be joining us soon."

I remember glancing back to Mab, who was smiling but had a look in her eyes that said, quite clearly, no more.

Kingston cleared his throat and took my hand. His touch was warm. He was in jeans and a worn Icelandic-style sweater, and there was a thick paperback on the table next to him. I tried to smile, but my heart was still racing from whatever it was that came before this. His touch wasn't helping any, either.

"Nice to meet you," I said.

For the first time in a long time, I actually meant it.

A few miles pass us by, and I'm starting to feel more awake. The caravan of trucks stops at a gas station around nine, and we all get out, stretch our legs, and head straight for the Dunkin' Donuts for coffee and sugar. Kingston's in there with Mel. They both look like they're coming off some bad trip, with dark circles under their eyes and a shake to their hands as they hold their coffee cups. In the fluorescent lighting, their skin looks like paper. The high from Penelope's revelation wears off. Here

I was, thinking I'd run in and do something brave and stupid like kissing Kingston without so much as a hello. But they both look like they're five steps from the grave. Not the time for large acts of desperation.

"You guys look like shit," I say as I walk up to them. "You feeling okay?"

"What do you think?" Kingston says.

He starts to leave, and Melody and I follow. We sit on a concrete bench out front, one overlooking the highway and the sun that's already burning through the haze of traffic. Kingston fishes around in his pocket and pulls out a pack of unmarked cigarettes. He takes one out and brings it to his lips, cups the other hand around it like he has a lighter, though I know it's just a feint. The smoke that curls out smells like cinnamon and brimstone. His eyes practically flutter with happiness, though he still looks bone tired. We watch the rest of the troupe mill around for a while. Lilith's near the dog park, doing somersaults in the grass while Poe stretches in the sun. When no one says anything, I speak up.

"I saw something last night." There's no one around, and Mab's still in her black Jag E-Type, but I'm whispering nonetheless. I don't care what Penelope was trying to hint at; these two are my only friends. "I tried to tell you after the act. But there was a guy in the crowd. Blond, seemed pissed off at everything." I look at Kingston but he's concentrating on his cigarette. He just doesn't want to admit he should have listened. "After you found Mab, she came out and took him backstage."

"So that's what you were doing," Melody says. I stare at her. "What? I was talking with Heath last night. He said you came in looking for Mab."

Are there any safe secrets in this troupe? I look at Kingston and remember Lilith's outburst. I wonder how long it will take for it to get back to him. I wonder if he'll still talk to me after he knows. I take a few sips of coffee and then continue.

"Yeah, well, I found her. She and this guy, they were talking out back. Something about some treaty being broken."

"They're always looking for some reason to shut us down," Kingston finally says.

"Who?"

"The Summer Court. Only other time we had to pack up like last night was '83. Mab was raging for weeks."

'83. So maybe Penelope wasn't joking about his love life. I can't help but stare at him and try to figure out if even his twenty-four-year-old body is one of his illusions. It's not something I have brain power to think about. Melody nods and takes another nibble from her doughnut. She's hunched over herself, elbows on knees, brown hair falling over her eyes. Give her some emaciated ribs and she'd easily pass for a junkie.

"But why?" I ask. "We're just a circus."

Kingston laughs and Mel chuckles, which once more turns into a hack she tries to hide behind a drink of coffee.

"*Just* a circus?" he asks. "You really think that's what this whole operation is?"

I raise an eyebrow. "What else would it be? We travel around the country in a blue and grey tent, putting on shows. Sounds like a circus to me."

"Viv," Melody says when her coughing fit's over. "We're talking about Queen Mab here. The Faerie Queen of legend, ruler of the Winter Court. You really think she just gave up ruling an entire kingdom to wander the mortal world and put on a show?"

I shrug. "Everyone gets bored, right?"

Mel shakes her head and shares a what-an-idiot look with Kingston. Then she looks back at me with a grin on her face.

"Time for a lesson in supply and demand," she says. "What do faeries live on?"

"I dunno. Honey?"

Kingston laughs again and continues where Melody left off.

"Not quite. Faeries live off *dreams*. Why do you think faerie tales exist in the first place? The fey are secretive as hell; if they wanted to remain anonymous, they would. So why would a group that prefers to stay away from mankind let mankind even know they exist?"

"I…"

"Right," he says. "You don't know. Faerie tales are like seeds." He waves a hand, and the smoke trailing from his cigarette curls into itself, forms a tight little nut-shape floating in the air. "We tell them to kids because it makes their imaginations run wild with thoughts of magic and the supernatural." The smoke-seed breaks open, tendrils sprouting wildly like vines. "Those thoughts feed the fey. Without them, they die."

I interrupt him. "What happened before humans?"

"I've never asked," Kingston says, an eyebrow raised. "The point is," he continues, the tree of smoke-vines before him beginning to fade and wilt, "over time, faerie tales started to lose their ability to inspire. Kids believed them, but adults stopped. Technology overtook the story." The smoke fades out entirely, blown away in a gust of wind. "The stories weren't enough. So, Mab decided to be proactive. A more in-your-face approach."

"She made us," I say.

"She made us," Kingston continues. "We spark people's imaginations, get adults dreaming of the impossible. And those dreams, all those hopes and fantasies, they feed the fey."

Melody spreads her arms wide. "We are the lunch ladies of the faerie world. The Dream Traders."

She chuckles and coughs again, which stifles the humor of her statement.

"Okay, I'll buy it," I say. "But if that's the case, why would the Summer Court want us to stop?"

Kingston gets an evil grin and takes one last, long drag on his cigarette, then flicks it to the curb. It turns into a moth and flutters away before ever hitting the concrete.

"Because," he says, "if you hadn't noticed, Mab's a woman of business. All those dreams we procure, all that magical faerie food? It's reserved. All for the Winter Court. Which, of course, means Summer is hungry. And pissed."

"Can't they make their own damn show?" I say.

"Come on," Kingston says. "Faeries are proud. The Summer King would never stoop to imitating his enemy."

"Besides," Mel says, "The name *Cirque du Soleil* was already taken."

We reach the new site a few hours later, in some town whose name I missed in between napping. It's on a beach, I get that much. The trucks park a few hundred yards from the shoreline in what looks like an old soccer field. I jump out of the cab and stretch my legs. Poe slinks beside me and vanishes under the truck; Lilith slides out behind him.

"Lilith," I say, quietly, once the door is shut. "What did Mab say to you last night? After you left?" She's looking at me with a blank expression on her face. "You know," I continue, "after she met with the bad man. We were hiding under the truck." I crouch down to emphasize the point. She smiles, and I try to smile too. Her smile quickly fades.

"You're mean," she says. The sober tone is back. "You help me, make me think you're my friend. But you want to take him from me. You're bad. Bad. Just like bad man."

Then she turns and runs off, cartwheeling toward the tide. I watch her go with a sinking feeling in my stomach. Just looking at her brings the scent of brimstone back to my nostrils. That, and the fact that when I looked into those green eyes, a part of me felt like I should be screaming.

CHAPTER SEVEN: BYE BYE BABY

The tent gets set up that night. I half-expect Mab to come out and demand that Kingston magic the tent back to standing, but much to my surprise—and Kingston's, apparently—he's been given the night off. Melody, Kingston and I sit on the beach and watch the moon rise over the water while behind us, lit by giant floodlights that turn everything the color of bone, the tent rises like a monstrous skeleton. The sound of the waves is accented with thuds and clangs and curses from the tent crew as they work their graveyard shift.

We don't really talk, the three of us. Instead, we share two bottles of red wine and sink back into the sand. After the day we've had, there's really not much space to say anything. All any of us are after is the calm that comes from good company and contented silence. Halfway through the first bottle, Melody lays her head in Kingston's lap and stares at the stars while he runs his fingers absentmindedly through her hair. Something turns over in my chest when I see that, some memory of comfort and love I can't quite place, but I don't say anything. Now that I know it's entirely platonic, I'm only filled with the hope that maybe, someday, he'll act like that with me. I'm already tipsy before I can start thinking how I feel about this, this sudden knowledge that I have a sliver of a chance with Kingston. I can't tell if it makes things easier or worse.

"I really don't know what's wrong with you," he whispers to Mel, and he seriously sounds sorry about it, like it's all his fault. She reaches up and touches his arm.

"Don't worry," she says with a small smile. "I'll be fine."

I turn back to watch the tide, my head filled with thoughts I wish I could share but can't bring myself to voice. The man from the Summer Court, Lilith's disapproving glare. My contract. It hasn't even been a month and I feel more confused than when I started, like maybe things were simpler before I came here. Whatever "before here" actually entailed. The wine is not making it any easier to think.

A few minutes later, I look back over at the two of them, watching him run his fingers through her hair. Mel's eyes are closed and her chest is rising and falling in rhythm with the tide. She looks peaceful like that, fast asleep. Even peaceful when she lets out a soft snore. Kingston's looking out at the moon, his eyes distant. I'd give anything to switch places with Melody, to have him run his fingers through my hair.

He looks to me and smiles. Just that is enough to make my stomach warm.

"Why do you look at her like that?" I whisper, the wine making me bolder than I should be. Melody doesn't stir.

"Like what?" he asks. He doesn't stop twining his fingers through her hair. Yeah, I'd give anything to switch spots.

"Like you're responsible for her."

"You wouldn't understand."

I huff and lean back into the sand.

"I could be here a while," I say. "You might as well get used to the fact that if I don't understand now, I will eventually."

"What do you mean?"

I think back to my conversation with Penelope, though the memory is a swirl of wine.

"I don't know how long my contract is," I say.

He says nothing to that, but he doesn't look away. It's me that has to avert my gaze; there's an intensity in those coffee-colored eyes I just can't match.

"I *am* responsible for her," he finally says.

"What?"

"Melody. I'm responsible for her."

"She's twenty-two," I say.

"Age is deceiving," he replies. I know he's not just talking about Mel. He looks away. "I found her, much like—" he stutters, "much like Mab found you. If not for me, she wouldn't be here." He brings his gaze back down and traces a finger along Mel's forehead. Maybe it's the drink, but I swear a faint blue light swirls beneath her skin, a pattern I barely glimpse before it's gone. "If not for me," he whispers, so soft I can barely hear it, "she wouldn't be getting sick."

"It's not your fault," I say, though the defense sounds weak. He doesn't say anything, so I try to make an actual point of it. "I mean, Mab brought me here and some crazy shit's gone down, but I don't regret it."

I look back to the tent, to the Shifters milling around. The sides are being pulled up now, the skeleton gaining skin.

"This is better than whatever I came from," I say, though even as the words are leaving my mouth, I know it's not true. I have no idea what I came from. I can't even remember what street I lived on. The thought infuriates me for a moment, makes me want to scream at the top of my lungs and rip everything apart. And then it's gone, and I don't know what I was thinking about in the first place.

He laughs, and I look over.

"What?" I ask. What were we talking about?

He's smiling. It looks genuine.

"You're cute," he says. "Drunk is a good look on you."

"I'm not drunk," I say. I realize a little too late that it sounds slurred. I chuckle and fall back in the sand.

"Get some sleep," he says.

I don't want to, but after all the running around today and the lack of sleep last night, it's hard to resist.

I close my eyes and listen to the waves as I sway with the heaviness of wine. I want to tell him he's beautiful, that he isn't responsible for everyone.

That Melody's lucky no matter what because she has him looking out for her. I don't say any of this; the words just won't piece together. I'm drifting when I feel something brush through my hair. I don't open my eyes to see if the fingers are real or just my imagination. *Melody's lucky she has you.* When sleep comes, it washes everything to grey.

❖

"Shit," Kingston says, and I'm pulled from dreams of nothing. The sun is just rising, the pale light making everything pink and purple and beautiful. But that's not enough to mask the screams coming from the tent. I sit up, sand stuck to every inch of me. Both Melody and Kingston are pushing themselves to standing.

"You don't think?" Mel asks, and Kingston closes his eyes. Although he looks much more well-rested than yesterday, there's a weariness around his eyes that seems to grow by the minute. If it weren't for the screaming, I'd be sorely tempted to tell him to go back to sleep.

"I don't want to find out," he says.

My heart is sinking into the dirt. A crowd gathers by one of the trailers, and the scene from a few days ago is playing on loop in my head.

"Come on," I say, and head toward the chaos.

The two of them are right behind me, and it's not 'til I'm running up the grassy slope toward the field that I realize Melody's lagging behind. I turn back. No, not lagging, limping. One arm is around Kingston, her face twisted with pain. She must have slept wrong or something. I don't slow down. I want to see this before Mab takes over.

When I reach the trailers and push my way to the front of the crowd, I'm immediately glad I haven't eaten anything yet.

It's Roman. He's naked, except for socks and boxers, like he'd been killed in his sleep. Except he was clearly awake for this; his eyes and mouth are wide open and his body is arched back, supported by six swords piercing his spine, the tips just poking out the front of his torso.

He's covered in thick blood that drips down his arms and pools on the grass below. His powder-blue mohawk is stained purple. Flies are already gathering.

I push aside the nausea and look around, scan the crowd, try to find someone who's missing, something out of place. But everyone's there, and everyone looks horribly shocked. Everyone except for Lilith, who's nowhere to be seen.

The crowd parts like a sobbing Red Sea the moment Mab arrives. She isn't even trying to look mortal, now. She glides over the ground like a wraith, the grass beneath her long, black, smoke-like dress turning to ice. Her green eyes are blazing, and I swear her nails are talons.

"What is the meaning of this?" she hisses, and the crowd draws back. She moves forward and reaches out, her hand hovering an inch above Roman's face. "Roman," she whispers, the intensity of her rage dimming with her words. "Who did this to you?"

She turns back to the crowd and points. Again, they part, all of them except Sheena, the purple-haired girl who was working the novelties booth two nights ago. She seems rooted to the spot, her eyes locked on Mab's. I can tell she's not afraid, but she looks wary.

"Come here, girl," Mab says.

As Sheena steps forward, the troupe looks at her with fear and anger in their eyes, and I feel my own pulse start to race. Mab's narrowed it down. Mab knows the killer, Mab is about to tell the world. My heart is hammering in my ears. It was Sheena all along. But why?

Sheena walks straight up to Mab and stares up into the eyes of hell, her head held high. I have to give it to the girl; she's keeping calm even though every single one of us knows she's about to turn to dust. Every nerve and muscle in me tightens, ready to fire as judgment is dealt.

"I should have done this the first time," Mab says. She raises a hand...

...and steps aside, leaving a space for Sheena to approach the body.

"My Queen?" Sheena asks.

"It must be done," Mab replies.

Something crosses Sheena's features, hesitation and loathing, but she nods anyway. Her eyes close, her fingers clench into fists. And then she changes.

It's not Shifter magic, which—according to Kingston—isn't really magic at all, but something else entirely. Sheena's body shivers like static on a screen, a flash of purple light and smoke, and then she's no longer there. In her place is a tiny hovering orb of violet light. It takes a moment for the truth to hit, but there's no mistaking that Tinkerbell-esque glow. She's a fucking faerie.

I expect some great wave of magic, maybe for Roman to start speaking in tongues from his bladed bed, or for sparks of lightning to shoot out. But nothing happens. There's a haze of smoke around the orb that seems to wrap around the body, but it's so faint in the light of day that I can't really see it. A few moments pass, and then I blink and the girl is standing there again, all purple hair and blue jeans. She looks down at the ground.

"I'm sorry, my Queen," she whispers. "I cannot divine. Someone has hidden his sight from me."

Mab hisses and the air around her grows dark, just for a moment.

"The Summer King," she seethes. "It must be him."

Sheena bows and steps back into the crowd. People edge away from her like she's diseased, but I see the flickers in a few people's eyes—the recognition, the longing. Sheena's not the only fey hiding in our midst, but she's clearly the only one who's been outed. For the life of me, I can't figure out why she looks like her dirtiest of secrets has just been aired. After all, it's not like Mab makes any attempt at hiding what *she* is.

"What is this?" someone asks, and I look over to see the guy next to me—one of the jugglers, the one I don't know—take a half step forward. "Mab, what's going on?"

She studies him for a moment. I can't stop staring at the blood dripping down from Roman's pinky.

"It would seem," she says, "that the Summer Court is trying to force us down. Which,"—she raises her voice—"Will. Not. Happen. Do you hear me, Oberon? My show *will* go on."

I expect thunder to crackle or clouds to gather, but there's no retaliation, no mark her words were heard. Everyone seems to be holding their breath, myself included.

"This...this wasn't part of the contract," the juggler continues. He takes a deep breath and looks around for support, but no one's looking him in the eye. He's sweating, but he doesn't back down. He's got guts. Mab raises an eyebrow. "You told us we'd be immortal so long as the contracts stood." He takes another breath and I can feel everyone's hackles rise.

Behind me, I catch Kingston whispering under his breath, "Don't do it, you fucking idiot. Don't do it."

"Sabina's dead. Now Roman. None of us are safe. Which means... which means our contracts are void."

Mab smirks, but there isn't even a drop of humor there. She takes a step forward.

"Is that so, Paul?" she says. Her voice is ice. "You believe your contract is forfeit?"

There's a curl in Mab's words that promises something horrible, but Paul isn't stopping now that he's gained steam. I have a sinking suspicion he's been waiting to say this since Sabina had her throat sliced open.

"Yes," he says. "Your part of the deal was immortality. I'm not going to sit around and wait for that to be proven false again."

Mab chuckles. "You have served me for ninety-two years, Paul. And you are due to serve another forty before your contract is up. But if you believe I have failed my end of the bargain, well, I am an honest businesswoman if nothing else. I follow my own rules. You are free to go."

The guy slouches visibly with relief.

"Thank you," he says.

She nods and he begins to turn away.

"But," she whispers. The word hangs in the air like an executioner's ax. "As you will clearly remember from line 76C, early termination of the contract for whatever reason also terminates the magic that kept you—what did you call it? *Immortal.*" Paul stiffens and looks back, his eyes wide. "Which means, my dear servant, that I can no longer protect you from the hands of time. Ninety-two years is a long time, Paul. And had you just waited another forty, you could have prevented them from ever catching up with you."

Paul opens his mouth, but no sound comes out. He reaches both hands up to his neck and makes a horrible gagging noise. No one goes to help him. We all just take a step backward and try not to flinch.

He drops to his knees as wrinkles etch themselves into his face and hands, his skin yellowing and sagging, his veins bulging blue. His hair turns white in a matter of seconds and falls to the ground like dandelion fluff, his teeth yellowing and following in stony suit. His whole body dries up from the inside out. His eyes roll back in his head as a spasm wracks him. He topples. And like a husk, he caves in upon himself, flesh eating skin, until all that's left is a pile of clothes and a few mounds of ash.

"A shame," Mab says, almost to herself. "I've lost two good performers today."

She looks straight at me. Her eyes pin me like a cobra's. "Vivienne. Can you juggle?"

"I—" Then I realize it's not a question and nod, my stomach sinking even further. Melody said I wouldn't make it here if I didn't learn to lie. I'm starting to think the opposite is true.

"Good," Mab continues, completely ignoring my lack of confidence. "You will learn your routine from Vanessa and Richard. If you are not onstage by this time next week, you will be fired."

She snaps her fingers, and Roman's body collapses in a cloud of blue dust behind her.

"The show *will* go on," she says again. "With or without the lot of you."

In a sweep of shadows, she vanishes.

CHAPTER EIGHT: YOUR LITTLE BODY'S SLOWLY BREAKING DOWN

No one says anything after Mab leaves the murder site, but as the crowd disperses, Melody and Kingston stick behind with me. The two other jugglers—Vanessa, who's short with a brown bob, and Richard, who's tall with wavy black hair and a heart tattooed on his arm—come up and say they rehearse three hours a day, between lunch and dinner, and they'll help me get as good as Paul in no time. They both look at Kingston when they say this, as though he holds the secret to success in his fingertips. When they leave, I can't help but feel like I've been roped into a losing fight. It's amazing how fast things can fall to shit.

"Come on," Kingston says. He glances back at the swords scattered on the ground. Although Roman's body is gone, his blood is still congealing in the sun. "Let's get out of here."

We head to a picnic bench on the edge of the beach. Melody is walking on her own, but she's still got a limp, and Kingston hovers by her side like he's waiting for her to collapse. When we reach the table, she leans back onto the wood and lies back to look at the sky.

"Remind me not to sleep on the beach again," she says. "I feel like sand should have asked me on a date first."

Kingston laughs but gives me an *I told you so* sort of look when she breaks into another cough. She's definitely getting worse. But even after our talk last night, I refuse to believe he can be responsible for it. Whatever *it* is.

"So," Mel continues, oblivious to the shared look. "A juggler, eh? Frankly, I pinned you as more of an acrobat myself."

"I'd rather not think about it," I say. "I've never juggled in my life. Anyway, what the hell's going on with you? Are you okay?"

She closes her eyes and the grin slips. "Nice diversion," she says. "I'm fine."

It would have been a convincing cover-up, if not for the hacking fit that immediately followed.

"Kingston?" I ask.

He sighs. "I don't know. I can't heal it, whatever it is."

"I'm still here," she says.

"I'm not saying anything you don't already know," he says. "Besides, Vivienne's a friend. She deserves to know."

And yeah, it's sick in light of everything that's happened in the last twenty minutes, but that statement makes me feel really, really good.

"Fine," Mel says. "Yes, Vivienne. I appear to be quite ill, and our all-powerful witch can't do anything about it. As you said, I'd rather not think about it."

"I was going to talk to Mab," Kingston says, half to me and half to Melody. "Whatever this is, it's not normal. But I don't know if she's in the right mood to be confronted with another loophole."

I sit down on the table and look back at the trailers. I wonder who's going to gather up Roman's swords, and who's going to take his place as head of the Shifters. I wonder if his blood will still be pooled on the ground when we go back.

"What do you think she's going to do?" I ask. "I mean, clearly this isn't a one-time thing. First Sabina, then Roman. If that Summer guy was telling the truth, we're going to keep getting picked off one by one until the show falls apart."

"I don't even know," Kingston says with a sigh. He runs his hands through his lank hair and looks out at the waves. "As far as I'm concerned, we're already falling apart. All the Summer Court has to do is pull the right thread, and we're done."

"But they can't, right? It's Mab. You heard her. The show will go on."

Melody answers, her words laced with bitterness. "Don't gloss over the details, love. *With or without the lot of you,* she said. She's only concerned with the show. I have no doubt that she's willing to accept a few casualties if it means she can keep playing ringleader. Never stopped her before."

She looks like she's about to say more, but Kingston glares at her, which shuts her up instantly. No one says anything after that. It's clear that she's overstepped a line in the sand I'm not supposed to see. Apparently I don't deserve to know everything. I can only hope that what I don't know doesn't get me killed.

As they promised, Richard and Vanessa find me at lunch that afternoon. I'm sitting across from Kingston while Melody rests in her trailer. I hadn't said much to him during the meal. What was there to say? Sorry one of your friends died like one of Vlad Dracula's victims, but hey, I hear you're single so maybe we can go out to dinner sometime? By the way, what is it that you're so obviously hiding from me, because I'm getting tired of waiting around, and I might be the next to go? There's nothing *to* say, and the silence just grows and grows between us. Not that anyone else in the troupe is talkative. Today's meal is even quieter than when Sabina was killed. So I just eat my salad and pasta primavera, and stare at Kingston's left arm, where the head of his serpentine tattoo has suddenly taken up residence.

Vanessa spots me first. She sits down on my left side, setting her tray with a half-eaten salad and juice next to mine. The distraction is an immediate relief that I know won't last long. She smiles at me, and I can't tell if it's friendly or laced with you-can-never-replace-him undertones.

It makes me wonder if she and Paul ever had a thing in those ninety-two years of service.

"So," she says, barely giving Kingston a second glance. "Do you actually know how to juggle?"

"Kind of," I say. I try to think back, try to remember juggling oranges in my kitchen or something like that. The images are there, but they don't seem to piece together quite right. It's like looking through someone else's childhood scrapbook. "I think so."

"Don't worry," she says. "If we can't train you, Kingston can always bewitch you into stardom."

Kingston coughs slightly. "You know it doesn't work like that, Vanessa," he says over his mug.

Vanessa waves her hand, "Fine, fine, whatever it is you do, then. I'm just saying, with my skill and your magic, we'll have no problem turning her into a young star."

"What do you mean?" I ask. Okay, I know I probably couldn't juggle if my life depended on it—and my life probably *does* depend on it—but I don't think I'm that hopeless.

"I think it's best if he explains," Vanessa says. "I'd just get it wrong."

"There's nothing to explain," Kingston says evenly. "How about you just do your job and train her. When that inevitably fails, come find me."

Vanessa opens her mouth, but Richard's arrival spares us from whatever she's about to say. He steps up behind her and puts his broad hands on her shoulders. He looks maybe ten years older than her; he's probably in his late thirties. But when she looks up at him, her face instantly becomes all smiles. If that isn't an I'm-sleeping-with-you look, I don't know what is.

"Hey, guys," he says. "Am I interrupting?"

"Not at all," Kingston replies.

"Good," he says. "I was hoping I could steal Vanessa. We're going to have to piece together a duo act for tonight." He turns to me. "Unless you think you'll be ready by then?" He grins.

I decide in that moment that if I had to choose to save either him or Vanessa from being eaten by sharks, I'd choose him. Neither of them act fazed by the fact that their partner was just aged to death in front of their eyes. Maybe Kingston was right; maybe everyone *is* only looking after their own asses.

"Only if you want it to be a clown act," I say. I can no longer remember if it was juggling I was good at as a kid, or unicycling. Or maybe I'd just *wanted* to be able to do them.

He chuckles and helps Vanessa to her feet. They walk off, leaving me, Kingston, and Vanessa's half-empty tray.

"Bitch," Kingston says the moment she's out of earshot.

"What was that all about?" I ask.

"She's still pissed that I slept with Richard a few decades back. In my defense, they hadn't been seeing each other for at least a year. Girl can hold a fucking grudge."

My stomach does a flip and I can't tell if it's because he just admitted to sleeping with a guy or because he just said he's at least a *few decades* old. Then again, after watching Paul turn to ash, the notion that Kingston is much older than he appears isn't as shocking as it should have been. My mouth is hanging open like a fish, which just brings a smile to his face.

"What? It gets boring here. You can't blame me for playing both sides of the field."

Which just makes me wonder how many people he *has* slept with. I mean, I can't judge. Even though I can't remember my sexual exploits— which doesn't speak very highly of them—I know I'm no virgin. But still...*how many?* I didn't even really care about the genders.

"I...That's not what I meant. What did she mean by that whole bewitching me to stardom thing?" I say.

"Oh."

Kingston picks at the food on his plate, then looks up at me and points his fork at my face.

"How do I put this? You've seen *The Matrix,* right?"

"Sadly." I'm not certain how that memory stands out, but it's there, swimming in the haze of my past.

He smiles, but his voice is serious. "Well, it's sort of like that. If necessary, I can…download, if you will, things into your memory. Make you know how to do things you couldn't do before."

"You what?"

"It sounds bad," he says. "But I don't use it if I don't have to, and even then, I only use it if the person asks. And *even then*, only if Mab allows it, and writes it into the contract. But she almost never allows cutting corners."

"So you could make me think anything you wanted."

Like making me fall madly in love with him. The moment the thought crosses my mind, I push it away. After all, if Disney taught me anything, it's that love can't be forced through magic. Thank you Aladdin.

He raises an eyebrow. "In theory, yes. In practice, no." His voice drops. "Consider me reformed."

Then he points his fork at Vanessa's salad and it bursts into flames, instantly disintegrating into ash.

"Don't fool yourself, Vivienne," he whispers, almost to himself. "I might have the magic, but the others…they'll get into your head way before me."

❖

Practice is a disaster.

I don't know what I was expecting, but it certainly wasn't the black eye and three bruises on my chest from missed passes. So after about twenty minutes of having clubs thrown at my face and torso, and subsequently missing every single one, Richard and Vanessa give me three juggling balls. They scoot me over to one corner, where I can practice without interrupting them and they can keep an eye on me.

"It's like trying to keep a beat," Vanessa says in a voice most people reserve for very small and very stupid children. "You have to imagine a rhythm, and throw at the proper time." She demonstrates by throwing the balls in the air, while saying, "One, two, three, catch."

They land in her hands like magic. I don't care that she's probably been doing this longer than I've been alive: I hate her for making it look so easy. "Keep trying," she says, and hands them back to me. She stands up to go and I stand with her, but she puts a hand on my shoulder and pushes me back down. "No," she says. "Don't move around. The balls need to stay in one plane. If you move, you won't learn anything."

Then she goes back over to Richard—who is, of course, practicing with knives. Eight of them. They're even on fire. I stay in the corner to fumble around on my own. I try. Over and over. But I don't have the coordination, and with every failed attempt, the image of Mab's angry face grows in my mind. Then I just start freaking out that in this case, getting fired might actually mean getting incinerated. An hour later, Vanessa tells me to head out before I frustrate myself. A bit too late for that. I drop the balls into their prop trunk and wander off, sorely tempted to find Kingston and have him *Matrix* me.

I don't, of course. Instead, I make my way back to the trailers and find Sheena sitting by herself under the awning of the dining area, a book in one hand and a mug in the other. I've only spoken with her once, in my first week here. She took me aside after dinner and asked to read my tea leaves. As I drank down the bitter tea, we made small talk about life and art and how nice it was to get away. When she read the dregs, her eyebrows furrowed, and she said my future was hazy, like my past. Then she started talking about all the indie bands she'd seen on tour, and asked what sort of music I liked. We hadn't spoken much since then, but she smiled at me whenever she saw me. For me, that made her my friend. I sit down beside her, and it's not until I clear my throat that she looks up and notices me there.

"Oh, Vivienne. Sorry." She holds up the book. "Got carried away."

"It's fine," I say. I've been trying to figure out how to broach the subject all day, and I still haven't gotten an idea. So I just ask straight out, "Why are you hiding that you're a faerie? I mean, you're in good company."

She does a little half-smile and puts the book down. It's then that I notice the coffee cup is empty, but she's still cradling it like it's the nectar of life.

"Well," she says. "That's a political matter. I'm kind of a refugee."

A few months ago, I'd have no clue what she was talking about. Now I was catching on.

"You're from the Summer Court," I say, because it's not really a question.

She smiles at me, and her cheeks dimple. "Yes," she says. "A few years ago, I found myself on the losing end of a deal with a satyr. My only option was to flee, but in Faerie, there's nowhere to go. Mab found me and offered me sanctuary in exchange for my services to the show."

"And let me guess: the Summer Court still has a warrant out for your arrest."

Sheena laughs at this. "I'd say *arrest* is a nice way of putting it. Eternal torture and servitude is more accurate."

"Thus the human disguise."

She nods, and her smile slips. "I don't know *how* you manage to do it. Human skin is so...suffocating."

"Are you worried?" I ask. "That someone will sell you out? Now that you're in the open."

"Not really," she says. The smile she gives me is horribly sad. "Mab and I sorted that out when I signed on. If I'm ever taken from the troupe against my will, my life is immediately forfeit."

"You mean your contract will kill you if you're stolen?"

"Yes," she says. "There are many worse things than death."

And now we're edging close to the subject I've wanted to ask her about all day. I still don't have a nice segue, so I just ask.

"Like what happened to Roman?" I whisper.

"Yes," she says. "Though his death was quick in comparison to what to my own fate would be. He was just a half-blood, not a traitor like me."

I pick the next words carefully. Sheena seems to be the first person who is honestly willing to talk about what's been going on. I don't want to mess this up.

"So...your safety's clearly important to Mab. Why would she jeopardize all that? What was she asking you to do?"

"Big questions," Sheena says. "And I can't answer the first because I truly do not know. As to what she wanted from me, well...in my contract, she has the right to call upon my skills whenever she deems it necessary. Today was such a time."

"And those skills are?"

"I'm a medium."

"You're like Miss Cleo?"

"No," she says with a laugh. "When I'm in my true form, I can communicate with the recently deceased, before they pass on. I can catch the last few moments of their life, ask them questions. In the case of murder, I can see who or what killed them."

"But you said you were blocked from Roman?"

"Yes," she says, and her eyes look down to the ground. "His spirit was there. I could sense it. But it was blocked. I couldn't reach it."

"I take it that's never happened before."

She laughs, "It should be impossible. Like everything else going on."

The show goes up that night without a hitch. Anyone on the outside wouldn't have noticed a thing. But for those of us within the troupe, well, it felt different. There's an energy before a show—an excitement and expectation—like every time has the potential to feel like the first. Not so this time around. The clouds came in shortly after dinner; the sky grew heavy, mirroring our mood. There was no pre-show circle and cheer. There was no pep talk from Mab to rally our spirits after the horrendous morning. No. She was absent, appearing only to introduce the show and to do her postintermission whip act. No one knew where she spent the rest of the time, and no one was about to ask.

I watched the jugglers from the side aisle. Vanessa and Richard flipped and cartwheeled and threw clubs and knives and flaming torches high in the air, cartwheeling around before coming together for the dramatic catches. Not a single club was dropped, and when they took their bow, their faces gleamed like they'd been a duo act all along. The entire thing made my stomach clench. There was no way in hell I'd ever be that good. No way. Not in a week.

When the magic show was up, Melody appeared onstage with a ton of makeup to cover whatever was ailing her, and Kingston played up his part of fumbling magician with panache. For their final trick, he waved his wand in the air, chanting a gibberish spell he told the crowd would make Melody grow ten feet tall before their very eyes. "A feat," he said, "defying the laws of her seemingly prepubescent nature." But rather than change height, she disappeared in a puff of pink smoke and laughing applause. Kingston bowed and walked offstage. I followed.

"How's she feeling?" I ask when I find him backstage.

"Horrible," he says. He flops down on a trunk and peels off the cape, tossing it onto the table beside him. This time, the serpent tattoo is curled over his stomach, the head nestled between his shoulder blades and the tail spiraled around his navel.

"Where is she?" I ask.

"Back in bed," he says. "I sent her straight back to her trailer. I don't want her getting any worse."

He bites his lip. It doesn't make him look cute or childish. It makes him look like every worry in the world is stacked on his shoulders.

"You really care about her, don't you?" I ask. I want to reach out and comfort him, tell him it will all be okay. But I don't, because I can't be sure about that, and I've already gotten myself neck-deep from one lie today.

"She's like a sister," he says. "I don't know what I'd do if she got hurt." His voice hitches.

That does it for me. I sit down beside him and, before I can think better of it, put an arm around his shoulders. He stiffens and then leans into me, his hair tickling my chin. He smells like talc and spice and I want to remember that scent forever. I don't want to have to let him go.

"She'll be okay," I say, praying it's not a lie. "It's just a cold."

"Don't you get it?" he says, but his words aren't at all harsh and he doesn't push away. He just sounds tired. "She *can't* get sick. She is contractually obligated *not* to get sick, just like the rest of us. She's being targeted."

Things click, things that I don't want making sense.

"You think she's next," I say.

He doesn't answer, just nods and takes a deep, slow breath.

"This is fucked up," he says. "We're just sitting around like ducks waiting to be picked off."

Something burns inside of me, and before I realize what I'm saying, the words tumble out of my mouth.

"I'll protect you. I'll protect both of you."

He leans away from me then and gives me a wry smile.

"That's cute. Heroic, even. But if Mab can't protect us, what hope do you have?"

Chapter Nine: Too Close

I'm wandering around a few hours after the show. The punters are gone, and the lot is empty of cars. A couple performers are outside at the pie cart having cake and coffee and trying to make light conversation, but I don't stick around very long to listen in. My feet feel antsy. The need to wander is tugging at me, but there's nowhere to go. Besides, I don't want to go far after this morning's horrifying reality check. The sky above is completely clouded over, and the air tastes like rain. Out of the corner of my eye, I see something flash, and I shrug it off as lightning. I kick the popcorn box at my feet, trying to convince myself to pick it up and throw it out. I'm still trying to figure out how, precisely, I'm going to protect everyone, and kicking this box around the big top is about all the answer I've found so far. Another flash goes up, this one a soft blue that lasts for more than a split second. I look toward it. Down at the beach, someone is shooting off fireworks.

The time it takes for my mind to decide between *popcorn box* and *fireworks* is infinitesimal. I head to the beach.

Once I've left the pitch behind and am halfway down the sloping lawn, I hear the music. It gets louder with every footstep, and the fireworks are growing more chaotic. Brilliant flashes and bursts are going up every second. But they aren't making any noise, and nothing's flying higher than the shrubs that are blocking my view. Must just be ground flares or something.

I slow down when I reach the shrubs. The music is loud—some pop song with a heavy dance beat that reminds me a bit too much of the music from Noir. I still can't hear any noise from the fireworks, even though I can't be more than a few yards from their detonation point. When I clear the shrubs, I stop.

Kingston is standing in the sand, barefoot and wearing a pair of dark cargo shorts and nothing else. There aren't any fireworks.

He's dancing along to the music, his eyes closed or half-lidded, the sweat making his body shine. His feet trace circles in the sand and his arms sweep around. One hand reaches out, stretching to the lake, and curls of light snake from his forearm and flare over the ground. He looks different, somehow. His hair is matted, sand is covering his bare calves. And that's when I realize what's different. His tattoo is moving.

The serpent is undulating across his skin, twining from neck to shoulder, curling around his arms, as sinuous as the dance Kingston is weaving. Lights pulse from his fingertips, arcing over his body. Every movement of his arms is traced by light, every thrust of his hand and kick of his leg throws sparks over the sand. He is wild and feral, yet his movements are deliberate and controlled, like some form of tai chi on crack. The music is pulsing, pulsing, and he responds.

I know I'm not meant to be seeing this. I don't really know what it is I'm seeing, but it seems personal, private, and the last thing I want is for him to open his eyes, see me there, and stop. I could watch him move all night.

Right before I tear my eyes away, though, he stops and cups his hands at his stomach. His head tilts back to the sky. The music is still throbbing wildly and I want to dance, want him to dance, but something's changing now. The serpent tattoo gathers at his stomach. As he pulls his hands up, the serpent moves, like he's holding it in his hands. He brings his arms above his head and the tattoo writhes up one arm, curls around his wrist, and, in a flood of silver-gold ink, spills into the sky.

I gasp. I can't help it. And that's when Kingston opens his eyes and looks straight into mine. He lowers his arms and the glowing feathered serpent floats in the air above him, curling like a snake in water.

"How long have you been watching?" he asks.

I can hear his voice perfectly, and it's only then that I realize the music has faded out. There isn't a stereo to be seen.

"What are you doing out here?" I ask instead. I can't keep my eyes off the creature hovering and twisting above his head. Its path leaves traces of light behind my eyelids every time I blink.

"Practicing," he says. He follows my gaze and grins. "Vivienne," he says. "Meet Zal."

The serpent-dragon-thingy turns to regard me. And winks.

"What is it?" I ask. I start walking forward, my feet sinking into the sand. I'm drawn to the apparition like a moth to the flame.

"My familiar," he says. The serpent drifts down and wraps around Kingston's outstretched arm, almost like it's perching there. "All witches have one."

I'm only a few feet away now. I can see every glittering scale on the thing. Its body is the palest gold, and the feathers sprouting from its head are teal and mint and dusty rose. Its eyes are golden yellow, like amber. They're the only part of the thing that seems solid. Kingston reaches his free hand over and strokes the snake's mane. I swear it purrs.

"But what *is* it?" I say again.

"A Quetzalcoatl," he says. "I found him while we were doing a tour in Mexico. Mab was in one of her better moods and said it was time I found my familiar. I'd only been with her for a year or two by then, and I still didn't really know what it meant to be, well, a witch." His lip twitches in a smile, as though he's still not used to the word. "Anyway, she took me...somewhere. First, we were walking down some back alley in Mexico City and then, bam. We're in the middle of a tropical jungle straight out of *National Geographic*. And right in front of us was this temple, older than old. Aztec, she said. And hidden from mortals by their priests. It looked like a pyramid, but the sides were entirely made up of steps and there was some sort of pavilion up top. She made me walk up alone. When I got there, I found him curled up on top of an obsidian mirror."

The serpent makes its purring noise again, rubbing its head against Kingston's pec. Kingston smiles and ruffles its feathers.

"The moment I saw him, I knew he was my familiar. It just clicked. He's been with me ever since." He glances at me and his grin widens. "You can pet him, if you want. He doesn't bite."

It's stupid how much I trust Kingston. I reach out and pet the thing without hesitation. It feels like warm static beneath my fingertips, just the barest amount of solidity.

"He's beautiful," I say, because there's really not much else to say when looking at something that probably descended from a god. "Why do you keep him as...why is he your tattoo?"

Kingston shrugs. "Keeps him nearby. A familiar is an animal extension of a witch's soul, so it made sense. Besides, people tend to stare when he's out."

I look from the golden creature to the space on Kingston's chest where it usually resides.

"I think people stare no matter what," I say. The words tumble from my mouth before I can stop them. My face immediately heats up in a violent blush. Thankfully, he just laughs while I desperately try to change the subject.

"Why are you out here?" I ask again, because I know in my gut he hasn't really answered.

Kingston looks down and kicks the sand at his feet like a little boy.

"When I practice...it's the only time I feel like I have any control over all this anymore. You know?"

I nod. I do know. It's the same reason I'm out here, the same reason my tired body refuses to give in and sleep. Someone we care about is in danger and there's nothing—*nothing*—we can do about it.

Kingston stares at me. Not in a quizzical way, and not in a joking way. He's looking at me like he knows precisely what I'm doing on the beach. Like that's throwing him for a loop. I'm suddenly all too aware of my pulse and how it's speeding up. What a first kiss this would be, standing on the beach and bathed in the light of his godly familiar. He catches the current and takes a half step toward me. My heart sticks in my throat. His heat is unbearable, the scent of his cologne fills me as he leans in.

It begins to rain.

And I'm not talking a romantic drizzle, I'm talking about a full-on downpour, like God decided to fuck with me and turn the tap on full blast. Kingston's head shoots up and Zal starts writhing around above his head again. I am soaked to the bone in seconds. When Kingston speaks, I can barely hear him through the din. He looks disappointed and also a little embarrassed.

"We should get you inside," he says, putting a hand on my arm. His touch is hot. I can practically hear the rain sizzling off his skin. "Don't want you getting pneumonia."

I bite my tongue. Go figure. Go *fucking* figure. But I'm not about to act desperate. Not now, not when his familiar's watching like an expectant house cat.

"Right," I say.

We don't say anything else as he guides me back up to the trailers, but his hand doesn't stray from my arm, not until we get back to my bunk and he opens the door. Once I'm inside, he snaps his fingers. I'm dry immediately.

I can't really describe how he looks, standing on the bottom step of my trailer, his hair dripping rivers down his soaked body, and every inch of him glowing in Zal's golden light. One hand is on the door frame, like he's trying to hold himself up. Or back. I'm not sure which. And I want nothing more than to lean over and kiss him goodnight, but I don't.

"Goodnight," I say.

"Goodnight," he replies.

Then he raps his hand on the frame once and steps down. I close the door before I can change my mind about the whole kissing thing. A part of me hopes that he'll knock. I even wait by the door a few breaths, just in case.

He doesn't.

I stay in my bunk 'til one, when the chapiteau is dark and everyone is definitely fast asleep. I'm still antsy after seeing Kingston, and my head is ringing with his words. *It makes me feel like I have some control over all this.* I may not have any magic or a divine familiar, but I'm not about to sit around and wait. No, I'm not going to be that person anymore. When my watch beeps at one, I don my raincoat and head to the pie cart to pour myself a mug of lukewarm coffee. I sit under the canopy of the dining area and watch the trailers. I try not to shiver and try not to look suspicious in case anyone braves the weather to use the Porta-Potties on the edge of the field. No one does. I'm alone for the first cup, and then the second. Kingston's trailer is dark, and I have no doubt he's asleep after our earlier encounter.

I check my watch. One thirty. I pull the raincoat tighter and head out, wandering over to the sparse woods on the other side of the trailers. I crouch the entire time, but no one's out. I find a place among the undergrowth where I'm pretty certain I can blend in with the tree trunk behind me, and I watch. Melody's trailer is right in front of me. I wasn't just being overzealous when I told Kingston I'd protect them. I keep my word.

I sit and I wait. I don't know what I expected when I psyched myself into guard duty, but it wasn't the reality of getting soaked to the bone and having pine cones digging into my ass. I shiver, but I don't move. I watch Melody's door and it's only when I check my watch and see that only twenty-three minutes have gone by that I start to wonder if this is even necessary. If Kingston suspected something, he'd be on guard and would have enchanted or hexed the door to make it impenetrable or something like that. Hell, maybe Zal was patrolling the woods right now, if he could do such a thing. Kingston was right; if Mab couldn't protect us—and if I didn't trust Kingston's magic—what chance did I have? Still, as uncomfortable as it is, I feel better sitting out here in the rain with the owls. At least I'm *thinking* that I'm doing more than I would if I were back in my warm, cozy trailer. I shove the thought away and try to shift my weight off whatever twig is getting a little too personal with my personal space. The rain pours. The trailers stay dark. Nothing happens.

I'm about to call it a night at 1:59 when something crosses my path. My heart leaps into my throat, but I keep quiet. A moment later, I realize it's not a person or Zal or a wandering faerie. It's Poe. The cat curls up at my feet and I reach out to stroke it. Its fur tingles like static under my touch.

"Lilith," I hiss into the rain. "Where are you?"

I can barely hear my own voice over the sound of water falling through the trees, but something above me snaps and I jerk my head to the branches above. There's a shadow moving around up there, though I can't really make it out. She says nothing, but I can tell it's Lilith. The figure waves, and I wonder if I've been forgiven for liking Kingston, or if she's forgotten entirely. At least we have the same idea of whom to protect. I settle back down and keep watch.

Time ticks by and the only things that move are the rain and Poe shifting around in front of me. The cat starts shying away from my touch, so I stop trying, keeping my hands shoved in my pockets to stay warm, and wishing either something would happen or the sun would rise so I could go to bed. I check my watch again. 2:43.

Poe stirs, stretches, and wanders off.

Something behind me rustles, and I assume it's just the cat chasing a waterlogged mouse. Then I hear voices, and my breath catches.

I turn, very, very slowly, and sink even deeper to the forest floor. I try to blend in with the undergrowth that I'm now thanking rather than cursing for making this entire stay uncomfortable as hell.

I can't see anything, not in the darkness. And through the rain, I can't make out distinct voices. Just words. I try to edge closer, every inch of my skin on fire with adrenaline. Someone's definitely out there, someone trying to remain hidden. I sneak closer, down an all fours, my stomach grazing the ground as I crawl. Then I stop, because I can hear them now, two voices. One of them, I'm sure, is the blond guy, but the other? Wherever she is, I hope Lilith's getting a better view than I.

"...can't back out now," the man's voice hisses. I can just imagine him, the shadow of him, standing only a few feet away. "You know what's at stake. The Dream Trade *must* stop."

The response is whispered, a mumble I can barely make out.

"Had *enough?*" the man says. "Too much blood on your hands?"

Another pause, and it sounds like someone's crying their words out. If I could get closer...

"No," the man says. "The next phase will happen, with or without your help."

Another sob.

"If you fail—" and then he pauses. I hear a snap as something moves closer to me. My blood is pounding louder than the rain, and the only thing I can think is *shit shit shit.* Then there's a hiss, and the man curses as Poe leaps from the underbrush.

"Damn cat," he says. Another pause. "Leave," he finally says. "And do your part."

I don't move. I don't know how I can tell, but the guy is gone, vanished like he had before. I don't dare move an inch in case he's hovering somewhere nearby. I stay there, crouched in the mud, waiting for him to put a knife in my back or for the other person to stumble across me. Nothing happens. Time ticks by, and every inch of me aches from stillness. The rain doesn't stop. Lilith doesn't appear by my side. There's nothing but rain and silence.

I don't leave, though. I don't move. Not if something is about to happen, not if there's a threat.

Only when the first streak of light brightens the rain clouds do I move away from my spot. Only when I'm positive Mel hasn't been taken, and that the people I care about are safe. I strip off my raincoat and scurry back to my trailer, stepping gently inside so none of the other bunks register the shift of weight. I dry off and curl up under the covers, hoping I'll get enough sleep to last the rest of the day.

I close my eyes and picture only cold and darkness and conspirators bathed in shadows, but at least my friends are safe. At least we're safe.

CHAPTER TEN: NOTHING FAILS

I don't think my eyes have been closed for ten minutes when someone's knocking at my door. There's bile in my throat and a cold that won't get out of my limbs, but I push myself out of bed and open the door. *No fucking way* keeps repeating in my head. Everyone's safe. They have to be safe. But somehow I know that's not the case.

It's Lilith. Not Kingston, coming to say that someone else has bit the dust. I highly doubt the girl has that sort of mental capacity. I could kiss her in relief.

She ducks under my arm and comes into the room, Poe gripped tight in her hands. Her clothes are dry and clean, but there's a smear of mud across her pale forehead and her eyes are just as shadowed as Melody's were yesterday.

"Bad man," she says the moment she sits on my bed. "Bad man, bad man's here. Bad man wants us."

I look out the door once more and make sure there isn't a commotion. No one is screaming about another death, so I close it and look at the kid shaking back and forth on my bed. She looks like a doll. One that walks around your house at night stealing knives and hiding your puppy in the freezer.

"The bad man," I say. "Yes, you saw him last night. Who was with him?"

"Bad man," she says. "Bad man chasing, bad man finding." She looks up at me. "You can't protect them." Her voice has turned eerily sober once more. "And they can't hide from him. She will die. And he will die. We will all die if the Summer Court finds us."

"Who?" I ask. "Kingston? Mel?"

But she's back in la-la-land, singing Kingston's name under her breath. I sigh. The only other person who saw what happened last night is as good as a vegetable. The sigh becomes a yawn, and I'm about to ask her to leave or at least make room on the bed so I can continue my nap, when there's another knock on my door.

I open it. Kingston. *Fuck.*

"It's Melody," he says before I even say hello. "She's not waking up."

We're out the door and walking toward her trailer in a heartbeat, Lilith at our heels. She's still singing his name, but Kingston doesn't seem to notice. I swear the world has slowed down; I can feel every footfall, every beat of my acidic heart pounding out its terrible truth. I failed. I failed. I failed.

"What happened?" I ask. No one's outside except for the cooks in the pie cart, and the air smells like bacon. "What do you mean she's not waking up?"

He gives me a look. "I went in to check on her. And she didn't wake up. What doesn't click for you?" His words are biting, but they aren't hitting home. If roles were reversed I'd be just as terse.

Lilith giggles at that. "Kingston's smart. Lilith's smart, too."

"Yes you are," he says in an offhand way. Then we're at Melody's door, and he opens it without knocking.

Her bunk is the same size as mine, with the same furniture setup, except the curtains drawn across the windows give the room the feeling of a crypt. The stale air and stench of sweat don't help. Kingston walks right up to the window and opens it, letting in light and fresh air. Melody is on her bed, the sheets tangled around her. I move closer and see the sweat dripping down her forehead. Her eyelids look like they've been covered in dark stage-makeup. She's pale—pale as her white sheets— and except for the slightest tremble of her lips, she's not moving.

Lilith sidles up beside me and stares down at Melody. Poe purrs loudly in her hands.

"Melody's sick?" she asks, like a child asking why Granny isn't coming home from the hospital.

"Very," Kingston says, stepping over to Melody and putting a hand on her forehead. A soft haze seems to flow from his fingertips, but it only lasts a second before he slumps to sitting on the bed as well. He runs his hands through his hair. Zal is once more twined around his arm, its head on the back of Kingston's hand. The ink is a little smudged, as though even the serpent's tired of trying to hold itself together.

"Lilith," he says. "Would you...would you please get Mab?"

"Auntie Mab?" Lilith asks.

"Yes," he says. He sounds so, so tired. "Tell her there's something wrong with Melody. Now, please."

Lilith puts Poe on the ground and nods, then turns and opens the door for her cat. They both slink out into the filtered light.

"You didn't leave her side last night, did you?" There's a thermos sitting on the desk beside her bed, along with a book I remember Kingston carrying around. "You stayed in here to keep an eye on her."

"Someone had to," he says, with more venom in his words than I expected.

"I was outside," I whisper. "In the woods. Watching."

He looks at me and there's a surprised smile on his lips, but it fades in a moment. "I don't know what's wrong. No one came in, nothing changed. Zal was patrolling just outside the trailer all night. I didn't sleep at all and now—" He leans back against the wall and closes his eyes. "Now I'm too tired to light a candle, let alone heal her. I failed her, Viv. She's going to die because of me."

"No, she won't," I say. "I think I know what's going on. Last night, I heard someone out in the woods. Well, two people, but I only heard the one. It was the Summer Court guy. He said something about the next phase needing to happen." I nod my head to Melody and whisper, "Do you think she's the next phase?"

"How could she be?" he asks. "She doesn't have any magic. She's just a girl."

"I thought she was—"

"She's not," Kingston whispers. He closes his eyes, like he doesn't want to witness what he's about to say. "She's mortal, like you. She just doesn't like admitting it."

I stare at Melody for a moment and wonder what got her into this mess. Was she an orphan like me? Or was she running from something else? I sit down on the other end of the bed and put a hand on her forehead. She's burning up. If she *had* been running from something, it looked like it was finally catching up. Knowing this…she looks so much tinier, so much more frail. I always expected her to have some magical ability she never let on, something that made her invincible. But she was normal, mortal, and Kingston brought her here. Why? I don't have time to ask him.

The door opens, and Mab walks in. She's in her sequined dressing gown, her hair loose and curling down her back. Her face is guarded, but she doesn't seem wrathful, at least not now. She closes the door softly behind her and raises an arm like she's throwing confetti into the air. The walls of the bunk glow gold for a moment—the slightest shimmer of light—and then are normal.

"Prying ears," she says, and steps forward, leaning in between Kingston and me to examine Melody.

For a moment, no one says anything as Mab traces Mel's outline with her hands. I watch Mab's face, but it gives nothing away, not a hint of concern or recognition or rage. She is a perfectly painted mask of obsidian eyebrows and crimson lips. When she steps back, she looks at the both of us.

"Which of you found her like this?" she asks, her voice a smoky whisper. It's exactly what she said when we gathered around Sabina. My stomach drops.

"I did," Kingston says. "I didn't leave her last night, after the show. She said she wasn't feeling well, so I decided to keep an eye on her." Neither of us mentions meeting on the beach. Neither of us wants to wonder if *that's* when she became so ill.

"And in the light of all that has happened, you failed to come to me?" Mab's voice has a dangerous edge, even though her tone is still perfectly civil.

"You had enough on your plate," Kingston says. He doesn't flinch from Mab's gaze. I've never seen the two of them interact before this, but somehow, there's no sense of a power struggle. They both seem to be on the same playing field. And that field is way, way above me. "I figured it was just a…a by-product."

There's a silence in the room, then, one that makes me feel they're sharing more than I can catch, one that makes me feel like I shouldn't be there. It makes me wonder if that's precisely why Kingston came and got me first. I'm the buffer to keep Mab's rage in check.

"Perhaps so," Mab says. "But whatever illness has taken her…it's not normal. She has been cursed."

"I know," Kingston says. "I can't break it."

"Nor can I," Mab says. "But that's precisely why you brought her in, isn't it?"

They both look at me.

"What?" I ask.

"I thought, perhaps—" Kingston begins, but Mab waves her hand and cuts him off.

"You put your love of this girl," she says, and a part of me hopes she means me, and not Melody, "before your obligations to the show. Under normal circumstances, you know what that would entail." She looks again at Kingston, and there's a sneer, one that says she's caught on to the game. "But these aren't normal circumstances, are they? You know I'll be kind."

Kingston doesn't contradict her. He just crosses his arms and stares at Mab like they're discussing politics over tea. Mab raises her hands and steps away from the bed.

"I've taught you well," she says. Then she looks at me. "Vivienne, if you please?"

"You want me to leave?" I ask.

"No," she says. "I call upon line 23B of your contract. I request that you break this girl's curse, or at least discover its maker so I may dispose of him. Though," she says, looking at Kingston, "I don't think there's much doubt that the Summer Court is at fault."

Something burns inside of me at her words, something that singes through my brain the moment she utters the word *contract*. I want to say I have no clue what she's talking about, but the fire is building and burning. And then I'm putting my hands on Melody's face, one on each side, and I'm closing my eyes. The fire inside is flash and thunder and everything is roaring, roaring, the world ripping apart and filing itself back together. It's nails on concrete fire in water trees on fire burning through suns and stars and emptiness circling the tunnel of falling, falling, falling into white. Then there's someone's words cutting through it all.

"I call upon line 23C. Forget."

And I'm back. There's only a ringing in my ears and a heat in my head, but there's no fire or thunder anymore. I'm sitting on Melody's bed covered in sweat and shaking. I can't tell if I'm starving or about to throw up. Mab and Kingston are both looking at me with blank expressions on their faces.

"Well," Mab says. "That was most…unenlightening."

"What, what was that?" I manage, though my words are sour in my throat.

"None of your concern," Mab says. She raises an eyebrow. "Nothing happened, you just aren't feeling well. Or don't you remember?"

"I…" But I don't remember. I just remember sitting in the trailer, listening to them talk about curses and Mel and then feeling faint. "What was I talking about?"

"Nothing," Kingston says, putting a hand on my shoulder. There's no magic, this time, but his presence cuts through the sickness anyway. "We should get you out of here, in case whatever Melody has is catching."

He helps me to my feet and squeezes me past Mab, who is still looking at me like an interesting specimen. Kingston opens the door for me and ushers me out, an arm looped around my waist.

"I...does Mab know what's going on?"

"Not yet," Kingston says. He speaks slowly, like the words are hard to find. "But we have a better idea now of what we're up against."

"And?"

He looks at me and tries to smile. It slips into a grimace. "And it isn't good."

Melody doesn't wake up for lunch, so Kingston and I spend the meal outside her trailer, dining and talking as the clouds from yesterday's rain slowly dissipate. He even brought a picnic blanket. It would be romantic, if not for the fact that we're both waiting for Mel to cry out and need us. I can't help but notice the way Kingston twitches every time there's a noise. I'm surprised he hasn't asked Zal to keep an eye out, but the tattoo is still wrapped around a bare arm. Maybe his familiar can only come out on special occasions.

"You going to practice?" Kingston asks, clearly trying to keep the conversation light. We can see the pie cart from here, and people are slowly starting to meander off to wash their plates and practice or take a quick run into town. I see that Richard and Vanessa have a table to themselves, and seem deep in discussion.

"I don't think there's a point in practicing anymore," I say. It feels stupid, worrying about learning how to juggle when one of my only friends is practically in a coma and we're all at risk of getting murdered. But, as Mab said, the show must go on, with or without us. Just the thought of being thrown back to the outside world makes my stomach flip. I try not to count the days I have left on my fingers.

He takes a deep breath. "If you want, I could help out."

The weight of what he says stuns me for a moment. Sure, I'd entertained the idea, but having him actually offer to mess with my mind makes me pause.

"I thought you said you didn't do that anymore."

He looks away, toward Melody's door. "I'll do what I have to to keep you around. Even if Mab said what she did in anger, she can't negate it. Faeries can't lie."

"It's not important," I say, though I'm touched by his words. There's more to this guy than I first thought. "I kind of think there are bigger things at stake."

He sighs. "Maybe."

"Why is it such a big deal?" I say. "The Dream Trade, I mean."

The question's been nagging at me ever since he mentioned it, and after last night's spying venture, it sounds like there's more to it than just sustenance. It almost sounded like some drug cartel, the way the Summer Court was willing to kill just to have it stop. But they're just dreams. Surely there are other ways of making people imagine.

Kingston takes a bite of his apple and stares up at the sun. "I told you, dreams are what keep the faeries alive. If people didn't dream about them, they wouldn't exist."

"So they're figments of our imagination?"

He chuckles. "Ask Mab that and find out. No, it's more like a symbiotic relationship."

"Last night when I was in the woods, the guy said the Dream Trade must stop. What if this isn't about killing us? What if the Summer Court just wants Mab to stop hogging all the faerie food?"

Kingston grins at me. "I'm sure Mab already thought of that, and it's really not so cut and dry." He tosses the apple aside and stands, reaching his hand down to me. I take it; his grip is warm and slightly sticky. He pulls me to standing. "It's time you saw the Wheel," he says.

I don't question. He doesn't let go of my hand as he takes me around to another trailer. His touch tingles, and I don't know if it's magic or my imagination or some combination of both. I half-expect him to take me to some invisible, hidden door, but it's just another bunk like any other. Door number zero.

"Now," he says, looking over his shoulder with a conspiratorial grin, "You can't tell anyone I showed you this. Technically speaking, Mab and I are the only ones allowed in."

I glance around. There's no one nearby—they're all at lunch or practice. I'm hoping my streak of rebellious bad luck isn't still with me.

"Maybe we shouldn't—" I begin. "I don't want her more pissed off."

"Pussy," Kingston says. He squeezes my hand, though, and pulls open the door, stepping inside and dragging me in behind him.

The door closes silently, and at first it's as dark as Mab's trailer. It smells of hay and barn wood and summer heat. Kingston snaps his fingers and a flame appears, balancing on the tip of his index finger.

The flame floats out of his hand and disperses to all corners of the room, lighting a couple dozen candles along the way. The room glows with warm light, its contents slowly coming into focus.

It's about ten feet square—much larger than the trailer, which makes me think we're not actually in the trailer at all—and the walls are wood. The floor is cobblestone with tufts of hay scattered across the smooth grey stones. The room is entirely bare except for a single structure in the middle of the room. It's wood and round and clunky and covered in threads. A loom.

It's so ordinary it's a letdown—not that I've seen any looms in real life. I could easily imagine Rumpelstiltskin sitting on one side, turning a pile of straw into gold. But there's no one there. Still, the giant wheel— easily my height—turns slowly on its own, pulling a myriad of strings into place, the shuttle sliding back and forth at a lazy pace. Kingston takes me around to one side, to where the completed pattern is working itself out and draping into a large wicker basket.

"This," he says, "is what all the fuss is about."

I stare at it.

The fabric the loom produces is beautiful, sure. It's a rainbow piece of cloth covered in twisting patterns and colorful swirls, but it doesn't look special. Probably not worth creating an entire circus for. Definitely not worth killing over. Sabina's and Roman's and Melody's bodies flash through my mind. All that suffering and loss, all for a bit of pretty silk?

"That's it?" I say. I can't help but sound disappointed. I was picturing some beautiful golden Wheel of Fate or something encrusted with diamonds. Something more up Mab's alley. This? This is just something out of a heritage museum. It's borderline pathetic.

"I knew you'd say that," Kingston says. "Which is precisely why I brought you here."

A pair of tiny scissors appears in his hands. The blades glint in the candlelight. He reaches down into the basket and snips, pulling out a tiny square of cloth. It's barely the size of a thumbnail.

"This," he says, holding the square with the scissor blades like a tiny morsel, "would sell in the Night Market for a minor favor or a day's worth of subjugation." He holds it out. "But I'll give you a taste for free."

"It's a scrap of fabric."

"Just touch it," he says. I reach out. He drops the tiny blue square of cloth in my palm.

Lights explode across my vision and suddenly I'm no longer in the trailer; I'm soaring through the clouds, light shining from the heavens. My arms are stretched out to the sides and I'm giddy, laughing, bubbling with happiness. I swoop down, break cloud cover and smile at the brilliant green fields that stretch all the way to the horizon. I bank right, coast into a beam of soft sunlight—

And I'm back. My arms are stretched out to the sides and there's a giant grin on my face. I quickly drop my hands and try to force away the dopey smile. Definitely not quickly enough.

"Flying dream, eh?" he says. "Should have thought as much. Blues usually are."

I look down at the fabric in my hand. The tiny bolt is now grey. The moment I move, it dissolves into ash.

"One use only, I'm afraid," he says.

"What was that?"

"A dream," he says. "Energy. Pure, creative, spontaneous energy. Mortals experience it as visions. For the fey, it's like oxygen."

I look at the loom.

"So this, what, converts dreams into fabric?"

Kingston shrugs. "Something like that. It solidifies energy, focuses it into something tangible. I've seen Mab store it in crystals and books and skulls, whatever takes her fancy. This is just easier to regulate. She can sell by the yard and make a killer profit."

"You make her sound like some sort of drug lord," I say.

"What's the point of drugs if not to dream?" he says, and I can't think of any way to counter that.

"Anyway, that's the Trade. Mab converts all dreams in the tent into this, which she then sells or distributes to the other fey. Her own Court gets a discount, while Summer is taxed. But they need it, so they pay. Mortals don't dream as much as they used to, and Summer's still putting all their effort into the publishing industry…which wasn't their best idea."

I watch the loom weave its slow pattern, imagining it working double-speed when the tent is full and imaginations soaring.

"I still don't see why it's such a big deal," I say.

"It's sustenance for them," Kingston says. He moves in a little closer. "Entire civilizations have been destroyed for less. Religion, ideology, love." He looks at me, a wild glint in his eyes. "Love is usually the one everyone feels is worth dying over."

"Have you ever been in love?" I ask. I don't know where the words come from. I only know I want him to answer without words, the way I'd like to draw him close and breathe him in.

"Have you?"

I reach out, my hand only an inch from his arm.

And then there's a knock at the door. Kingston jerks back and walks over to it. *Damn* my shitty luck.

"Should I hide?" I ask. Even as I say it, I know there's nowhere to hide in the space.

He just looks at me and shakes his head with a smile that makes me feel idiotic. He opens the door. It's Lilith. She barely gives me a second glance as she steps into the room.

"Saw you, saw you come here," she says. "Important, important." She goes up on tiptoes to whisper something in his ear, something that makes his eyes go wide. If he looked pale before, now he looks positively ghostly.

"Show me," he says, and jumps out the door. Lilith goes right after him. Neither of them look back to see if I'm following, but I run over and hop out the door into the blinding sun. They're already sprinting toward the chapiteau. I follow.

Lilith takes us around to the far side of the tent, the one facing the woods. Poe is sitting beside one of the support stakes, staring at the blue wall panel with a bristle to his fur. Lilith slows down when she gets there. It takes me a moment to figure out what caused Kingston to raise a hand to his mouth. Then I see it. There, in the seam between the blue and grey panels, is a rip. Not just a tiny tear, but a good eight-foot gash that starts just above arm's reach and stops a few inches above the grass.

"No," Kingston whispers over and over, like a terrible mantra. I look away from the rip and stare at him. Lilith is kneeling at his side, one hand out to pet Poe, the other reaching up to lace around Kingston's fingers. He looks mortified.

After a moment of standing there, I ask the question digging at me. "What's the big deal?"

He looks at me like I've just spoken the worst of heresies.

"Get Mab," he says through his fingertips. "Get her. Now."

I know that look, 'the sky is falling' darkness, and I turn without question and run straight toward Mab's trailer.

Mab's door opens immediately after the first knock.

She stands before me in a leather vest and a black mesh undershirt that reaches her knee-high leather boots. Her leggings are black leather as well, and her waist is cinched with a belt of tiny silver skulls. Behind her, the trailer is swathed in shadows and candlelight and the scent of moss and pine. She leans out the door toward me. I step back, almost dropping into a curtsy.

"Mab," I say. "Kingston…Kingston told me to get you. The tent—"

"What about the tent?" she asks, cutting me off. She steps down and the door closes behind her. "What else could possibly go wrong today?"

"There's a rip."

She actually flinches back at this, as though I've slapped her across her rouged cheekbones. One hand goes to her chest, the other reaches out and grabs me by the shirt. She pulls me in close. "Show me."

I lead her across the grounds, over to where Kingston and Lilith are still standing. Neither of them has moved. Even Poe is transfixed by the rip.

Mab releases my shirt and steps past the two of them, one hand just barely touching the tent, her fingers flinching back as though it's on fire. She hovers there a moment, her face unreadable, and none of us dares to breathe, let alone ask what's going on. *It's just a fucking rip in the seam,* I want to say, but clearly there's more to it than that. Like most things in this company, I have no doubt there's more to this than meets the eye.

"We tear down now," Mab says. Her voice is quiet, and there's a waver in her words. That note of fear is enough to make me believe the worst. She was calm for the murders, for the confrontation with the Summer Court's herald. Whatever this is, it's worse than all of that, and I have a terrible feeling it's only the beginning of the end.

CHAPTER ELEVEN: SOONER OR LATER

I can bring you somewhere safe," she said. She offered her hand, and I took it. I don't remember why I had been in the alley, and I don't know what had brought me to listen to a strange woman in the middle of Detroit. All I remember is that when she smiled, I believed her. Nothing could have been worse than what lay behind me.

She led me down the street, not saying much. People passed by us with umbrellas and raincoats and didn't look at us twice, even though we should have looked out of place. They may have been dark shadows moving through the mist and rain. But Mab and I, we were something darker, something hidden in the corners of sight. When I think back, the one thing I remember is the greyness, the melancholy, and the splash of crimson that was Mab's dress. Then we turned the corner and stepped into another world.

The tent rose above us in the neon-lit park, all blue and wild and vibrant, Cirque des Immortels *roaring in acid-green lights. It was color and sound, reds and blues and yellows, tufts of fire and spinning clubs. Music cartwheeled through the crowd that laughed and pointed in the broad avenue leading up to the tent. I stopped, speechless, and watched as giants on stilts trundled past, stared at the woman clothed in only a python standing beside a sign for a freak show. Mab put a hand on my shoulder, but she didn't make me move. The place smelled of popcorn and cotton candy and something else, something that defied scent. Something that smelled like energy and excitement.*

"Welcome," she said. "Welcome to your new home."

❖

There's a pause after Mab's declaration. She stands there, staring at the rip in the tent, and none of us dares to breathe. Finally, she turns around and crouches low so she's at Lilith's level. Poe prowls around her feet, rubbing against her leather boots. She ignores him.

"Lilith, baby," she whispers, "Auntie Mab needs you to tell the Shifters to come at once. When you've done that, I need you to go into my trailer with Poe and hide until I find you."

"Hide?" Lilith says, cocking her head to one side like a broken bird.

"Yes, sweetie," Mab says. She reaches out and pets Lilith's head. The exchange makes me cringe. "I fear the bad man might be nearby, and we don't want him finding you."

She stands as Lilith scampers away, Poe at her heels. She looks at Kingston and me, takes a deep breath, and then hesitates. Mab never hesitates. Mab is assured, confident, powerful. Once more, I feel the end drawing near. In spite of the heat, my skin is covered in goose bumps. I want nothing more than to grab Kingston's hand for support, but he still looks shell-shocked and worlds away. Besides, I can't show weakness. Not now. Not in front of Mab.

"Kingston," she finally says. "It is becoming increasingly clear that someone is trying to destroy us. I fear we may have a spy in our Court." Am I imagining it, or did her eyes flicker to me? "After teardown, you will go ahead to the next site. Take no one, tell no one. Once there, you will use every enchantment at your disposal to make the ground hallowed. Do I make myself clear?"

Kingston swallows hard and nods.

"Vivienne," Mab says, turning her serpent's gaze to me. "I am putting you under surveillance. You will be placed under Penelope's watch until this situation has been sorted and your name cleared. Yes?"

"I..." I falter under her gaze, but there's a feeling of indignation in me that flares for just a moment. *She's* the one that brought me here. *She's* the one who promised I'd be safe. And now *I'm* the one she suspects is behind all this? "Why?"

Mab takes one slow, dangerous step forward. She is taller than me by only a few inches, but her anger makes her taller.

"Given your past," she says with a decided twist to the word, "you are a suspect individual." Her eyes bore into me, and I have the sense she's seeing something I can't. Memories seep into my head, the color red on my knees the day she led me here, the feeling of needing to run, to get as far away as fast as I could. I clench my fists. Was I running from myself?

Then she steps aside and begins to walk away and the train of thought derails into nothingness. "Besides," she says, not even turning back. "Lilith has already told me you were sneaking around last night. If you don't want to be a suspect, I propose you refrain from suspicious activities."

The fire in me wants to run after her, wants to grab her arm and demand she tell me what the hell she's talking about. But before I can make what would probably be the worst—and last—mistake of my life, Kingston puts his hand on my shoulder and the rage dies down.

"Come on," he whispers. "Let's get out of here before the Shifters arrive."

With that, he draws me away from the tent and leads me toward the pie cart.

❖

"I always find problems are easier to deal with over coffee," he says, handing me a mug. I didn't miss the slight hand-wave over the rim as he passed it over, so I'm more than suspicious as I take a sip. Unlike the last time he magically spiked my drink, this one doesn't taste like battery acid. I try not to wince as I take a few long gulps, hoping either the caffeine or magical alcohol helps settle my nerves. Neither does.

"What was she talking about?" I finally ask. "What did she mean, *given my past?*"

I watch Kingston as I ask this and can't help but notice that he's studiously looking away.

"I don't know," he finally says. "It's *your* past, after all." Maybe I'm just getting better at lying or he's getting worse, but I have no doubt whatsoever that he isn't telling me the truth.

Up until then, it hadn't really bothered me that I couldn't dredge up the details of my past. It was one of those things that just seemed better *not* to think about: high school, sitting bored in math class, driving lessons, summers at the public pool or playing video games. It was all there, but it was all coated over, hazy almost. And as far as I was concerned, that was probably a good thing. The trouble was, it was all so plain, so generic; there was nothing there that would make someone suspicious of me.

Except for those times when, looking back, I could have sworn there was blood on my jeans the day Mab found me. Blood that wasn't mine. But even that memory is slippery. Maybe it was just a dream.

I run a hand through my hair and close my eyes. There are worse fates than being put with Penelope for a few days. Much better than a sword through the gut or half-decapitation. At least, that's what I try to convince myself. Some doubt lingers in the back of my head, though. What if it *was* me? The deaths happened at night…what if I sleepwalked or was under a spell or something?

A moment later there's a hand on my arm, and then Kingston's leaning in. He smells like cologne and coffee, a mix that's oddly comforting.

"I'm sorry," he whispers. "I know how unfair Mab can be, but she's just scared."

"I'm not the killer," I say. *At least, I don't think I am.* "I almost saw them, last night."

"Well, if it's any consolation, I don't think you're the killer either."

I open my eyes and look at him. He's looking right at me, his face only a few inches away. How many times have we been like this? Half a step away from leaning in and kissing, a second away from doing what my heart's been begging me to do since I first laid eyes on him. If I wanted to, I could end the streak; I could lean in and kiss him here and now.

"Why not?" I ask.

"Because," he says. His comforting smile turns wicked. "You're too much of a wimp to kill anyone." He taps my nose with one finger and pulls away, hops off the table, and stands, stretching back like a cat. I can feel myself blushing. Another moment lost. I'm hoping it's not some sort of karmic trend.

"I better be off," he says. "Mab would skin me alive if she knew I was still waiting around."

He turns to go and then stops, looks back.

"Keep yourself out of trouble," he says. His face is serious. "I mean it."

"You too," I say.

He winks. "Me? Never."

Then he's walking away, and I'm left with a cooling cup of coffee and the sense that nothing's going to get easier to deal with, not anytime soon.

❖

"How is your practice going?" Penelope asks. We're once again in her trailer as the rest of the crew does the grunt work. I can see the tent from the window; Mab is out there with a few Shifters. They're carefully folding up the ripped panel like a flag. It doesn't touch the ground once.

"What?" I ask, not looking away. There's a steamer trunk at Mab's feet, and the two Shifters are gently placing the panel inside of it.

"Your juggling practice. I assume you've been training night and day." She talks as though that's clearly the only thing I should be concerned about, as though there's nothing going wrong. Maybe she really does spend all of her time secluded away in her trailer, lost in her own little world. I can't really blame her for it. Outside, Mab closes the lid and latches it.

I turn my focus back to the computer. Penelope's at another laptop, figuring out losses and gains and ticket sales. Once more, Mab's refunding the tickets for tonight's show and donating to nonprofits so people won't be too pissed for missing the sold-out performance. And I'm the one sending out the notification emails, each one personally addressed because Mab likes things to have that personal touch.

"Practice? Not good," I say. "I wasn't made to juggle."

Penelope sighs and taps away at her keyboard. She looks tired, like the rest of the troupe, with a light layer of makeup and a faded *Cirque des Immortels* hoodie. I hate to admit that she makes even that look attractive.

"Mab's always like that," she says. "I should know. Always making rash decisions she can't get out of later."

I shrug and go back to emailing Mr. Carson, apologizing to him and his two lovely daughters for having to refund the tickets but promising to donate to St. Jude's to offset the harm done. Somehow, Mab has more than just his contact details on file. There's a full paragraph of his family history, his employment status and income, and even a line at the bottom that I hope is a joke. *What the customer dreamt of becoming as a child.* Mr. Carson, apparently, wanted to be an astronaut. Now he's the general manager of a local Taco Bell. If she has this much information about her customers, I can't help but imagine what she has on file for the rest of us. Which makes me wonder...

"That memory you showed me...you said that you were with her before that, before the circus got started?" I ask.

"Indeed," Penelope says, not looking up from her work. "I was with her for the very first show. It was just her and me on tour, then. I was but a child. The Only Living Fiji Mermaid, she called me." Penelope looks up at me. "Not exactly the way a girl should grow up, though there was *some* glamour on the road. When we weren't at Court, she and I would stand on the busiest boulevards in the biggest cities: London, Paris, Berlin. She would erect a fish tank and set me inside of it. I would wave and smile at the crowds and she would collect the gold."

"Why did she need gold?" I ask. Mr. Carson's been sent out, and now I'm staring at a photo of Miss Jessica Meyers, thirty-two, who once wanted to be a ballerina.

"She didn't," Penelope says. "It was the attachment she needed. People gave us money because we had inspired something within them, got them dreaming of the impossible. That infused what they paid us. It was, if nothing else, a very crude beginning to the Trade."

How long has this been going on? But that's not what I really want to ask her.

"So how long is your contract?" I ask.

She doesn't answer right away. She looks at me for a long moment, seeming to study whether or not I'm worthy enough for the answer.

"Life," she finally says, her voice filled with a resolute sadness. The word fills the room.

"But I thought...I thought we couldn't die? It's in the contracts."

"Now you're finally catching on to the way Mab works." She looks back down at the computer.

"So...you're here forever."

"Perhaps," she says. "There's always an exit clause."

"What is it?" I ask.

"If you're trying to keep your head down after being accused of murder, my dear, asking about the termination of people's contracts isn't the way to go about it."

I blush and look back to my screen. I start tapping in Miss Meyers's name, apologizing for the horrible inconvenience, and saying we've booked her a ticket for the ballet that's coming through next month. I can feel Penelope's eyes still settled on me.

"Besides," she finally says. She goes back to typing. "What you should really be worried about is your own exit clause. No one wants to run away forever, not really."

"I don't know it," I say. "I don't remember what I signed, or why I even did it. It must have seemed worth it at the time."

Another pause.

"You remember nothing at all?" she asks.

"No. But apparently it was enough to make Mab suspect me of killing everyone." I hadn't said it aloud before this, but the words spill from my lips and hang in the air like bloodstains. It's like signing my own death warrant, and I can't help but wonder if telling this to the gossip queen of the troupe is a terrible mistake.

"Interesting," she says. She gives me a considering glance. "You don't strike me as the murderous type."

"Try telling her that," I say. I lean back in the chair and try to block out everything swarming around in my head. There's no way in hell I'll be able to get a juggling act together for Friday, no way I'll be able to clear my name even if I do. The only way around it is to find the real killer, which isn't going to happen with Penelope as my new guardian. And there's another reason I need to find the killer. I need to make sure it's not me. I mean, I *know* I overheard the Summer Court dude talking to someone else. It *can't* be me. But a small part of me is saying that stranger things have been happening.

"Mab wouldn't listen to me," Penelope says. "You know how she is." A brief pause. "We all have pasts we wish we could run from, Vivienne. The trouble is, they always manage to catch up with us in the end, no matter the magic attempting to keep it at bay."

"What are you saying?" I ask. There's a nervous quake to my heart, like maybe she knows more about me and my history than I do, which, I'm starting to realize, wouldn't take much.

"I'm just observing," she says. "As I said, I've been with the troupe from the very beginning. I've seen numerous performers come and go, their past sins atoned for. But not one of them left happy, I can tell you that."

"Why?"

"Because what they were running from—all of them—was something from within. They may have joined to escape incarceration or execution, but their demons never left."

"I don't have any demons," I say. I'm not liking where the conversation turned. Mainly because I'm not convinced anything I say is true.

"Darling, everyone has demons. Yours have just gone quiet."

"Maybe that's a good thing. Maybe it was part of the contract."

"Perhaps," she says. "But where has that gotten you?" She gestures to the room. "You might not know, but Mab does. And it sounds like your demons need reconciliation rather than ignorance."

I don't say anything to that. Her words sink down into my bones, binding themselves to memory. She has a point. Whatever I was running from is still there, still haunting my movements. I rub my hands together and try to force out the uncertainty. For the first time since I came here, when I think back to my past, deep inside I feel unclean.

Mab wasn't lying when she said I'd be put under Penelope's custody. I'm not allowed to leave her trailer except to use the Porta-Potty on the edge of the grounds, and even then, Penelope goes outside her trailer to keep an eye on me. It weirds the hell out of me the first time I go to pee and realize she's timing me, but when I get back to her bunk she acts entirely nonchalant, as if she was just outside enjoying the sunshine. She even opens the trailer door for me and waits a bit before coming in herself. That said, there's one freedom I want that I'm strictly denied. I'm not allowed to go check in on Melody.

"She's fine," Penelope assures me as she boils the electric kettle for afternoon tea. "If anything was amiss, we would know." She smiles warmly. "Trust me, in a company this small, it's impossible for the welfare of another to slip through the cracks. Now, English Breakfast or Earl Grey?"

By the time the tent's been torn down and packed away, I've emailed all of the refunded tickets and spent a good chunk of time staring at the Internet, hoping it would entertain me. Any other day, I'd have been overjoyed having an afternoon of sitting in the AC, wasting time online.

Except now, I'm realizing that I can't really enjoy myself online because all these little things are adding up in ways that make my skin crawl. I don't know what my email address is. There aren't any blogs I know I read regularly. I don't remember my Facebook account or anything else. Did I even *have* an email address? I take a deep breath and try to stay calm, try not to worry. Maybe I was just too cool to use social networking. Maybe I'd grown distant from all my friends and stopped communicating with them. I try to think back, try to remember chatting with someone—anyone—online, but the memory doesn't come. I stare at the home screen and try not to have a panic attack. With a calculated slowness, I type my name into the search bar. Hit enter. Nothing comes up. Nothing whatsoever. Somehow, the search is completely, entirely blank. I stare at the white screen and wonder how no one in the world shares my name, how there is no trace of me out there whatsoever. Something about the wrongness of it makes me want to gag, or throw the laptop out the window. My hands are shaking.

When Penelope closes the lid of the laptop, I'm almost relieved to be torn away from the damning screen. I blink a few times and stare up at her. What was I just looking at?

"Time to hit the road," she says.

By the time we're in the cab of one of the trucks—just her and me, this time—I can't even remember what I'd been worrying about.

We reach the next site at midnight. We've driven halfway across the Midwest, down interstates clogged with cars and back roads that seemed more mud than concrete. Now, we're somewhere in Nebraska, on a plot just off the edge of the highway. As our truck heads down the dirt road toward our site, I catch a glimpse of a farmhouse and a few tractors. We really are in the middle of nowhere this time. How the hell does Mab expect to sell tickets all the way out here? The caravan stops at the edge of the cleared field and Penelope parks. The cars are parked facing the same way, lights still on and many engines still running. There's a crowd of people assembling in the headlights, a mob of performers silently staring at the dark field.

"What's going on?" I ask. I reach for the handle but then realize that Penelope isn't moving. Her knuckles are white on the steering wheel, and in the green light of the dashboard, her face looks even more sallow than this morning. She doesn't look terribly beautiful now.

"It's him," she whispers. "He's here."

I look back out, almost ask what she's talking about. Then I see him.

There's a man standing in the middle of the cleared plot. His hair is so blond it's white, his skin is just as pale, and he's in a sharp grey suit with lines like razors. It's the man from the show, the man from the Summer Court.

And one of his arms is looped around Kingston's chest, the tip of a dagger pressed to his throat.

Chapter Twelve: Burning Up

I don't wait. I jump out of the cab and run the short space to the mob of performers. All I can see is Kingston. All I can see is the tiny line of blood dripping down his neck. My world goes red. Someone tries to grab my arm as I run forward, but I push him off.

"Get off him," I growl.

I stand at the front of the assembled mob, a few steps ahead of everyone else. My white-knuckled fists are clenched at my sides and there's a burning in the pit of my stomach that threatens to overwhelm me. I am half a second shy of going ballistic on a guy who could probably kill me with a thought.

He glares at me.

"Who, child, are you?" he asks. His voice is deep. Precisely the same as I remember when I was hiding underneath the semitrailer, listening to him and Mab argue.

"Someone you don't want to fuck with," I say. I don't know where the words come from. The man's got a knife pressed to Kingston's throat; I'm in no position to play chicken. My skin tingles as the fight or flight response kicks in, all gears shifted to fight.

"Vivienne," Kingston whispers. "Please, don't . . ."

The bastard pulls him in tighter.

"Vivienne?" he mutters into Kingston's ear. Then he looks at me with a devilish grin. "Ahh, I see. The wicked witch has a suitor."

"Fuck you," Kingston says, which just causes the man to dig the knife in deeper. Another line of blood trickles down his neck. His chin is raised high, as though he can squeeze his way out of this. That's when I notice that Zal, too, seems to be pierced from the knife. The tattoo is squirming underneath the blade, stuck like a butterfly on a pin.

"And he likes her!" he calls out with a laugh. "The witch fell in love."

Kingston squeezes his eyes shut and says nothing.

"You weren't listening to me," I say. I take a half step forward. The tingling in my hands grows stronger, feels like pins and needles coiling beneath my skin. "Let him go."

"Now, now," the man says. He turns the knife just a little bit. "Let's not be too hasty. I'm not here for him. I'm waiting for…her." He looks past me, past the troupe, to where Mab is pulling in.

The black Jag pulls up beside one of the semis. Her headlights go out. Then, the headlights of every truck in the lot blink out, one by one, until we're all standing in complete darkness. Even the moon and the stars above seem dimmed. The only thing I can hear is the wind and Kingston's ragged breath. Everything else seems to be waiting for the storm.

Mab appears from her car in a haze of blue light that stretches out across the ground like talons. She is shadow at first, then darkness made solid, a presence I can barely see but can feel with every nerve of fear in my body. She hovers as she moves forward, her skin pale and glowing, her black dress twining itself out of and into the night air. Glowing ice forms in the grass around her, crackling out in thunderbolts. Her image flickers, and she's suddenly standing beside me. The man's and Kingston's features are outlined in the glow of the demonic Faerie Queen.

"What is the meaning of this?" Mab asks, her voice colder than frost, darker than midnight.

"You have broken the Blood Autumn Treaty," he says.

"Bold words, Senchan," Mab says. Both of their voices carry over the field, both as clear as crystal. "Once more, you come onto my land—"

"Ah ah," tsks the man—Senchan. He wags his free finger. "You see, that is where you are wrong. This land is *neutral*."

Mab takes in a sharp breath that seems to hiss from the cornstalks around us.

"You *dare*." She says. "You *dare* spy on my Court and impede my plans."

"Your plans are moot," Senchan says. "You know the price of your insurgence. You will give the girl up, or we will hunt you down and flush her out of hiding."

Kingston gasps as the knife goes deeper.

"Release him," Mab says. "And we will talk."

"Not until you've promised me safety from your dogs," he says, nodding toward me.

Mab doesn't even glance over.

"I swear that none in attendance shall harm you. Release him."

Senchan hesitates. Then he withdraws the dagger and knees Kingston to the ground. Kingston stumbles. I hold out a hand, reach forward to help him up, but then he's standing, and before I can do anything, he runs. Not into my arms. But toward the trailers.

Senchan looks at me with a smirk on his face.

"Maybe not in love then, after all," he says.

"Enough," Mab says. "Come back to my trailer. We will speak there."

"No chance, Queen," he says. "We will stay here. On neutral ground. With both your and my Courts as witness."

Mab doesn't even flinch at this. "Let me guess, your kin are hiding like snakes in the grass," she says.

The man bows, mockingly. "I learned from the best."

"Vivienne," Mab says. "Check on Kingston. Make sure this beast hasn't hurt him."

I nod, not entirely sure I want to run after him when he clearly didn't want my help in the first place. But I also have no desire to stay here in the crossfire. Now that Kingston is safe, the fight impulse is dying, the heat in my hands faded to a faint tingle. I turn and head through the crowd, straight toward Kingston's bunk.

The bunk numbers are barely visible in the darkness, but I finally find 13. Kingston's. I don't even knock; I just open the door and step in.

The only light is coming from a green candle on his table. He's on his bed and barely looks up at me coming in. Then something slams into me, pushes me to the wall. A hand clamps over my mouth.

"Are you?" my assailant asks. "Are you bad man?"

Lilith.

I shake my head, and she steps back.

"Oh. Vivienne."

Then she steps away. She goes over to the bed and puts one arm around Kingston. That one small action makes my blood boil. I want to protect him, but I can't tell if that's protecting him from Senchan or from Lilith's arm around his waist. *He's mine,* something in me hisses, even though I know it's not true.

"Bad man hurt Kingston," Lilith whispers. "Hurt him bad."

"I'm okay," Kingston says. He looks up at me. There's something in his eyes that tells me his words couldn't be further from the truth. For one thing, I've never heard his voice waver before. The wound is still dripping a smear of blood down his neck. Zal has disappeared from sight. "I'm okay now."

"What did he do?" I ask. The fire in me builds. I want to kill Senchan for doing this to him, whatever it was. My fists are clenched and I can hear the blood in my ears grow louder. It takes everything I have not to yell at Lilith, to force her out of the trailer so I can take care of him. But I don't. For some reason, a part of me knows Lilith needs to stay.

"Nothing," Kingston says. "I mean…I'm not hurt. But he has my magic." His voice cracks at this.

"What?" The roar grows louder.

"He…when I got here, he ambushed me. And I don't know how, but he took it." He holds up his hands in a begging posture. "That's why

I couldn't enchant the place, couldn't make it part of Mab's territory. He stole my powers. It's all my fault."

"I'll kill him." The words echo in my ears, and that's when I realize I wasn't the only one saying them. Lilith is staring at him.

"I'll get your magic back," she continues. "Mab be damned, I will kill him for hurting you." She looks at me, and there's a fire in her eyes, a literal glow of red and gold that makes me edge further against the wall. Her gaze makes my skin go hot, like standing over the edge of a volcano.

"Vivienne," she says. Her voice is cinder and ash. "We must kill him. Together. Tonight."

I'm not a killer. I'm not.

She holds out her hand.

I'm not a killer.

I look at Kingston. The blood still trickling down his neck. The lost look in his eyes. The bloodlust in me hums.

I'm not a killer, but I'd kill for him.

I nod at Lilith. Senchan will pay for this. Senchan will die. I take Lilith's hand. The world explodes.

Fire and fire and
blood
and   fire
scream fire blood fire   body burns fire fire
faerie
kill
kill
kill
kill
kill
fire   fire   fire
fire fire
kill
Senchan
Mab
Lilith walks to Senchan
Poe
Kitty kitty kitty kitty
curls at Mab's feet.

Poe watches.
Kitty kitty

Lilith walks

fire burns

in   her eyes
two   coal eyes   brimstone sulfur burning

Lilith walks
past
the troupe
Senchan stops talking.

Lilith. Get back inside, sweetie. **Mab says.**

Please.

Lilith walks to Senchan.

You hurt him.

You hurt Kingston.

**Fire burns fire blood
fire blood faerie fire fair faerie blood**
Yes.

Senchan says. *I hurt him.*

*And I will keep
hurting
everyone
you love.*

Until you come with me.

Or until this show is in flames.

Lilith, please. Get back inside. **Mab says.**

No.

Lilith.

Let her play. **Senchan says.**

*Let her see
what happens
when those she loves get hurt.*

**Senchan reaches
down
He picks up Poe.**

Poe **hisses**

growls

spits

**Senchan holds the cat
by one leg
with one hand
the other**

Don't—

    Don't—

              s n a p s
            the cat's leg
                in
              half

      Lilith
      burns

fire   fire   fire   fire
fire breathes fire eats fire fire   screams   fire   fire
    fire howls fire   fire burning fire
      blood and   flame
                          Senchan screams
                       fair faerie blood
                          on fire
                    Senchan burning

fire flaming blood
Lilith, stop!

          Fire fields
        fire burn corn burn
     smoke burning faeries burning
        Lilith on fire
        eyes bright
       blood in darkness
     fields   burning
        Lilith burns
        everything
            burns.

   "Vivienne, please, wake up.

         wake up.

           wake up."

CHAPTER THIRTEEN: AMNESIA

I f I wasn't one hundred percent certain we didn't have animals in our show, I would have blamed the elephants for trampling over my head. There's no other explanation for the pounding in my temples and the fact that every joint in my body feels like I'd been sent to boot camp. I roll over in bed, and try to visualize happy, healing light spreading all over me, easing away the pain. Then someone puts a hand on my forehead, and that's exactly what happens.

My eyes flicker open. There's Kingston, leaning over me, a sad smile on his face. No sign of tears or blood, just his usual shadow of stubble and a tiredness in his eyes. I wish I could kiss his exhaustion away.

"You got your magic back," I mumble. His touch is ice water over flame, the perfect dose of Vicodin.

"What do you mean?" he asks. He pulls his hand back and the sensation goes away, though now the pain isn't as bad.

"Last night," I say. I try to think back, but it's mostly a blur. I just remember him in the trailer and Senchan and Mab in the headlights. Something about Lilith...a flash of pain makes me wince. I close my eyes and burrow my face into the pillow.

"What about last night?" he asks. His words are slow. Deliberate.

"You were hurt," I mumble, leaning my head to the side. It feels like trying to string together a dream from two weeks ago. I know it's there, but I can't bring it up. "After...after the guy from the Summer

Court took you. You said he took your magic." It even sounds stupid once I say it.

He takes a deep breath but doesn't speak.

"What?" I say. Maybe I'm still asleep. Maybe that's why everything's slurring together in my brain.

"You really don't remember?" he asks.

"Remember what?" The memories are swirling along with the trailer now. The last thing I want to do is try to remember anything but the solidity of this bed.

"Last night…gods, I can't believe this." Another deep breath on his part, and I look up in time to see him press his face into his palms, like he's about to deliver a death sentence. "You passed out last night."

"I figured," I mumble, trying to motion to the bed but failing. Even thinking of moving a limb hurts. "But I saw…."

"Honey," he says, and he reaches down to pull the covers off me. *Honey.* The word makes me melt. "You nearly died last night." I look down to where he's pointing. There, on my calf, are two red scabs, the skin around them puffy and pink. "You were bitten by a rattlesnake a few minutes after getting out of the truck."

"But the Summer Court guy. Senchan."

He pulls the covers back over my leg and gives me a no-nonsense sort of stare.

"Who's Senchan? You must have hallucinated. You got out of the truck and were bitten by a rattlesnake. Then you started convulsing and passed out. Everyone saw it." There's a finality to his words that make the room stop spinning. Only I know that's not what happened. I think I know that's not what happened… Right?

"But…" My thoughts are racing, burning like wildfire. "The fire. Lilith." My head throbs. "Lilith set everything on fire."

"Lilith's just a little girl," Kingston says. "I'm the only one with any real magic in this troupe. There *was* a fire, yes. But that was the bonfire the Shifters had last night—some embers set part of the field on fire. *I* put it out."

"But—"

"You passed out, Vivienne. I've never seen someone have such a bad reaction to snake venom." He bites his lip and closes his eyes for a moment. When he opens them, he's looking out the window.

"Last night was a shit show," he says, finally. "But what you're talking about never happened."

"I saw you," I say. I push myself up even though it hurts like hell. That inner fire is back. I *know* it wasn't a hallucination. He had been held captive. I fought for him. I *saw* it. "He had a knife to your throat. You were bleeding and helpless because he took your magic."

Kingston leans in close and lifts his chin to the ceiling. His skin is perfectly smooth.

"See?" he says. "No blood, no cut." He looks down at me and tries to smile. It's almost successful, too, but there's a waver in his eyes, an uncertainty. He's lying. "I wasn't in danger," he says. "But it's kind of cute that you think I could have been. Did you save me? In your dream?"

He's close, oh, so close, but right now, I just want to smack him. I lie back down instead and stare up at the ceiling. When I close my eyes, my memories sift around. I still remember him in the headlights, his face pale and terrified. I still remember Mab confronting Senchan, and I remember meeting Lilith in Kingston's trailer. Taking her hand. I swear I remember it, even though it's blurring around the edges, fading the more I hold it up for examination.

And there's another memory, a shadow of doubt. I remember the sharp pain in my ankle as I walked to join the troupe at the bonfire. I remember the pain, the nausea and spasms, as the world spun and fell away. I squeeze my eyes tighter and bring a hand to my forehead, try to block out the images. What I saw—Senchan, Kingston, Lilith—had to have been real. It *had* to. So why is the rattle of the snake I stepped on just as real? Why is that pain just as sharp?

"You need to sleep," Kingston says. I don't open my eyes, but I hear him stand. He puts a hand on the side of my face. His touch is still cool, even if there's no real magic in it now. I can feel his fingertips shaking. "I just wanted to make sure you were okay."

Then he leaves, the door clicking quietly shut behind him.

I'm not okay. Not even close to okay. I'm on another fucking planet from okay. But for the first time in a long time, I'm beginning to doubt if he'd be able to make it better.

He's lying. But why? Why would he lie to me?

I thought he was on my side.

Now I'm wondering if that was the biggest lie of all.

I don't sleep.

I have this terrible feeling that the moment I close my eyes, the truth—*my* truth—will fade away like a dream. It's easy to believe I made it all up. The pain in my ankle is real enough, and the more I let it, the more the memory of being bitten becomes tangible. I just don't *want* it to be real. The memory of the confrontation is taking on the same hazy feel as everything else in my past. So I keep my eyes open and watch a few bands of sunlight slide down the wall of my room. I consider standing up, but the bite burns like acid. I don't move except to get more comfortable. I try not to think of having to pee.

The door opens a few hours after Kingston's departure, when the sun is turning the inside of my bunk pink. I glance up, both hoping and not hoping it's him. Instead, it's Penelope. I sink back down into the mattress and try not to frown.

"How are you feeling?" she asks. Her voice is barely a whisper.

"Better," I say, which is true. Physically, at least. My head doesn't hurt nearly as much and the ankle is just a throb. I'm still holding the memory of Kingston in danger like a sanity anchor. I can't let it go. I can't let myself believe I'm delusional. Sanity is about the only thing I have going for me anymore, and even that's not saying much.

She walks over to the desk beside my bed and sets a tray down. There's a steaming bowl, a mug, and a few thick slices of bread. The sight of it makes me want to gag. How can they expect me to do something as normal as eat when everything in my life is spinning upside down?

"A simple meal," she says, noticing my glance. "We don't want to add any more poisons to your system."

"Thanks," I say. I force myself into sitting up and she places the tray in my lap. I pick up the spoon but don't start eating. The scent makes me nauseated. She's still standing there, watching.

"Are you sure you're okay?" she asks.

I open my mouth, almost tell her the truth, that I feel like my brain's been put through a blender and the people I trust are out to get me; I don't. Never trust the gossip queen. High school taught me that.

I think.

"I'm fine," I say. "Just...beat."

She nods. "Well, I'm just glad you're all right. If you need anything, my trailer's parked right across from yours."

I laugh weakly. "So I'm still under your watch?"

"Yes," she says. "So it would seem. Get better soon. I know Richard and Vanessa were hoping to up your training this site."

"Right," I say. "That." I've completely lost track of the days. Is it tomorrow I'm meant to be onstage? Or sometime after?

Penelope doesn't say anything. She just looks me over one more time, opens her mouth like she wants to ask another question. Then she turns and leaves.

I can't remember the last time I ate, but there's no way in hell I can stomach anything right now. I put the tray on the desk and curl back up under the covers. I'm not going to fall into that trap, the idea that things could start to return to normal. When I close my eyes, I don't really care if sleep comes. Maybe this whole thing—juggling included—would be better off as a dream.

I'm woken up by Kingston the next morning. He knocks on my door and steps inside without waiting for my answer. The sight of him washes away whatever nothing I'd been dreaming, and makes me panic for a moment, wondering who's just been killed. Thankfully, he's smiling as he walks in, a tray of food in his hands. He looks entirely casual—in gym shorts and a sleeveless shirt. Zal is wrapped around his bicep, its body hidden around Kingston's back.

"Sleep well?" he asks as he nudges aside my uneaten dinner and sets his tray down.

"Yeah."

"How's the ankle?"

I stretch my foot under the covers. No pain. When I pull the sheets back, there's only the slightest of red marks to show I'd be been bitten.

"Excellent," he says. He sits down in my chair and puts his bare feet up on my bed. "Looks like you'll be ready for practice in no time."

"Thanks for reminding me," I say. I reach for the coffee, which is already making my room smell like a caffeinated heaven.

"I talked with Mab," he says. The declaration comes out of the blue, makes me pause before taking a sip. I don't say anything. "She won't let me help you with juggling."

"Why not?" It's not like I enjoyed the idea of Kingston prodding around in my mind, but it was better than being thrown out.

"She said it's cheating and against your contract. No magical shortcuts."

"That might have been nice to know."

"You'll be fine," he says. His tone isn't even remotely convincing. There's a pause, and when he speaks again, he sounds tentative. "As for yesterday…"

"It's okay," I say. "I can't expect your enchantments to ward off snakes as well. There's no need to apologize."

He smiles at me. "I'm glad to hear it," he says. "You had me worried for a bit there."

An uneasy silence threatens to come between us, so I pick the first question out of my mind I can think of.

"How's Mel?" I ask.

"Better. Much better. She's out of bed today."

"That's good," I say.

What had I been worried about earlier? I look at him and feel a distant sense of betrayal I can't quite place. Why would I feel that about him? He's the one taking care of us, all of us. Still, the usual butterflies are out of place. Something just feels *off*. I try to place it, but the idea doesn't come, so I just pick up my spoon and start to eat.

He leaves a few minutes later, after inspecting my ankle and throwing a little more magic my way. I should be fine to walk around, he says. Just watch where I step. The door closes behind him and I eat my cereal. Every once in a while, I stare down at my ankle to make sure it's still there. The puffiness is gone, and there's only a tiny pink scar from the bite marks.

Every time I look at it, something in the back of my mind stirs, some wisp of fire and pain. Then I look away, and the memory vanishes.

❖

I leave the trailer shortly after breakfast, when it's clear putting weight on my foot won't make it fall off and my bladder can't take another moment's hesitation. There's barely even a limp as I head to the Porta-Potty at the edge of the field. The sun is high and the sky is clear. All around us are sweeping cornfields that vanish into the blue haze of the horizon. It's already sweltering, and the inside of the Porta-Potty is exactly what you'd expect from a small box of excrement sitting in the blazing sun. If Mab had ever mentioned the outdoor toilets when I signed on, the harsh reality must not have sunk in at the time.

I pause on the return trip, feeling infinitely lighter, and stare out at the tent and the trailers spread before me. There aren't that many people about—a few performers are lying on their backs on lawn chairs, others are taking shelter under the canopy by the pie cart. Penelope is nowhere to be seen, which makes me wonder if maybe I'm no longer such a threat after being felled by a snake. Everyone else must either be inside or in town, wherever that is. The ground beneath my feet is grey, and when I bend down to inspect it, I realize it's ash. That's when I notice the char marks on some of the corn, the blackened stalks and crispy husks. *The bonfire.* We were lucky the tent wasn't set up when the blaze went off. I'd heard enough horror stories of old tents going up in flames. After the rip in the tent, we didn't need any more disasters.

The thought makes me wonder if Mab's already gotten the side wall replaced. I head over to the tent to inspect. Sure enough, every one of the grey and blue panels is intact. Whoever she got to fix it must have worked pretty damn fast.

"Looking for something?"

I turn around and see Melody standing there. She's in shorts and a loose shirt with a tree sprawling across the front. Her brown hair is messy and her eyes are still shadowed. But she looks better. Thin, but better.

"It lives," I say, grinning. Seeing her up and about makes me feel like maybe things are finally on the upswing.

She smiles as well and walks the few steps over to me, looping an arm over my shoulders. "I could say the same for you," she says. "I don't think I've ever seen someone foam at the mouth before."

I wince and look down at my ankle. "I was foaming?"

"Like a rabid dog," she says. "Still, that Kingston's a miracle worker."

I nod. "How about you?" I ask. "How are you feeling?"

"Meh," she says with a shrug of her shoulders. We start walking toward the pie cart. "Still feel like I've been run over by a truck a few hundred times, but it's better than before."

She pours herself a cup of water from one of the Gatorade containers when we hit the pie cart, offering me one as well.

"Any plans for the day?" she asks, sitting back on a wooden table still littered with a few bowls of half-eaten cereal.

"Juggling practice," I say. The words feel like a death sentence. "What about you?"

Her grin widens. "There's a swimming hole nearby. An honest-to-God swimming hole with rope swings and tetanus and everything. I think a couple of us are heading over after lunch."

"That sounds amazing."

She nods. "Don't tell Kingston I'm going, though. He'd probably say I'm not well enough. I say, however, the promise of gorgeous girls in bikinis is cure enough for me." She raises her glass in mock toast and takes a drink.

"Yeah, well, at least one of us should get some action."

She raises an eyebrow, her smile going wicked.

"Not like that," I say. "I mean...you know what I mean."

"Who is it?" she teases. She looks around conspiratorially and leans in. "C'mon, love, you can tell me. Let me guess. Uma."

"Who?"

She sighs. "Not Uma, then. How long have you been with us? She's the Shifter with all the piercings."

The name's familiar, but I can't place it. She must have read something in my blank expression. "Oh, come on, I know you've seen her. She said you dropped into her tent a few nights back. You know"—she raises her hands to her chest and cups her hands—"piercings everywhere. And I mean, *everywhere*."

Then I remember Uma. I blush at the memory of seeing her onstage swaying like a belly dancer to the sounds of violin and shivering metal. What had I been doing there? I was looking for something...

"Ah, *now* she remembers. Pierced nipples usually jog the mind." She chuckles to herself, and I punch her on the shoulder.

"Bitch. No, not Uma. I don't swing that way."

"Can't blame me for trying," she says. Her voice sobers. "Don't tell me you've got a thing for Kingston."

I don't answer right away, which makes her jump off the table and spin on the ground, one hand covering her mouth to hold back the laughter.

"Oh, no," she says. "Please, please not him. He's like my brother." She looks at me and sees I'm not smiling. If anything, my face has gotten redder.

"Seriously?" she says. Her grin drops.

"I know," I say. "I don't have a chance in hell, do I?"

She runs a hand through her hair.

"Not really," she finally says.

"Comforting," I say. "Aren't you supposed to be giving me friendly advice?"

"Yes," she says, nodding. "And here it is: don't date within the circus."

"That's it? That's your good advice?"

She holds up her hands.

"That's my honest advice. Think of it this way: what did you do when you broke up with your past boyfriends?"

"I..." But then I realize, I don't remember any past boyfriends. I know they should be there, but the idea's just...blank. She doesn't seem to notice the stutter in my memory.

"You move on," she continues. "You stop calling or texting or whatever you do, and you see other people like a normal girl. You can't do that here."

She gestures around.

"You fuck up a relationship in here and you're stuck with an angry ex for the rest of your contract. And trust me, Kingston isn't someone you want pissed off at you for a few dozen years."

"Why would I be pissed?" Kingston says from behind. I nearly jump. *How long was he standing there?*

"Speak of the devil," I mumble. Clearly, even getting bitten by a rattlesnake wasn't enough to clear my shitty karma. I try to visualize my face not being red and turn around. I know it doesn't work. "We were just talking about you."

"I thought I felt my ears ringing," he says. Apparently, he doesn't care to know what we were saying. He walks over to Melody and puts a hand on her face, uses a thumb to lift an eyelid. "Shit," he whispers.

"What?" we both ask. My heart immediately drops.

"Still nothing in there."

"Ha ha," Mel says, swatting his hand away. "Nice to see you too, dickhead."

Kingston turns to me. "Feeling better?"

I nod and take a drink of water. If he was listening in, he didn't catch much. I hope. God, do I hope.

"Good," he says. "Vanessa was asking after you. Apparently, you aren't allowed dinner until you can manage eight three-ball passes in a row."

"Fantastic," I say. "I'll just start gorging myself now, lest I starve for the next few days."

Kingston reaches over to a bowl and snatches a few pieces of cereal.

"Better start practicing now," he says, and tosses them in a high arc toward me. They ignite in midair, flaring into three soft, red juggling balls. I manage to catch one. The others fall to the ground. Melody chuckles.

Some part of me can't help but feel like this is all forced, though I have no clue where the notion's coming from. Kingston seems too casual, Melody too quirky. Something is going on, something that neither of them wants to admit. Either that, or I'm getting paranoid.

One of the balls rolls under a table, so I bend down to grab it. That's when I see Poe curled up beside a bench leg. The ball is right next to him. He stirs as I reach out, opening one eye and then rolling up to stretch before limping away.

There's a miniature white cast on his front paw. Memory burns, but then Kingston taps me on the ass with his foot. I stand and chuck one of the balls at him, missing by a mile. I'm smiling, but I can feel it slip. Something digs in the back of my head, something pulling itself up to consciousness. It smells of brimstone and fear.

Chapter Fourteen: Gimme More

When the rest of the troupe leaves for the watering hole—
Melody as well, since Kingston saw some benefit in her
getting out for a bit—I sit inside the main tent, legs
crossed, with a pile of juggling balls beside me. It's a bit cooler in the
chapiteau, and with the lights off, everything is a muted blue from the
sun diffusing through the walls. The bleachers are empty and there's a
thin stream of light coming in from the back curtain. I can still practically
feel the ghosts of crowds past. Being in here without an audience seems
wrong, somehow, much emptier than it should be. I've got my MP3
player on to drown out the quiet, trying to keep a rhythm with the balls.
One, two, three, catch, one, two, three, catch. I succeed every couple of songs.
It's easier to practice without anyone watching me, judging, or waiting
for me to do it right. I even cheer when I manage three successful passes
in a row. Then I drop one of the balls. It rolls away, toward the ring curb,
where it's stopped by Kingston's foot.

I pull out one of my earplugs as he bends down to pick it up. A faint
voice inside of me is saying I should feel strange right now. I should be
holding something against him, but I can't remember what. I let whatever grudge I had go. I just don't have the energy for that sort of drama.
Not when my job and everything else is on the line.

"That was good," he says, rolling the ball around on his palm. I watch
him for a moment as he moves his hand back and forth, twists it over and
under, the ball seeming to hover in one spot as it rolls across his skin,

then up his forearm. Zal is wrapped around his neck, the tip of his tail just protruding from Kingston's shirtsleeve. After a few more moments of contact juggling, he pops the ball into the air and catches it. He winks when he sees my stare and slightly dropped jaw. "Years of practice," is all he says.

He walks over and sits down next to me, then tosses me the ball.

"How's it going?" he asks.

"I think I'm getting the hang of it."

"That's not what I meant."

"Oh."

We sit there a moment, and I'm acutely aware of how close he is. Even in the heat, his presence feels cool, and his scent is sweat and spice, something exotic and dangerous and alluring, all in one. I can practically feel the static between us, my bare arm hardly an inch from his.

"Well," I finally manage, picking up the balls and trying again. *One, two, three*—but the ball flies far and I miss the last catch. Taking my mind off juggling certainly doesn't help my performance. "I guess, all things considered, I'm doing okay."

"All things considered?" he asks.

I pick up one of the balls from the pile and try again.

"Well," I say, making the first pass. "I was bitten by a snake, I'm a million miles from home, and, oh, yeah, three people have died in the last week, and no one knows who did it, so naturally Mab suspects me. On top of that, if I don't learn how to juggle by the next site, I'm on the street. Again."

Kingston nudges me, which makes me fail the catch.

"You're being melodramatic," he says.

"Really? Because from where I'm standing, I'd say there's more than enough drama outside of myself."

"Welcome to circus life," he says. "Never a dull day."

"You don't seem to care if I stay or not," I say. The words grate against my pride, but I can't help but voice them.

"You know that's not true," he says.

I put down the balls and look at him. He's looking at me, a slight smile on his lips. Is it just my imagination, or is he looking at me differently? It's almost as if he's looking at me like he knows I have some sort of secret. Like I'm worth noticing for more than comic relief.

The words I want to say sound childish in my head, but I don't care. I'm tired of not knowing.

"Why?" *Why do you care? Why is this happening? Why does everyone seem to be against me? Why am I suspected of murder?* A thousand other questions are also left unasked. But I know he can't or won't answer.

He looks away.

"I know it's hard," he says. "The first couple weeks. The troupe's been together for years and we're cliquey as fuck. But that doesn't mean people don't care about you."

People like you? I want to ask.

"I highly doubt anyone else in the troupe has had the same welcome. Being suspected of murder isn't exactly friendly."

He looks at me.

"You don't really believe that, do you?"

"What?"

"That Mab suspects you."

I throw up my hands and can't help but laugh. "What are you talking about? Of course she does. Why else would she say she suspects me? Why else would she put me under house arrest and threaten to kick me out of the troupe if I don't learn how to juggle? She *hates* me. And what if she's right? What if I *did* do it? I can't remember my past! What if I'm blacking out the memory of killing everyone as well?"

It's a thought I wouldn't let myself entertain before, one that shakes the very core of who I think I am. What if I really *am* the killer? Like one of those Russian sleeper cells, just awaiting activation.

Kingston shakes his head.

"You're not the murderer. I wouldn't believe that for a second. Do you really think Mab—cunning as she is—would put her cards on the table like that?"

I don't say anything. I haven't been here long enough to have even the slightest idea of what Mab would do. And I have a feeling that that wouldn't change even if I stayed here another thousand years. Which might be a very strong possibility.

"She's using you," he finally says. His voice is flat, like he's not entirely pleased with it himself. "You're a diversion."

"A diversion?"

"Of course. If she places the blame on you, the real killer might think they're off the hook. They'll get messy."

"Yeah, well, they only have a couple days left. After that, I won't be around to play scapegoat."

"I won't let her kick you out," Kingston says. There's a promise in the way he says it. As much as I want to laugh it off, I don't doubt for a minute he's telling the truth. I've seen him go head-to-head with Mab. He could hold his weight. But could he hold his ground while defending me?

"Why?" I ask again.

He doesn't answer. For a moment, all I can do is stare at him, wonder if he's really willing to be my knight in shining armor or if he's just being macho. The desire to reach out and touch him slugs me in the chest, but I hold back. There's still that inkling that I should be royally pissed at him.

"Have you ever killed someone?" I ask.

He leans back. "Why the hell would you ask me that?"

"Because I wanted to make sure you wouldn't burn me alive if I ever tried to kiss you."

"Funny," he says, and he picks up one of the balls, starts rolling it around in his palm again. *Smooth*, I think. There goes that moment.

"Sorry."

"Don't worry about it."

Neither of us says anything for what feels like the longest while. But he isn't standing up to leave. Maybe I didn't fuck it up entirely. Maybe he's just making sure I meant it.

"I take it that's a no on the kiss, then?" I finally say. I try to keep my voice light, but—to continue his metaphor—now that my cards are on the table, I feel horribly exposed. Besides, isn't this supposed to be his role? Shouldn't *he* be the one trying to win over me?

"I'm too old for you," he says. The statement is fast and well practiced, so smooth it doesn't sound genuine. It also isn't an answer.

"You don't look like it."

"Yeah, well, that's Mab's magic for you. All glitz and glamour. Nothing real." The bitterness in his voice is overpowering.

"So," I say. "How long do I have to wait?"

"Until?"

"Until I'm old enough for it not to be so creepy."

He actually laughs at this, an outburst that sounds like half a sob. He looks at me.

"You're serious?"

I nod. I'm not smiling. It's the most honest I've been with him since signing on to this venture.

"I'm three hundred and forty-one."

The numbers drop like guillotines, but he doesn't look away from me as he says them. Clearly, he's judging my response. I try to keep my face composed, and my response is as witty as I can make it.

"You don't look a day over two hundred," I say. "Must be all the popcorn."

He shakes his head, but he's smiling nonetheless. Again, he looks at me like I'm amusing. But there's something else behind it. Surprise?

"What did you do?" I ask. "Why did you join?" *Most of our performers were in a bind,* Mab had said. What could Kingston have done?

"Well," he says. "I used to live in Salem."

"Oh."

He takes a deep breath and stares off at something past the bleachers. "Yeah. *Oh*. A little over three hundred years ago, I was being burned at the stake. I'd accidentally lit someone's pig on fire, which sounds much funnier in hindsight. At the time, when I didn't realize I actually *was* the type of person all the menfolk were burning, it freaked the shit out of me. I was found out, given a trial befitting the times, and found guilty.

"So there I am, bound to a pole in the town square, getting called every possible name for a bastard heathen. I was crying because I knew I was guilty and going to hell, but I didn't want to die. But that doesn't really mean anything to them, you know? Anyway, Mab must have been watching for some time, because a minute or two after they lit the kindling—bitch let me roast for what seemed like eternity—everything just...stopped."

He pauses and looks at me, clearly making sure I'm still following along. I am. Either he's a good storyteller or I've got a vivid imagination: I can practically smell the wood smoke.

"I mean, it's like being in a movie. Everything's on pause. I still remember there was a rotten tomato hovering like a foot away from my face. And then *she* appears out of nowhere in a puff of black smoke. Didn't look anything like she does now. She was in her PVC boots and mohawk phase, even had a British flag as a belly shirt. Think *Tank Girl* but infinitely more badass. Certainly made the right impression."

I let the image of Mab dressed as a true punk seep in. It's quite at odds with her current glamorous self.

"She offered me a job then and there. Work for her and she'd not only set me free, she'd let me get revenge and teach me how to use my powers. I accepted, of course. I mean, it wasn't much of a choice: burn an agonizingly slow death, or get out of jail free. At the time, I thought I was just hallucinating because after I'd agreed, everything started back up again. People were yelling, the tomato missed me by an inch. Then I realized the ropes on my hands were gone, and the fire didn't seem so hot. That's when the fire turned blue.

"Everyone started screaming and trying to run away, but there were demon eyes in the flames and I heard Mab's voice in my head. *This is your power. Do with it as thou wilt.*"

"And?" I ask.

"And I killed them," he says, tossing the ball into the air. "All five hundred and forty-three of them. Men, women, children. All burned, just like they would have done to me."

I stare at him. My mouth is open, I'm sure, but I can't close it. If he notices, he doesn't pause to point it out.

"It wasn't until later, of course, that Mab set out the actual terms of my contract."

"Which was?"

"One year for every life lost. So, yeah, I've killed before. And I'm paying dearly for it. Circus freak for life," he says with a sigh.

"I don't remember any of that in the history books," I say. Here I was, freaking out because I might have killed three people, and he's killed hundreds. He doesn't look like the type who'd have blood on his hands. But then I remember the way his eyes flashed when doing some of his more dangerous tricks. *Not everything is as it seems.* His words. He was definitely talking about himself.

He just shrugs. "Mab's good at misdirection." The look he gives me is loaded, but I'm too wrapped up in the idea of him fricasseeing small babies to let it sink in.

"Do you regret it?" I ask, shaking off the image. "Joining? Your contract?" In other words, killing all those people.

"Hell, no," he says, standing. "I'd do it again."

He tosses the ball into the air. At the top of its arc, it explodes in a burst of sparks and flutters away as a pearl-white moth.

"You don't fuck with a witch," he says. "Ever."

With that, he strolls out of the tent, a slight, cocky bounce to his gait. I know I should be looking at him differently. He's a killer. He's here because he murdered a town. But then, I can't say I'd have done much differently if the roles were reversed. Kill or be killed. Wasn't that the most basic human instinct? Besides, it's not exactly like I could crucify him for his past when I couldn't even remember mine. He's still the guy who promised to keep Mab from kicking me out, the guy who takes it upon himself to make sure Melody and everyone else is safe and happy. He's still the guy I fell for at the start. I pick up the balls and then realize one thing: he never answered whether or not he'd kill me for trying to kiss him.

❖

A couple songs later, I stand up and leave the tent, dropping the juggling balls in a props basket backstage. There's no one around—no one at the pie cart, no one in lawn chairs outside of their trailers. Everyone must either be inside their air-conditioned bunks or out at the watering hole. Hopefully, Mel found some of the eye candy she was after. I wasn't kidding; one of us deserved some action, and since I clearly wasn't going to be getting any from Kingston for quite some time, it might as well be her. Was there even anyone else in the troupe who was gay? Or was her only hope at getting laid outsourcing?

As I head to the pie cart for water, a shape dodges in front of me, then another shadow close behind. Poe chasing a mouse.

The cat pauses in front of me and turns its yellow eyes up to mine, the rodent forgotten. His front paw is still in a cast. Something in my memories shifts.

"You can't have him."

I spin around.

Lilith's standing behind me. She's in a lacy white floral dress that makes her look like a doll, her head tilted to the side in that lost-bird manner she often has. There's even a pink ribbon tied in her hair. The sight of her makes the air feel warmer, makes me take a half step back.

"What?" I ask. Poe slinks around from behind me and curls around Lilith's feet. She bends down and picks the cat up, then stands and looks at me dead-on.

"You can't have Kingston. He is too good for you. He is mine." There's nothing vapid in her voice. The contrast between her words and her appearance chills me to the bone. *Not everything is what it seems here.* Then what the hell is Lilith hiding?

"I...I don't know what you're talking about," I say.

Her eyes narrow.

"I won't let you steal him away. I won't let you do what the bad man did to him."

"Bad man?"

"Bad man Senchan."

Her words fill me with fire, and as her brown eyes turn red, my vision burns. Smoke fills my nostrils, screams and crackling as Lilith is there on the field, burning the man from the Summer Court. Burning the fields and the Summer Fey within. Lilith, flames looped around her in cords, flames of her fingers, fire and wrath, and Senchan burning and screaming and cracking apart with corn-husk skin. And then Mab's there, covering Lilith in a hug, and the fires die down and she's whispering. *My baby, my baby, stop now, please.*

I take a deep, shuddering breath. Bile rises in my gut. I drop to my knees and vomit, my hands clenching the ash-covered earth. *Senchan, burning. Senchan, screaming. His ash is everywhere.*

"What...what did you do?" I manage.

"Bad man," Lilith says. There's a smile in her words that twists my intestines. Pride. Sheer, contented pride. "Bad man gone."

She kneels down at my side.

"You don't look so well, Vivienne. You look weak. Kingston despises weak women. Which is why he will always choose me. Always."

She puts Poe on the ground beside me, and together they run off, disappearing into the cornfield like the damned.

❖

Mab opens her trailer door after the second pounding knock.

She's in a black velvet-and-rhinestone blazer and velvet leggings. Her hair is bleached white today, and her green eyes spark at the sight of me. The air around her seems to shiver with shadows, but I stand my ground. Her trailer is completely dark; no candles, no walls, just shadow.

"Vivienne," she says. "I thought I left you under Penelope's watch?"

"I remember," I say. The words come out as a croak. My throat is on fire and every breath is sandpaper and flame. There are two worlds battling in my head, and my body is splitting apart at the seams. "I know about Senchan. I remember."

I don't know how I expect her to react. Shock? Anger? Whatever it was, I wasn't expecting her to smile and step back into the trailer.

"Come in," she says. Her tone grows motherly in an instant. "Let's talk."

I step inside the trailer. The door closes behind me and all is black, black and empty, save for her hand on my back. Then a cool breeze blows past me, smelling of ice and dust, and a faint blue light flickers in the distance, then another. One by one, a host of candles blaze into life, their flames the blue of a summer sky. Her office materializes from the dark in tendrils of fog, wisps that solidify into an ancient wooden desk, four walls, two chairs, and a bookshelf that covers the entire back wall.

She guides me into the seat and settles herself in the plush velvet chair behind her desk. Memories of my first time in this very chair settle on my shoulders, but there's no time to feel at home. Something is wrong, very wrong, and I'm not going to be kept in the dark any longer.

"So," she says, leaning back to prop her stiletto boots on the desktop. "Talk."

The words are tumbling around in my head but I can't seem to pick one to start it all off.

"I know," I say again. "I remember him. Senchan. The Summer Court." I take another shuddering breath as I try to think back without losing it—either the memory or my lunch. "I know Lilith killed him. I saw what Lilith is."

Mab smiles.

"I find that highly unlikely," she says. "But pray tell, what, exactly, did Lilith do?"

"She burned him. There was fire. A lot of fire. Lilith burned Senchan alive. And all the fey in the fields. She killed them all."

Something flickers across Mab's eyes, but it's gone in an instant.

"That is quite a statement," she says. "Especially since you seem to be the only one who saw such a thing."

That's when reality dawns on me, the memory of Kingston not quite meeting my gaze when I woke up with snake venom coursing through my veins and dueling memories in my head. He knew. Worse, he knew that I was supposed to be in the dark. He lied.

"You had him erase the memory," I whisper. "From everyone."

"Apparently not," Mab says. She eases her boots off the table and leans in closer to me, fingers laced together under her chin. "You seem to remember everything. Which is especially odd since—if we are to be completely honest now—you were passed out in his trailer when the incident took place."

"I…" I try to remember. She's right. I know I'd been in Kingston's trailer. I remember the blood trailing down his neck. I remember him shaking. And I remember Lilith, the two of us swearing to kill Senchan. Taking her hand…"I had a vision," I say. The words taste strange on my tongue, almost tingling as I speak.

"That," she says, "is impossible."

"Why?" I whisper.

"Because. Your contract expressly forbids your visions to manifest. That's why you joined us in the first place."

I sit there in silence as she studies my face. *Visions? I'm supposed to have visions? What happened to just being normal? Mortal? Or was that just a lie, too?*

What am I?

"What are you talking about?" I finally ask.

"Well," she says. She leans back and snaps her fingers. "I suppose that now the cat's out of the bag." From the bookshelf behind her, a massive volume slips down and glides over to the desk. It flutters open in front of her. My name is at the top of the page, beneath the words *Official Contract*.

Her finger slides down to one of the bullet points.

"Paragraph 1C," she says. "As part of her agreement, Vivienne Warfield shall have no recollection of her powers, past, present, or future, unless deemed necessary by Queen Mab or…"

She pauses.

"That isn't right."

She looks up at me and her eyes are blazing.

"You've been in my office."

"What are you talking about?"

"You've changed your contract."

"What? I—"

"You are lucky I still have use for you," she whispers. Her voice is poison in the air. It fills me with fear and magic. "Otherwise, I would make you beg for mercy. What else have you done?"

"I don't know what you're talking about."

"Get out," she says. "And stay out of my sight until I call on you."

I don't move.

"Out!" she shouts. The entire room shakes at this, a minor earthquake, and the chair I'm in whips around and topples me to my knees. I stand. I don't hesitate. I reach for the door and jump out into the sunlight, Mab's rage a claw sinking deep into my skin.

Chapter Fifteen: Guilt by Association

My first impulse is to run. Not just away from Mab's wrath, but out of the circus altogether. The moment the idea crosses my mind, however, I feel something like iron clamp around my lungs. I stagger and fall to my knees, desperately trying to choke down air. My lungs burn, my eyes fill with stars. Then the idea floats away, and so, too, does the constriction in my chest. I gasp as oxygen floods me. I roll over onto my back and stare up at the blue, blue sky, breathing in deep lungfuls of oxygen.

"Let me guess," he says. A shadow falls over me, and I peer back to see Kingston standing there with his hands in his pockets. "You thought about dodging your contract."

My fists clench at my sides. I turn over and jump to my feet so I'm facing him eye to eye.

"Contracts?" I say, my voice barely holding in all the rage and fear now cycling through me. "You want to talk about contracts?"

He takes a half step back.

"Whoa, easy tiger. I don't know what Mab said but—"

"I know," I say. "You don't have to lie anymore. I know you know about me. My visions. Lilith. Senchan. I know everything was just an elaborate lie."

The moment I say it, I wish I could take it back. Because I know there's more to the lie than just messing with my memory. *That* part

I'm somewhat okay with—if I signed up for it, at least I had some say in the matter. It's the things I can't change, the things I didn't agree to. Kingston pretending to care, toying with me. Melody pretending we were friends. Everyone in this godforsaken troupe pretending to be a family when we were all just watching our own backs. It's all broken down now, shattering to the ground in fragments I'll never be able to recover. No one cared. The only reason Kingston pretended he wanted me to stay was because Mab still needed me. Not because he liked me. Because I was *useful*. The thought makes my blood boil.

Kingston's usual smirk drops.

"She told you?" he says. "What did she say?"

"I think you know," I say. My words tremble and I can barely contain the anger that wants to spill through. "You've been fucking with my memory. You made me forget Lilith and the fire. You've been messing around in my head!" The last bit comes out as a yell, the words echoing around the empty site. I half expect Mab to come out and escort me off the premises, but she doesn't. No one comes.

Kingston holds up his hands.

"I only did what you told me to," he says.

"I never asked for you to erase my memory."

"You did," he says. "I was there, when you signed your contract. When we laid out every single term and condition, you wanted it all gone—your past, your visions, all of it. You begged me to take them away. I was there holding your fucking hand."

"No," I say. His words open a floodgate.

I shake my head, try to force out the new memories flooding in. Kingston, standing beside me at the desk, one hand on my shoulder. *Are you sure about this?* It wasn't Mab who asked, it was Kingston. I put a hand to my head. The vision flickers in and out, fighting with the old memory, trying to fill in holes I hadn't realized were there in the first place. There's a ringing in my ears like a train coming down the tracks. And I'm pinned to the rails, waiting for it to strike and blow my mind to bits.

"So you don't remember everything," he whispers.

"Shut up," I say, because every word is another memory, another lie to cover another lie.

"I was the one who found you, Vivienne."

I drop to my knees and try to drown out the images, but I can't, I can't: Kingston walks down the street while I'm sobbing in an alley. He walks in, his clothes soaked but he's still gorgeous with his faded jeans and deep brown eyes. When he sees me, he kneels down in the puddle beside me and asks my name, asks why I'm crying in an alley, and I can't answer. He doesn't wince at the blood on my jeans that turns the water pink, or the blood on my hands and in my hair. He puts a hand on the side of my temple and his touch is cool in a way that makes the pain feel better. His eyes go wide and he whispers, *Oh*.

"No," I say, my voice cracking. "What...is this?"

"It's what you wanted," he says. He's there at my side, I can tell. I can feel his shadow in the sun and his voice so much closer. "It's what you asked for."

"How much did you erase? Why would you change my memory, make me think I was bitten when it was Lilith who nearly killed everyone?"

"I had no say in that," he says. "Lilith's secret is written into everyone's contract, except for mine. Mab decided it was safer that way. And I swear to you, I only erased the memories you wanted gone. I couldn't change the fact that you wanted to forget all of them."

"Why? Why would I ever want that?"

"Because of your visions. They drove you here. You wanted to forget." His voice is soft, so soft. I curl in on myself and try to block out the burning in my head, the screams of memories fighting to the surface. I don't want them. I don't want the pain that's clawing itself to consciousness. The train is closer, the rails shaking. But I don't want to lose this truth, either—I don't want to keep hiding from myself. Whatever the cost.

"What are they?" I whisper, the burning growing to a wildfire. "The visions? Why me?"

"It's who you are; you get glimpses of what was, or what's yet to come. Whatever you saw before coming here made you want to lock them away. But…you can't hide from them forever. Not even my magic can change what you're born with. I can only hold the power off."

He gently puts a hand on my shoulder. I want to flinch but I can't move. "Take a deep breath," he says.

"Don't," I say. I want to. I want to fall into his arms and I want to trust him. I want all of this to go away, to forget it all because I was happier not knowing. But I can't. I can't go back to that. I can't keep hiding, even though I wish I could.

"Trust me," he says. I feel the first brush of magic easing the pain away…

"I said don't!" I shove him aside and push myself up to standing. The fire in my head is raging and screaming and I want to rage and scream as well, I want to tear this all apart.

"You lied to me," I growl, backing against the trailer like a cornered dog. "You lied to me all along. I fought for you. I wanted you, and you fucking lied!"

He's standing now, hands raised in defeat. I expect someone to come around the corner and see what's wrong, for someone to see what all the shouting's about, but no one does. It's just me and him and the inevitable breakdown.

"You knew all along," I say. "You knew everything about me—my past, my contract—hell, you know more about me than even I do."

His eyes are wide and his hands are dropping, and I know I'm hitting my mark, so I dig deeper. There's too much pain in me, too much for one person. In that moment, I want nothing more than for him to feel it as well.

"How can you live with yourself?" I whisper. "Three hundred years of fucking everyone over, messing with their minds. How many people have you manipulated like that? How many people have you forced into loving you?"

And I'm sick with myself for saying it, but I can't help it. I was fine knowing I'd run from my past, was fine thinking Mab knew more than I did. But I'm not okay with this, with knowing that Kingston had changed everything around in my head and had made me forget that he'd done it in the first place.

Worse, I hate knowing that I was most likely right. How could I trust my feelings for him when he had been playing in my head? How could I trust anything anymore? I close my eyes and squeeze my hands against my temples. The ringing won't stop. I wish I could force it into *him*, make him see how it felt.

"I had no choice," he whispers. His words barely cut through the din in my head. "You asked Mab to erase it, all of it. You signed the contract. I had to do it."

"You didn't have to lie about it."

"About what?"

I want to sink into the side of the trailer, want to disappear entirely. The rage in my head is dying down, sinking back below the surface, but the ache is still there. I'm tired, so tired, and this feels like a fight I'll never win.

"Liking me," I manage.

There's a long pause before he speaks.

"You think I lied about that?"

I don't respond, don't even move. The images in my head are still warring for control, still trying to piece themselves back into place.

That's when I feel his hand on the side of my face. His touch is cool, tingling. It melts the pain away, even though I know he isn't using any magic. It takes everything I have not to reach out and touch him as well, not to pull him close and lose myself in that touch. The rage allows me to keep that one small dignity intact.

"You're right," he says. My heart knots. *He lied. He lied about everything. No one could love you. No one would want you to stay.*

"I told you I didn't need someone," he continues. His hand traces my jaw and I want to break apart. "I played with you because you were cute and funny. But you fought for me when no one else would. No one does that around here." He laughs softly to himself. I feel like I'm a yo-yo. Just that sad little laugh makes me want to hold him, even if it is all a lie, even if he was just using me. In the middle of all this crashing pain, the idea of comfort is intoxicating. I force the feelings down as he continues.

"You were my savior. When Senchan had me, you tried to save me when everyone else stood and watched the show. And then I had to erase that from your mind, too." He sighs. "Do you know what that feels like? Knowing you tried to save my life and would never remember? That I'd never be able to repay you because you wouldn't know of my debt?"

I can't open my eyes. I know there are tears straining to come through but I won't let it happen. I won't. *This is just a game, too. I did remember, and this is how you repaid me.* I reach up and take his wrist, gently, and draw it away from my face. I don't want to—no way in hell do I want to—but I refuse to be toyed with. I'm done being the fool.

"How do I know?" I whisper. "How do I know this isn't another lie? How do I know this isn't because you need me to do something for you?"

He sighs.

"I do need you," he finally says. His words break apart the shell around me. "But not like that."

Then his hands are once more on my face, and I open my eyes to see his lips inches from mine. His brown eyes are like coffee, like mocha, and in that one glance, I know that he's telling the truth. I can see the hurt and desire, and I reach up and thread my fingers through his long black hair. He closes his eyes and smiles and then his lips are on mine. The world melts away.

His kiss is soft and hard and tastes like cinnamon and need. His hand slides behind my head and my hands are reaching around his neck and I'm kissing back as all the fury and fear turns into something else, some great passion I can't control. I pull him close and he leans in and every inch of my body is pulsing with heat and electricity and desire. The beast inside of me is roaring for a different reason. I could fall into this fire and burn forever.

"No."

The word, that one word, and he tenses up. We both freeze. Then he pushes me away, wipes a hand across his mouth like that could make her unsee everything.

"Lilith," he says.

But it's not just Lilith. Penelope stands behind her, her hands on Lilith's shoulders. Her expression is impossible to read, but Lilith's is plain—rage and hurt. She looks at me, and I can't help but flinch, remembering the fire that flew from her fingertips only nights before.

"You," she says. "You're as bad Senchan. You try to take him. You cannot take him. I love him."

I take a deep breath and wait for the flames to come. I wait for her to kill me, to burn the whole world down. But she doesn't. Her head drops when she's done talking and then she runs off, hiding somewhere out of sight.

"Well," Penelope says. "That was…unexpected."

Kingston stands and takes a half step forward.

"You knew," Kingston says. "You knew how she felt about me. Why would you do that to her?"

"I was merely bringing her back to Mab," Penelope says, holding her hands up in defense. "She had run off. Again." She turns her gaze to me. "And I have enough on my hands keeping *this* one out of trouble. Which is clearly not working."

"You're a heartless bitch," Kingston says. Then he runs off in the direction Lilith went, calling her name.

Penelope looks at me.

"You were supposed to be practicing," she says.

"I was."

She sighs. "You mustn't let your emotions get the best of you," she says. "In this world, show any sign of weakness, and it will be turned against you."

"What are you talking about?"

She smiles one of her sad, lost smiles. "Let's just say, for people like you and me, love, freedom, happiness...well, unless we're very specific from the beginning, they just aren't in the contract."

She turns and begins walking away. But as she goes, I catch her mumble something. It sounds like *for now.*

I close my eyes and slide against the trailer. I can still taste Kingston's kiss on my lips, can still feel the tingle of his fingers in my pulse. Underneath it, though, is an anticipation, a sort of fear. The way Mab paused, the catch in her words. The sudden rage. Someone's been messing with my contract.

Someone is targeting *me.*

Chapter Sixteen: Monster

It's dinner time when Kingston comes and finds me again.

I'm in my trailer, reading a book and trying not to think of everything that happened that afternoon, which isn't really working because now that I know my memory's been tampered with, that's all I can think about. How much did Kingston hide from me, and why the hell did I want it hidden in the first place? Why the false memories? Why the grand illusion? And, perhaps most importantly, what landed me here to begin with? I try to think back and am met with only haze and grey and patchwork moments that could have been pulled from anyone's life: walking to school, watching movies with friends whose names I can't remember, eating dinner with my mom whose voice I can't hear. Nothing remarkable. Nothing that would put blood on my hands and visions in my head. Nothing spectacular. What *was* I?

The worst part was, every time I closed my eyes, those weren't the only thoughts coursing through my mind. Every blink, every moment of darkness, and I felt his lips on mine, tasted the cinnamon of his tongue and felt the heat of his breath. Every blink, and I was back, crushed against his chest. Every blink, and I wished it would have lasted longer.

But that was the trouble. It was just a moment. Moments were easy to erase or change. How long would he let me keep this before he turned around and blanked it out? A large part of me didn't want to trust him, wanted to be pissed at him for toying with my past. But the rest of me knew. I had asked for that. I'd signed the contract. It was the things I hadn't asked for that sent me reeling, the things he could take away at any moment. How long did I have before he got tired of me and made me believe I was tired of him? I kept closing my eyes, reliving the moment over and over, waiting for the inevitable shoe to drop.

So when Kingston knocks and lets himself in, it's almost a relief, almost like stepping up to the executioner's block. I know what he's going to say. And I'm not going to wait around for it.

"Kingston, listen," I say, "about today—"

"Not now," he says, walking past where I'm sitting on the bed to stare out the window. Then he steps back and closes the curtain. "They're back." There's panic in his voice that makes my skin go cold. Everything I wanted to say drains in an instant.

"Who?"

"The troupe," he says. It's almost a relief. We're not under attack by the Summer Court or anything horrible. Just the troupe back from the watering hole.

"Oh."

He must note my relief, because his hands clench at his sides and when he speaks, there's more anger than before.

"No, not *oh*. They're back. But Melody's not with them."

"Maybe she got lucky?" I start, but this clearly isn't the time for jokes. "Come on, Kingston, she's not a kid."

"No, she's not. She knows not to leave the troupe." He's pacing back and forth. "This is bad, this is really, really bad."

"Why? She can take care of herself."

Then he stops and takes a deep breath. "If you tell anyone, I'll kill you," he whispers. He turns to face me.

"Melody's not like us. Remember when I said she was human? Well, it's more than that. She doesn't have the same immortality clause that we do, and she's only twenty-two. Like, actually twenty-two. And without her, we're all fucked."

"What are you talking about?" I say.

"I can't explain," Kingston says. "Contractual obligation." He runs his hands around his neck, as though the very thought of telling me is choking him—a feeling I know all too well.

"So let's go find her," I say.

"We can't," he says. "We have no idea where she is and no way to find out. And if we tell Mab, she'll go after her herself."

He slouches down on the chair.

"Would you just tell me what's going on?" I say. "Why is it a bad thing if Mab looks for her?"

He makes a noise that sounds like gagging and shakes his head, looking up at me with a sad grin.

"Damn these contracts," he says. "Don't you see? This is precisely what they want."

"Who?" I'm getting tired of this cat-and-mouse game of information.

"The Summer Court. They took her. They must have. I can't tell you why, but I know they did. And you're one of the few who understands the danger."

"I do?"

"Don't be stupid," he says. "You saw it. You saw Lilith on the field, you saw her kill Senchan and the other Summer Fey. One of them must have escaped and told their king. They know about Lilith. They know what she is. The Blood Autumn Treaty is broken. Now, we're at war."

"Why would they care about Lilith? She's just..." But I can't finish the sentence because she's clearly not just a little girl.

"Do you remember Sheena?" he asks.

I nod. It's hard to forget watching a purple-haired girl turn into a floating orb of light.

"Lilith's...Lilith's like that. Kind of."

"She's a Summer Faerie?"

He shakes his head.

"No. Different. But the Summer Court...they want her dead. And if they know she's here, they'll kill everyone around her 'til she's gone.

That's why they took Mel. Why Mab can't go. That's what they want—
they want us to be weak."

There's no clashing outside, no fires or screams. The only noise is the
rest of the troupe laughing, the sound of music as the chefs finish up the
evening meal. It doesn't sound like war.

"Now do you understand? If Mab leaves, we're more defenseless than..."
He coughs. "Guess I'll just leave it at that. Mab can't know. But the barriers
between this world and Faerie are weakest at dusk. If we don't get Mel back
before then, we're dead. The Summer Fey will kill us all."

"So what do we do?" I ask.

"I don't know," he says. "Mab will find out soon enough, but...there's
something we're not getting. There's something missing."

"What do you mean?"

He sighs and runs his hands through his hair again.

"We've been set up," he says. "The deaths, the tent, all of it. They
weren't just warnings, they were trying to weaken us. But that should be
impossible. Contractually, we can't die. We can't be weakened."

"That's it," I say. Mab's reaction is suddenly making sense, the wid-
ened eyes and accusing stare. "The contracts."

"What?"

I stand up and walk past him, pacing because it feels like the right
thing to do.

"Before we...before I saw you, Mab was showing me my contract.
She got pissed off and yelled at me for something. Said I'd changed it.
I hadn't thought about it 'til now—"

Kingston stops me.

"You *changed* your contract? How?"

"I didn't," I say. "But she thinks I did."

Kingston's nodding, now. "That makes sense." He chews the inside
of his lips as he thinks. "Someone's been changing the contracts. Little
changes at first, so we wouldn't notice. An injury here, an accident there."

He snaps his fingers, a small spark igniting and burning out.

"That's it. That's how people are dying. Someone's changing the contracts to make them vulnerable. It all makes sense."

"But how?" I say. "The contracts are in Mab's trailer. She'd never let anyone touch them, let alone rewrite them."

Kingston's face darkens.

"Of course," he whispers. He pushes past me and opens the door, but I grab his arm before he can pull it open.

"What?" I ask.

"Who does Mab trust above all others?" he says. "Who's been with her the longest?"

Realization dawns.

"Penelope," I whisper. *The woman chained here for life.*

He nods.

"Bingo. That's why she placed you under Penelope's care. It wasn't so she could watch after you, it was so you'd keep an eye on *her*." He pulls open the door. "So let's go find that mer-bitch and make her talk."

We jog to Penelope's trailer, past the troupe now standing in line for dinner. We don't knock, just pull open her door and rush inside.

She's sitting in front of her mirror, brushing her long red hair and staring into the placid depths of glass. She doesn't even start when we burst in, just keeps brushing her hair.

"If you are looking for a new place to fornicate, I suggest picking a trailer that is unoccupied," she says.

"You have one minute to talk before I burn you to a fucking crisp," Kingston says. As if to accentuate the point, the air around his palms shivers with heat.

"It is quite rude to enter someone's trailer without knocking," Penelope says, as though she's oblivious to the fact that Kingston's on the edge of burning the whole trailer down. "And even more rude to threaten their life. Tell me, to what should I be confessing?"

She watches us from the reflection in the mirror. The heat from Kingston grows and I step a little to the side.

"Don't play dumb," Kingston says. "I know you've spent your life pretending to be a daft bitch, but I'm on to you now. You've been changing our contracts. You're the reason everyone's dying."

"That, my dear, is an awfully strong accusation." She draws the brush through her hair one more time, then sets it down. "Do you have any proof?"

Kingston opens his mouth, then closes it.

"Precisely," Penelope says. She reaches for a tube of lipstick and glides it over her lips, making the perfect pucker in her mirror. "I suggest you come back when you have more concrete evidence. Or evidence of any kind, for that matter. " She sets down the tube and turns around in her chair. The fire in Kingston's hands is simmering, but I can tell he feels precisely as I do; there's no doubt that Penelope did this. If anyone in the entire troupe would be looking for a way out, it would be her—it explained her reaction to seeing Senchan in the field, her talk of finding an exit clause. But who would believe it? She was just so *perfect*.

She stands and walks over to us.

"If you don't mind," she says. I don't step aside. I want to punch her.

"Melody is missing," Kingston says through clenched teeth. "If you have any humanity left, you'll tell me where she is."

A look crosses Penelope's face, the mildest of concern.

"I assure you," she says, "I have no clue where Melody is. But the tent's still in one piece. Take comfort in that."

Then she steps past us and opens the door. It slams behind her, leaving us alone and aimless.

"Fuck," Kingston says. He punches the trailer wall, making the whole thing shake.

"What do we do?" I ask.

"She's right," Kingston says. "There's nothing we *can* do. We have no proof."

I glance around the room and something clicks.

"Maybe we do."

He looks at me in confusion as I walk across the room to Penelope's nightstand. I'm praying that she didn't think ahead, that she wasn't thinking we'd storm in here like this. I open the drawer. There, nesting in a little brass bowl, is the necklace. The black diamond glints like a raven's eye.

I pull it out by the chain and hold it up.

"What is that?" Kingston asks.

"I don't really know," I say. "But according to Penelope, she can store her memories here. If what we need is a confession, it's probably in here."

Kingston's eyes go wide as he crosses the short space between us.

"You're a genius," he says. I blush. A beat passes and I'm staring at his eyes as he stares at the necklace. "How do we use it?" he asks.

I take his hand and turn the palm up.

"I think we just ask," I say, and drop the diamond into his palm, clasping both our fingers around it at the same time.

The room spins.

Shadows are everywhere.

There's a man in the shadows. A man with white hair.

"I want out," Penelope says. She stands in the shadows, too, her body pressed against the trunk of a tree. She's in a dark cloak that hides every inch of her, but her voice is clear.

"Out?" Senchan says. "Is that why you called me here?"

Penelope hesitates. "I've been under Mab's control for centuries," she says. "I cannot bear it another day."

Senchan smiles sadly. Is it moonlight filtering through the trees, or is he really glowing like that?

"I feel your pain. Truly I do. But I'm afraid things just don't work like that. Your contract is quite binding. In order to break it, well, you'll have to do something for *me*."

"Anything."

Senchan's eyes widen. "A bold promise. You would truly give anything for your freedom?"

"I have nothing else to live for, nothing left to give. Everything has already been taken from me. Name your price and I will see it met."

Senchan takes a deep breath.

"We want the Trade to end."

"You know I don't have the power to shut down the show."

"No," he says. "But that is our price. End the Cirque, and you will be free. We don't care how you do it, only that you deliver. Unless you think the price is too dear…"

"No," Penelope says. She glances around. "I may have a way."

"Yes?"

"Kassia."

Senchan takes a step back, as though Penelope punched him in the gut.

"Kassia is dead."

"No," Penelope says. There's a fervent heat in her words. "She's still alive. I have seen her. Mab is hiding her."

"If that is true, then the Blood Autumn Treaty is broken. The circus would be forced to shut down."

"I would not lie."

"We cannot attack until there is proof," Senchan says.

"If I give you proof, if she reveals her true nature, will that be enough?"

Senchan nods and holds out his hand.

"Expose Kassia and Mab's treachery, and you shall have your freedom. A good bargain, if I do say so myself."

Penelope reaches out her hand.

"You will tell no one," he says. She nods as they shake.

Light pours out between their fingertips. The light fills my vision.

❖

I blink and I'm back in the trailer. Kingston is staring at me with his eyes wide and lips open.

"That's it," he says. "We have her."

"Who's Kassia?" I ask.

Kingston shakes his head.

"I can't say. Contractual…"

He pockets the necklace, turns away from me, and takes a step toward the door. Then he turns around and pulls me toward him, presses his lips to mine in one quick kiss that fills me with fire. He pulls away and smiles.

"You're a genius," he says. Then he's out the door. I follow right behind.

We're not even a few steps outside the trailer when we spot Penelope. She's not in line with the rest of the troupe. She's standing near the edge of the chapiteau, staring out at the field beyond. Kingston pauses and stares at her. The air around him shivers.

"Kingston, no," I say. "Let's just go tell Mab."

"No," Kingston says. "I'm going to make the bitch pay." He stalks toward Penelope and I stand there, torn between running to Mab and running after Kingston. The choice is easy; I run to Kingston's side and take his hand in mine. His touch tingles.

Penelope turns when she sees us. Her gaze takes us in, the linked fingers, the set in our eyes. She smirks and turns away.

"Back for another round of false accusations?" she says.

"We know," Kingston says. He holds up the diamond necklace. "We know everything."

I expect Penelope to gasp, to yell, to do any number of things the bad guys do in movies when they're found out. Instead, she laughs.

"Well done, Vivienne," she says. "I was hoping you'd remember that. This would have been so anticlimactic otherwise."

My heart drops. Penelope looks over her shoulder at my silence.

"What?" she asks. "You truly believe I accidentally left you in my trailer? Please, I'm not truly a—what did you call me?—a *daft bitch*."

Kingston drops the necklace in his pocket.

"Why?" he asks.

"Because I want you to understand that my intentions were never to hurt people. I just wanted freedom. This was the only way."

"If you've been changing the contracts," I say, "why not just change yours? End your contract early? Why kill everyone?"

"You saw what happened when Paul's contract finished early. Time is a force no magic can change. I couldn't take the chance that the same would happen to me. No, the only sure way to be free was to end the circus. Then, I wouldn't be dodging a contract. The contract would simply no longer exist." She almost sounds sad about it, like she's upset she had to get her hands so dirty, but Kingston and I are far beyond pity.

"Where's Melody?" Kingston hisses.

"Safe," Penelope says.

Fire ignites around Kingston's fingertips. The heat is blistering and I drop his hand.

"Talk," he says through gritted teeth. "Talk or I'll make you beg."

"Ahh, you see, that is what I was hoping for. It would have been disappointing to go to all that trouble for nothing."

Neither of us say anything, but I can see Kingston's resolve falter. Clearly, that's all Penelope was after.

"I call on line 89F, point three."

Kingston gasps and crumples to his knees. The heat in his palms vanishes.

"My, Kingston," she says. "Whoever would have thought that a few words could quench your fire?"

Something snaps inside of me. I leap toward Penelope. The only thought in my mind is the image of punching her square in the face, of making her bleed and beg and suffer like everyone she's hurt and killed in her quest for *freedom*. My arm pulls back, aims straight for her pretty jaw.

Then stars explode across my vision as something slams into my gut. I smack face-first into the earth and roll on the ground, clenching my stomach as iron binds itself around my insides. I can't breathe, can't move, can't get the pain to go away.

"As you can tell," Penelope says, "I've quite thought of *everything*. Your contracts expressly forbid harming me."

She steps over and kicks Kingston in the ribs. Kingston gasps.

"You, on the other hand, have no such safeguards. Perhaps this will teach you to be more careful with whom you choose to confront."

Kingston groans. I can barely see him as darkness inks itself around my vision.

"Oh, and one more thing," Penelope says, her voice perfectly calm. "I think you'll find that speaking of this to anyone else is a very, very bad idea." Her words turn simpering. "Contractual, you know." Then she walks away, humming happily to herself.

The moment she's out of sight, my lungs expand and I suck in a breath so sharp it's painful. I scramble over to where Kingston's sprawled out on the ground, his hands clutching his ribs.

"Are you okay?"

"She blocked me. My powers are gone." He takes a deep breath. "That must be how Senchan did it. She worked a containment clause into my contract and told the bastard the line." With a wince, he pushes himself to standing. I'm there, helping him up, looping his arm around my shoulder. Zal is wrapped around his arm. The serpent is smudging like mad, now, like those *Mom* tattoos slowly bleached off bikers' biceps.

"How could she do that?" I ask. Penelope's disappeared into the tents and trailers. Even the thought of chasing after her makes an ache creep through my skull. "How can she change the contracts?"

"I still don't know," Kingston says. "It shouldn't be possible; Mab's the only one who can dictate the terms."

"So Mab can change them back? Now that she knows what's wrong?"

Kingston shakes his head. "You can't just negate magic like that. Power goes in cycles. She won't be able to change our contracts 'til the next new moon."

"So there's nothing we can do."

He doesn't answer. Just the thought of yelling out that Penelope's the traitor makes my throat burn and sting.

"If only you hadn't signed your stupid contract," Kingston whispers.

"What do you mean?"

"Your visions," he says. "They're the only way we could find Melody. If she was here, we'd be fine. But Mab's the only one who can get you to use them."

Another click. The shock in Mab's voice when she read out my contract: *unless deemed necessary by Queen Mab or…* There was another. Penelope had changed my contract to allow someone else to summon my powers, someone who couldn't be linked back to her.

"No," I say. "There's another. That's what set Mab off. Someone else can access my powers." My mind races. Then the scent of fire and brimstone fills my head, and it's all horribly clear.

"It's Lilith," I say. "When I touched her, I had my vision. I thought it was just a reaction, but maybe…maybe she's the other one on the contract."

"Then we better find her," Kingston says, staring up into the sky. The sun is getting dangerously close to the horizon. We only have a few hours until dusk.

He doesn't waste any more time. Before I ask where he thinks she could be hiding in this vast cornfield, he's running across the lawn toward the eight-foot-tall stalks. I'm right at his heels. The tent and all its inhabitants disappear behind us the moment we cross over, the world suddenly becoming heavier, more humid. Kingston runs full stop in front of me, navigating through the corn as though he's got it all mapped out in his head. I don't bother asking where we're going. After a few minutes, he stops so fast I nearly bump into him. He puts up a hand and glances back at me, a definitive *say nothing* look on his face. Then he takes a few steps forward and motions for me to follow.

We emerge into a small clearing that could have been cleared by a UFO. It's a perfect circle of trodden corn stalks, maybe twelve feet in diameter. In the center is Lilith, humming to herself and playing with a figure made of grass. Poe stalks the perimeter, staring at us with flat yellow eyes.

"Lilith," Kingston says softly. "Lilith, it's me. How are you?"

Lilith looks up at the sound of his voice, her face practically glowing with happiness that Kingston came to see her. She opens her mouth, then catches sight of me standing behind him. The happiness turns to disgust.

"What do you want?" she grumbles, going back to playing with the stick figure in her hands.

"We need your help," Kingston says.

"Why?"

Kingston hesitates, and I wonder if it's because he can't find the right words or if he simply can't speak them under Penelope's new rules.

"It's Melody. She's gone missing. And we need to find her."

"Tell Auntie Mab," Lilith says.

"We can't. Mab can't know." He kneels down at her side and puts a hand on her shoulder. "Please, Lilith. We need your help. *I* need your help."

"Why should I?" she asks with a pout. She looks straight at me as she speaks. "You don't like me. You just like her. Not me. Her. She'll hurt you."

I take a step forward but Kingston puts up his hand again without even looking back.

"Lilith," he says, cupping her chin in his hand. "You know that's not true. You know I like you."

"You kissed her."

"It was a mistake."

The words come as a punch in my gut. It takes everything I have not to just drop to my knees right there. I can't believe it, don't want to believe it. *He lied to you about everything else. He could have lied about this, too.*

"Prove it."

He doesn't hesitate, doesn't take a breath or ready himself or anything. He just leans in and pulls her lips to his and kisses her. For a brief moment, Lilith's eyes flicker to mine and the corner of her mouth turns up into a grin. Then she closes her eyes and leans into the kiss.

It goes on for an eternity, the two of them sitting in the middle of the circle in the amber light, and I can't help but wonder if maybe this is how it's meant to be. Both of them are powerful, immortal, ageless. What chance did I have with someone like that? What hope did I have *against* someone like that? I don't cough, don't interrupt the moment. And I don't turn away. I won't give her that satisfaction. Anger and betrayal and a hundred other emotions roil in my stomach, but I don't give in. I won't be weak. Not now, not ever. Not again.

When Kingston pulls away, he doesn't turn back to me to give an apologetic glance. Lilith doesn't look at me either. She just smiles at him, totally lucid, and puts a hand on his cheek.

"Kingston," she whispers. "What can I do?"

Now he hesitates. "It's Vivienne," he says. "She has visions. But she's under contract not to use them. We think…we think you can access them. It's the only way of finding Melody."

Disappointment battles across her face, but then she drops her hand and looks at me. That lost little girl is gone, and in her place is a creature I can't even begin to come to grips with.

"What must I do?" she asks.

Kingston motions me over. I go and sit beside him, doing my best to stay composed, to not feel that mixture of rage and shame that are coiling around in my chest. I want to call him every name for bastard, want to run off before it gets any worse. *Fuck them, fuck this show, fuck everyone.*

But I know I can't leave, not until Mab's done with me. If they go down, I go down, too. And I'm not going down without a fight.

Someone's going to pay for all this.

"Repeat after me," he says. "I call upon the contract of Vivienne Warfield, Line 17A. I summon her powers of Vision. Seek out and relay the location of Melody Bonaparte."

Lilith nods, and begins to repeat his words, but the moment she speaks there's a rushing in my head, a fire and wind and fury I can't control, and I'm falling, falling, the wind screaming through every inch of me, and it's only white and grey, white and grey, white and grey and screaming.

When I wake up again, I'm alone in the middle of the field. The sky is pink and orange and spread out wide above me, the cornfields alive with the sound of cicadas and wind. I push myself to sitting, try to force the ringing out of my ears. That's when I realize I'm not actually alone. Lilith's sitting on the edge of the circle, stroking Poe and watching me. Both of their eyes gleam in the fading light, Lilith's green, Poe's a dusty yellow. I feel like a victim in one of those horror movies, just woken up from a chloroform stupor to find myself in some basement-turned-torture-chamber.

"Where is he?" I manage to say. The words make my head throb.

"Kingston is searching for Melody," she says. Her voice is so calm, so controlled. Poe mewls in her lap and she looks down and smiles. "Your vision told him where she is, and now he is gone. He will not return before sunrise. Melody is far, far away."

"Why didn't you go with him?"

"He told me to stay here. Keep you safe." She looks at me and cocks her head to the side. "Weak, Vivienne. You are very, very weak."

I struggle to standing and sway on the spot. I ignore her words and scan the field, though I can't see anything past the edge of the circle.

"Where is he?" I ask again. "I have to find him."

"You won't," she says. Everything in her voice says that this is precisely where she wants me to be. Dread creeps through my veins like ice. Is she teamed up with Penelope? Was this just some elaborate ploy to get me out of the way?

Lilith puts Poe on the ground and stands in one fluid motion. Even though she's still in her white dress, even though she hasn't grown and her hair is still tied back with a ribbon, she looks different, looks more in control of something I can't place. And whatever that is, it's terrifying. She steps right up to me, staring up into my eyes, pinning me like a serpent. "He told me to keep you here. Keep you safe. Safe with me." She sings the last bit, the childish tune frighteningly at odds with her somber stare.

Rage boils inside of me, burning away the fear. Anger at him, anger at her, anger at all of them for fucking me over. Everyone's been playing with me. Everyone. I'm not going to be played like this any longer. Fire burns.

I don't think. I swing.

My fist connects perfectly with Lilith's cheek, knocking her backward a couple steps. She staggers and Poe is hissing at her feet, but Lilith flicks a hand down in a *shut up* sort of gesture, and the cat goes silent. When she looks back at me, she's actually grinning. The trickle of blood from the corner of her mouth makes her look positively demented.

"There's the fire," she says. "Let's watch it burn." She lunges forward and tackles me.

She knocks me to the ground and we roll. Stars flash across my vision as she punches me in the face. I gag as her knee connects to my gut. For having a twelve-year-old's body, she fights like a heavyweight. But the rolling momentum carries and then I'm on top of her, slamming my fist into her face over and over before she flips us over and elbows me in the jaw. In one frighteningly smooth motion, she pins my arms to my chest. There's more blood on her face, but she's laughing. There's a madness inside of her that makes my rage flicker. I know that look. There's no amount of pain in the world I could inflict on her; she will always, always come back for more. Until one of us is dead.

"Oh, Vivienne," she says. "This is why he'll never choose you. You're nothing. Mortal. Weak." She sniffs and stretches her neck. "It would be so easy to fake your death, you know. A tragic accident. Wrong place, wrong time. He'd never even suspect."

I try to swallow the blood in my mouth but the iron makes me want to gag. She leans in close to my ear. "You are very lucky we are currently on the same side. Otherwise it would be so, so simple to dispose of you."

Poe hisses by our side and Lilith jerks her attention to the field. Something rustles in the undergrowth. Something chuckles. The sun has set, the horizon fading to hues of fiery pink and orange.

Then, something takes flight, a streak of fire that arcs high overhead. We both watch it fly, watch as it curves to the other horizon. There's a flash of light when it falls out of sight and then another flies a similar path. Then another. Arrows.

Lilith and I look at each other. Her eyes go wide and the fire inside both of us vanishes.

The Summer Fey have arrived. We're already too late.

CHAPTER SEVENTEEN:
'TIL THE WORLD ENDS

We run through the corn, Lilith in the lead, me right behind her, cutting a straight line toward the tent. As we get closer, I can hear the screams. We burst from the field into a scene that makes my blood run cold.

The chapiteau is in flames.

Streaks of arrows are flinging down toward the tent like burning birds, the whistle and howl of arrow and flame growing louder by the moment. The grey and blue canvas is peeling and ripping as flames eat it alive. Lilith and I stop and stare in horror. Arrows are ricocheting off the trailers, sticking into the ground like fiery voodoo pins. Others have found flesh. There are two bodies in flames on the ground, but we aren't close enough to see who they are. I don't want to know. I don't want those memories burned into my head.

Everything is chaos. Everything is fire.

Then I hear a voice, one that roars over the inferno and turns the air to ice.

"WHO DARES?"

Mab appears in front of the tent in a swirl of blue light and smoke. She hovers above the ground, easily three times her normal height, the top of her head level with the flaming pinnacle of the big top. Shadows swarm around her in a serpentine dance and her eyes are emerald coals.

She is every nightmare combined. Just the sight of her pulls at the darkest corners of my imagination, makes my skin crawl and fills my blood with the need to flee. I nearly drop to my knees.

"WHO DARES ATTACK THE COURT OF QUEEN MAB?"

A gust of wind answers, the sound of chimes and summer breezes.

I turn around to see a golden apparition floating above the cornfield, a man made of liquid light with a halo of brilliance behind his head. His eyes are sapphire, and when he speaks, I feel my veins pulse with life, feel the very earth shiver with expectation.

"I am Oberos, prince of the Summer Court. I am here on the king's behalf to deliver this message: Queen Mab—you and your Court are under direct violation of the Blood Autumn Treaty. You have knowingly harbored the daemon known as Kassia. As such, the Treaty is broken, and your Court shall pay in blood until Kassia is released or killed."

Kassia. I glance at Lilith as things click. Lilith in flames. Lilith losing control. And Mab trying so, so hard to keep her out of sight. Why the hell is she so important? Lilith glances at me. She's no longer in control. Her eyes are vacant and Poe is clutched in her arms, his fur sticking straight up.

"IF IT'S BLOOD YOU WANT, IT'S BLOOD YOU SHALL HAVE. WE WILL NOT REST UNTIL THE FIELDS ARE SOAKED IN SUMMER'S TEARS."

The sky above us darkens at her cry.

"So be it," Oberos says. The fields erupt in screams and howls.

More arrows fly through the air, but Mab's on top of things this time. She raises a hand to the sky, flames of blue shadow leaping from her fingertips and dancing above the tent. The arrows strike the shield and vanish. A second later she disappears from the sky, appearing in front of me in the blink of an eye.

"Where is she?" she asks.

"Who?"

"Melody!" she yells. Her face is pale as a skull and her teeth are razor sharp. I want to curl up and die.

"I don't know," I say. A Summer Faerie leaps out of the corn behind us, humanoid and stick-like, a sickle in its hands. I duck as it swings for my head, but in a flash of light, Mab freezes it solid. It shatters in a thousand pieces when its foot hits the ground. "Kingston…he went after her. He used my visions to find her."

Mab's eyes flare in anger and I wait for the finishing blow. It never comes.

"We'll speak of this later. If you survive," she hisses, and then vanishes.

Next thing I know, there's another mob of Summer Fey scrambling from the corn behind me. I don't wait another second; I run. Lilith's right ahead of me as we gun it toward the trailers and the illusion of safety, though I have no doubt in my mind that we are royally fucked. The Summer Court is closing in on all sides, fey of every sort running toward the troupe with bloodlust in their eyes. They take all shapes, from centaurs and twiggy dryads to floating balls of light and winged pixie girls. Even the ones that look like they should be stuck in someone's garden have bloodlust in their eyes and make my blood run cold. We're outnumbered. Horribly.

Mab floats high above, locked in combat with the glowing form of Oberos. He wields twin scimitars of liquid sunlight, she her whip that slices the sky in lashes of midnight. Every stroke of her whip sounds like thunder, every slash of his swords blinds like lightning. They are twin titans, and they are nearly impossible to see in the light of their fury. Lilith and I run past the pie cart, where a small huddle of our troupe is forming.

The Shifters are the first to leap into action. One girl drops to all fours and quivers. Scales erupt from her flesh, her entire body twists and contorts and grows, and leathery wings sprout from her spine. With a roar that sounds like every nightmare I've had come to life, she leaps into the air as an enormous red dragon, flames dripping from her maw like lava. The other Shifters follow suit, twisting themselves into every manner of mythical creature: three-headed chimera, twenty-foot-tall medusae, and a monstrous, lumbering cyclops that rips one of the telephone poles from the earth and wields it as a grisly club. I race under the body of a thirty-foot-tall tarantula that had once been a concessionaire, and notice a few other performers leaping into the fray, wielding powers I never knew they had.

Vanessa and Richard stand side by side, throwing daggers of ice that materialize from thin air. Maya, the tightrope walker, hovers a few feet above the ground. For a moment, she just floats there. Then her eyes glow blue and she lets out a scream that flings the approaching fey back a hundred yards. Lilith and I duck behind a trailer and lean against the side, panting. The sky is roiling above us and all I hear is screaming, the sounds of the dead or dying. We're outmatched, there's no question. We're going to die. We're all going to die.

Then something new comes crawling forth, something definitely not mortal and definitely not from the Summer Court. The shadows beneath the trailers quiver, ooze like oil. Then they change. Dark shapes pull themselves from underneath, their forms indescribable save for the terror they send reeling through my chest. One shadowy creature stretches out by my feet—a beast half-spider, half-man, with talons and fangs and hundreds of darting black eyes. I nearly scream. It stands and regards me, and I hear its voice hiss in my head: *We fight for the same queen, Oracle. You need not fear us.* The creature does a jerking sort of bow and then runs off, joining the other throng of black nightmares that stream toward the Summer Fey. I don't have time to wonder what they are, but something tells me these are the Night Terrors Mel warned me about.

Oracle?

Blood pounds in my ears as the old fight or flight response wells up inside of me. This time, though, there's a new sensation, a tingling that makes my fingers ache. A power like an electrical surge races along my skin. My hands feel alive with energy. Lilith chatters at my side, barely comprehensible over the roar of fire and screams.

Our solace doesn't last.

I've barely caught my breath when a group of Summer Fey appears at the end of the trailer. Half of them look like walking saplings, with sprig-like appendages and berries for eyes. The other half are more sinister: drowned-looking things with seaweed for hair and long, rusted scimitars. They spot us and rush forward, yelling a gibberish battle cry. Lilith drops to the ground in the fetal position with her hands over her head. There's nothing around to use as a weapon, and as they run toward me I want to close my eyes and just let it happen, pray that it will be a quick death.

But then something takes over, something that I can't control. The tingling in my fingers courses through my blood, fills my limbs. I crouch low as the fey approach, adopting some sort of battle stance, all the while screaming inside my head. *What the hell are you doing? Run! Run!* But I don't run, I just wait for them to crash upon me, a smile slashed across my face.

The first dryad reaches me, one clubbed arm raised to smash against my skull. Before it can splatter my brains across the trailer walls, I lunge forward, driven by a feral hunger that turns my world red.

I grab the creature's arm and spin, snapping it in two and ripping the wooden appendage off entirely. The dryad screams, but not for long. As I rotate, I bring the severed arm up and over my head, shattering it against my attacker's skull. The dryad explodes in a burst of leaves and butterflies, but my victory is short-lived. The others are upon me. I duck under the blade of a naiad and toss the dryad's arm aside, sweep one leg out to knock over my opponent and smash my fist into another dryad coming in from the side. I grab the scimitar from one of the water-monsters and make to slash off another head, only to have my thrust blocked by a vine that bursts from the ground. More tendrils snake from the earth and twine themselves around my calves and wrists, pinning me in a half-crouch. A naiad smiles at me, his waterlogged eyes red and bulging. He raises his scimitar over my bare neck.

The energy in my fingers turns to fire.

White light surrounds me, fills me, burns me with a thousand tiny suns. I see through half-closed eyes the vines disintegrating from my wrists and calves, see the shocked face of the naiad as he dissolves into nothing. Light fills me, blinds me, roars through me like the angry howl of a god. Bright, white, like a strobe illuminating the whole world, and then it's gone.

I drop to my knees and shudder with newfound cold as the power leaves me. That's when I realize that the mob of fey is gone. Only Lilith is still there, cowering in the alley between the trailers, arms wrapped around her head.

I stare at my hands. I swear I see faint traces of silver etched into the lines of my palm.

"What the fuck?" I whisper. Was this part of the contract as well?

I don't have time to think. Another wave of Summer Fey bursts onto the scene, a new mix of dryads and will-o-wisps and creatures I have no name for. The bloodlust is gone. So is the tingling. I'm not about to test and find out if there's enough power left over for round two. I reach down and grab Lilith by the shoulder, pull her up to standing, and duck into a trailer.

It's not until I've slammed the door behind us that I realize where we've landed. Mab's office.

It's dark. The air has that cold, dry sensation of a cemetery on an autumn night. Lilith huddles at my side. I fully expect to hear the Summer Fey clanging against the aluminum door, but all is silent. Just the sound of me and Lilith breathing and the hammer of our hearts.

Then a light flares into being, and then another, cold blue candle flames that glimmer out of skull sconces. The office emerges from the dark like a beast surfacing from a midnight ocean—first the desk, then the chairs, then the bookshelves. And then another form appears in a wash of mist. We aren't alone in Mab's study.

Penelope.

She turns the moment she becomes visible, as though Lilith and I were the ones who just appeared from the gloom. In her hand is the book of contracts.

"Lilith," she says. "I'd hoped Mab would send you here. Though I wasn't expecting an escort."

"What are you doing here?" I ask, my hands clenched at my sides. No tingling, this time, no power. And no chance of hurting her. She already saw to that.

"I could ask the same," she says. "Though I'm pleased you're here safe."

"Auntie Mab won't be happy," Lilith says. She's stroking Poe— I hadn't even seen the cat get inside—with that distant tint to her voice. "She doesn't like her book to be touched. No, no, not at all."

Penelope shoots her a venomous glance.

"After this," she says, "*Auntie* Mab won't have a book." When she looks to me, her eyes soften. "Vivienne, don't you see what I'm doing? I'm saving you."

I take a half step forward.

"*Saving* me? By bringing the Summer Fey here and getting us all killed?"

"I haven't killed anyone," she says. Her eyes go wild in that moment, as though I'm not the only one she's trying to convince.

"You're full of shit," I say. "What about Sabina? And Roman? Hell, Melody's probably dead now because of you!" The rage inside of me is growing, a white-hot anger I want to throw her way. But there's still no power in my fingertips, no growing pulse of magic. Even if there was, I know there'd be no point. The very thought of harming Penelope is enough to make my chest constrict.

"I had no hand in their deaths," she says. Her voice drops to a whisper. "My only task was to alter their contracts, to make them mortal again. I can only assume the Summer Court arranged for their execution. As for Melody, I have never touched her terms."

"What about her illness, then? Why did she get so sick?"

She opens her mouth, but she doesn't say anything. Not for a moment. "Melody's fate is different from the other performers of this troupe," she says. Her words are careful, as though every one is a chore. "She has always been mortal, and her fate has always been tied to the health of this show."

"What did you do to her?"

"You already know," she says. "I had her taken far, far away. The only things that can sever her bond to her duties are distance or death." She pauses and looks at me. Her voice goes soft. "You may call me what you like, but I am no murderer. It was my choice to have Melody hidden away. Senchan would have had her killed. I saved her, so I could save all of us."

"You're insane," I say. She's completely lost it. She doesn't seem to realize that outside the trailer, people are burning and bleeding— the very family of performers she's deluding herself into thinking she's saving.

"It was the only way," she says. "It's the only way we can be free. Our contracts will only be void when the circus is over. You and I, we should be working together. We're the same."

Then, before I can ask what she's talking about, she places the book on the table. It's open to my name.

"You see?" she says, and points to the very bottom line. "Section 72A: The duration of this contract is valid indefinitely, or until Vivienne is deemed to have served her purpose, whichever transpires first." She looks at me with true sadness in her eyes. "Your contract has no end. I didn't believe it at first, couldn't imagine Mab would try the same trick on you as she had on me. But she did. You're in this forever."

Her words send my mind into a haze, a heaviness I can't shake. I expect the memory to crash back upon seeing the evidence before me, but it doesn't. No remembering signing my life away, no reason to have done such a thing. I glance at my hands. The light, the power, the visions…

whatever it was, that was what I was running from. Whatever it was, it was bad enough to want it locked away for eternity.

"At first," she says, her words barely above a whisper, "it sounds like an okay fate. But that's now. That's only after a few weeks. Imagine how it will feel when you watch a hundred years pass you by, a thousand. The world changes, empires crumble. Friends die. And you know that every day you will wake up and see the sun rise, and you will put on a show, and then you will go to sleep without even a dream to help you escape. Never aging, never dying. Oh, yes, it sounds okay now, but when you are as old as I, the torment is unbearable."

I close my eyes and force myself to stay standing. What she's saying is impossible to fathom, but the idea of it is trying to sink in. I keep seeing the print, *this contract is valid indefinitely.* I had wanted to run away, but had I really wanted to run away forever?

"There is only one way for this madness to end," Penelope whispers. "If the show is over, our contracts are moot. If the Dream Trade stops, she has no more use for us. We will be free."

I take a deep, staggering breath and open my eyes.

"What about her?" I ask, pointing to the girl.

"Lilith?"

I nod and look at her. If she's paying us any attention, it doesn't show. She's nuzzling her cheek against Poe's face.

"I needed a reason for the Summer Court to intervene. She was the perfect ploy. Once they have her, Mab's reign is over for good."

"But why?"

She just smiles. "I'm afraid I can't say. Quite literally." She taps the book in front of her, then closes it and begins to walk around the desk. "You should be thanking me," she says. "I've done all I can to keep your friends safe from harm—even that *witch* of yours. When this is all over, you three will be free to come and go as you please."

She walks by me, right within arm's reach. I should grab her, should stop her. But her words have a weight. Sure, the circus is fun now; performing every day, seeing Kingston and Melody. An eternity of evenings under the stars and circus lights, endless nights of applause. But what happens a few years from now? Twenty? Fifty? What happens when Kingston and Melody's contracts are up and I'm left here alone, day after day, without even Kingston's magic to help me forget the years that edge by? Kingston's image fills me with regret; I can't even tell if he's worth staying for. I've been living off lies the entire time I've been here. What Penelope's saying sounds like the first bit of truth.

"Mab's trailer is protected," she says. "It leads straight into the heart of the Winter Court, which no Summer Fey can enter. Stay in here until this little war is over and you will have your whole life ahead of you. A normal life. One worth living." She puts a hand on my arm. I don't flinch. I can't make myself move. Endless nights, endless lies…"I'm on your side. Really."

The trouble is, I believe her.

"Come on, Lilith," she says, holding out a hand. Lilith takes it without a pause. "It's time to go meet your new friends."

"Friends?" she asks.

"Yes," she says. She opens the door; outside, all I can see is a silvery haze. "They've been waiting a very, very long time to meet you."

They step out and disappear in the fog. The door shuts.

I don't move.

There's a war going on outside the trailer and I don't move a muscle. The adrenaline is gone, the incredible power has faded. I stand in Mab's trailer, alone, the silence deafening. I don't even feel like a coward. I just feel helpless.

The book of contracts sits before me. Just looking at it makes me feel naked, vulnerable. I know without a doubt that if I were to take a few more steps, I'd have my entire life laid out before me. I'd know why I came here in the first place. I'd know more about these powers and visions. But as I look at it, I can't bring myself to move closer.

Somewhere, there's a small voice in the back of my brain that doesn't want to know. Knowing hurts too much.

I could stay here.

I could wait out the battle and let Penelope hand over Lilith. Then we'd be free. Tomorrow would come and Kingston and Mel and I would be together and we could head off and make a new life. No circus, no contracts. Freedom. We'd age together, live normal lives, get an apartment, and get real jobs. We'd laugh and fight and flirt and everything would be like in here, but more real. It wouldn't all feel like some grand illusion just waiting for the final curtain to fall.

I could stay here.

I could wait.

But then I imagine their faces when I tell them what happened, when Kingston pulls out the truth and learns I let Penelope win, when he realizes it's my fault that Lilith was lost and everyone's death was in vain, and no one was avenged. He would hate me. They both would. The scorn nearly tears me apart. I stare at the book on the table and feel the weight of this press on me with its terrible burden. If I do the *right thing*, I'll save the circus but eventually lose everyone I care about. I'll be stuck in here forever, or until I've served whatever purpose Mab has for me.

If I let this happen, if I let Penelope win, I'd lose everyone a hell of a lot sooner.

It's not even a decision.

I turn and run from the trailer, hoping I catch Penelope before she reaches Oberos.

Chapter Eighteen:
Destroy Everything You Love

The world explodes into focus the moment I leave the trailer. Flames leap across the sky and turn the entire world a sickening mix of yellow and red. Bodies litter the ground, some in flames, some mangled. Humanoid or overtly fey, the carnage is the same. The silence of the trailer gives way to the sounds of roars and screams. Even the earth heaves with tremors as the colossal Shifters and shadowy Night Terrors make battle with the Summer Fey. I look left and right and catch sight of Penelope as she drags Lilith to the edge of the cornfield. The battle rages around them, but their path is clear: no Summer Fey dares to attack them. I don't have time to hesitate. I run.

I duck and weave against the throng of Summer Fey that surround the tent, trying to make my way toward Penelope. Lilith is walking calmly at her side, Poe right behind them. It's almost like watching it in slow motion, the way they just keep getting farther away, the way everything moves like a dream. Then something clubs me over the back of the head and I yell out, stars bursting across my vision as I drop to my knees. Penelope doesn't hear it, doesn't stop. The cat does.

I can't move, can't bring myself to my knees as I call out for Lilith to come back, to fight. Another hit, to the side of my head this time, and I sprawl sideways across the ground. Warmth trickles from my skull. I taste blood. I watch them get farther away, watch Poe sit there and look between me and his master. They're getting away. Penelope's going to win. Something grinds into my ribs.

Then I see the Summer Faerie—an elf in leaflike armor with a giant sword—run past Poe. The elf stops, looks down, and with a sneer that makes my world go still, lops the cat's head off.

Everything goes silent. All sound sucks from the world; a great void that hangs on one improbably long gasp. Rather than blood, rather than death, the cat just disintegrates in a cloud of red and grey ash. The only noise in the deafening quiet is the sound of burning.

Lilith drops to her knees.

Penelope stares at Lilith, then back. Her eyes lock on the elven knight, whose expression is slipping quickly from victorious to confused. She sees the puff of cinders, sees me on the ground. All this in a heartbeat. Then she screams.

That one noise seems to jump-start everything back into motion. I watch in horrid fascination as the ash that was once Poe flutters over to Lilith, swarming around her like moths. The dust settles on her skin, coats her entirely. Penelope backs away, but Lilith is quicker. Her hand darts out and latches on to Penelope's ankle. Penelope screams again at the touch, screams like hell is trying to pull itself from her lips. Her ankle smokes, her jeans sear away under Lilith's hand. The dust motes sink into Lilith's skin, turn her even more pallid.

"I know what you would have done, Penelope McAllister."

At first, I don't register who's speaking. The voice seems to come from everywhere. It burns inside my head, a simmering fire that heats my blood. It's ancient. Powerful. Pissed.

Penelope's still screaming, struggling, trying to get away, but Lilith's grip doesn't waver; her arm is still as stone.

"You would have had me killed." Then I realize it's Lilith. The memory of her prior outburst burns through my mind, the fire and chaos, and it all makes sense. Poe had been injured then, and Lilith went berserk. Now, Poe was dead. I didn't need to know what was going on to know one very simple fact: whatever power Lilith had been hiding was now set free. Now, there would be nowhere on earth to hide from that hell.

Lilith's hand twitches and Penelope's ankle snaps. She jerks, nearly collapses, but before she can hit the ground her screams turn to gagging, and it's not blood pouring from her mouth, but lava. It burns down her lips and shreds down her shirt, the scent of burning clothes and flesh heavier in the air than I'd ever thought possible. She stiffens, seizes. The gagging cuts short. Flames lick across her body as every inch of her incinerates. The process is fast and efficient, as though she's made of oil-stained paper. Lilith slowly moves her hand away and stands, Penelope's burning corpse casting her body in an eerie glow.

She turns.

Slowly.

So slowly.

And then she is facing me. She looks above me, past me, raises her arms to the sides as fire lances around her, flickering from the naked air in tongues and tendrils. Her next words echo in my head, make me wince with pain.

"I know what all fey would have done."

Lilith goes insane.

The air around her turns white and red, flames billowing up in curtains that stretch toward the heavens. I can see her, barely, within the whorl of heat. She rises into the air like a fiery goddess. And when she reaches the peak of the chapiteau, she unleashes her chaos.

Flames lance down from her, spearing into the horizon, igniting the cornfield, filling the sky with heat and hungry fire. One pierces down toward me, and I don't even have time to shield my eyes as my world explodes in heat and light and then…silence. A quick glance around and I realize I'm still alive, completely untouched. All that's left of the fey who attacked me is ash. I look up at Lilith and she catches my stare, nods slowly, then dips her head back to the heavens as the flames around her grow brighter. I don't know if she saved me because, as she said, *we're on the same team* or because she wants to kill me herself. I don't want to find out.

The fields alight. There's no more room for sound beyond the crackle and roar of fire, not even the dying screams of the fey. I push myself to standing and see the chapiteau curling in on itself, peeling off in long ribbons of burning fabric that float away, like burial shrouds dissolving into the sky.

Lilith's reign doesn't go unchallenged for long. Arrows fly toward her, along with sparks and magical missiles and bolts of lightning, but they all vanish, all become nothing the moment they hit her cocoon of fire. And every shot at her receives a counterattack, a lance of flame that folds back to the assailant. I watch in horror as elves and fey burst into flame, some alive just long enough to scream and try to beat out the flames, others disintegrating on impact. Then another light fills the sky, a pure golden counter to Lilith's fire. Oberos.

The two meet, brilliant sun and burning dark star, and the words of Oberos ring through the air.

"So, it is true. Kassia the daemon has been kept in hiding by the Winter Court."

For a moment, I wonder if Oberos had killed Mab, but then she appears at my side in a swirl of shadow. Not a feature of hers is out of place—no sweat, no blood, not a stray hair. She could have stepped straight off the runway. Only her eyes are wild. She puts a finger to her lips and pulls me back, hides me against the wall of a trailer. Together we stand and watch in silence.

Oberos raises his scimitars out to the sides; they glow bright, like horns of sunlight. Lilith just laughs.

"You think you can take me, son of Oberon? I, who made rivers bleed and heaven weep with faerie blood?"

Oberos glows brighter. I wince, but keep my eyes open. I won't miss this, even if it kills me. I doubt I'll be making it out of here alive anyway.

"I will avenge the deaths of my kin," he says. Is it my imagination, or did his voice falter?

"When I am finished," Lilith says. "None will be left to avenge yours."

Lilith attacks. In the blink of an eye she's on top of Oberos, hands reaching around the Summer prince's neck as flames leap about both of them. I can barely see them in their halo, can only make out the faintest blur as flame meets sunlight. The sky roils, the fields burn. No one else moves.

"When Oberos is dead," Mab whispers to me, "we will have very little time. Kassia will come after me next. When she does, you will have to stop her."

I pry my stare from the battle above and look at her, my eyes wide.

"What the fuck are you talking about?"

She looks at me with those blazing green eyes, her hair a wild nest of black. She actually, amazingly, looks frightened.

"There isn't time to explain," she says. "Just be prepared."

"I can't fight *that*," I say, looking back up to the sky. The ball of flame surrounding them is alive, twisting and writhing with their struggle. It doesn't take an expert to realize that Oberos is losing: his light is dying, and the red flames grow brighter.

"You have, and you will." Her words are dark as prophecy.

I don't have time to ask what the hell she's talking about. With a roar that shakes the trailers and makes the sky fall, Lilith's red flames completely consume Oberos. The Summer prince screams and struggles, but he's locked tight in Lilith's grasp. Arrows once more fly from the fields as the Summer Fey try to rescue their prince, but it's too late. I watch in horror as Oberos's bright body burns from the inside out, sinister black and red flames spilling from his sapphire eyes, snaking from his lips. Lilith doesn't let go, not until Oberos lets out a final scream and explodes in a flurry of sparks and burning butterflies.

Silence.

Then I feel the heat of Lilith's gaze as she finds us.

"Auntie Mab," she calls out, a mocking imitation of her usual child-like tone, "It's time we talked."

In the blink of an eye she's there, standing right in front of us. The flames around her are gone, but she still radiates heat. Inside the shell of flickering heat waves, Lilith floats, somehow transformed. Her skin is grey, her eyes are red, her ripped dress hovers over her body like a cloud. When she smiles, it cracks her skin like fissures on pavement, small lines of red light streaming out.

"You thought you could hold me," she says. "You thought I'd be your prisoner."

Mab stands her ground.

"I protected you," she says. "You would have been killed."

"No," Lilith hisses, the grass under her feet igniting. "I cannot be killed. Not until every faerie has died for what they did."

"I will give you one more chance," Mab says, her voice calm. "Relinquish this battle and serve me, and you may live."

"Never."

"Then you leave me no choice." Mab takes a deep breath. "Vivienne," she says, and I jerk my glance back to her. *No, no, I don't know what you—* "Line 13."

Light fills me. Brilliant, shimmering white light that makes my skin dance. I can't see, can only feel the blaze of radiance that pulses in my blood, the light that is blood. My hands are fire, celestial fire, and all I hear is a single word, Lilith's word—Kassia's word—and that is *no*.

Kassia screams and is on me, her hands burning, reaching toward my throat. Deep in her eyes, I see hell blazing, feel its heat digging into my bones as she screams and tries to burn me, tries to tear me apart. But the light inside is brighter, brighter, and that's when I realize my hands are on Kassia, too. My hands are locked on her shoulders, and I'm flipping her over, pinning her to the ground, the grass below her burning and flickering in our combined light, and she's screaming, struggling as the light grows brighter, as it burns us both. And then I'm screaming, too. I can't stop it, can't stop the pulse and flare of the stars that rush through my veins, out from my fingers and into her skin. The world goes bright, bright, whiter than light.

White, white, then black.

Chapter Nineteen: Alive Again

D eath hurts.

It's not the release everyone says it is, not the light at the end of the tunnel. Death is falling down a staircase in the dark while covered in thumbtacks.

I open my eyes and try not to wince at the faint light that sears into my brain. A few blinks and I realize the cool blue light is from candles. Candles in crystal skull sconces. Death is classy.

"So," Death says, her voice smoke and grave dirt. "The dreamer awakens."

I push myself up, numb in spite of the needles shivering under my skin. A fine Oriental rug is below me. *Very classy.*

"Where am I?"

Death appears at my side as a shadow. Her eyes are jade, her lips crimson, her face pale gravestone.

"Where do you think?"

And then I see the desk, the bookshelf, all plucking themselves out of the blackness in puffs of fog. I see the chairs, and the open book.

I'm not dead after all.

Mab reaches down and I take her hand, let her help me up to standing. She leads me over to the desk and gently helps me into the chair. Then she sits opposite me. She wears only smoke, though her whip is coiled on the desk beside the book of contracts. The tip is covered in shining golden blood.

"I'm alive," I say. My voice feels strange in my throat, like I'm using someone else's lungs.

"For now," Mab says. She leans back in the chair. "What do you remember?"

I think back. I remember the battle, the tent burning. Oberos. Lilith. And I remember white, white light streaming from my hands...

"What did you do to me?" I whisper.

She just chuckles.

"I told you your gifts would flourish in time," she says.

"What gifts?"

"Hmm, I'm afraid I can't say." She leans forward and points to the page. My name is at the top. "After all, you were the one who requested not to know."

I make to lean closer but she pulls the book back.

"No spoilers," she says, and closes the book shut. It rises from her hand and inserts itself back onto the shelf.

"Trust me," she says, twisting her words like she'd twist the coil of her whip, "you don't want to know the specifics. You locked that part away for a reason."

I try to ignore the shiver that wants to race up my spine, the eerily familiar tingle in my fingers—the touch that destroyed the fey and somehow subdued Kassia. Who is she protecting from my past? Me, or herself?

"Does this mean...does this mean I'm one of you? Fey?"

She shakes her head. "You asked never to know the specifics, and I refuse to break your contract. There's been far too much of that lately for my liking." She says it like we've just been stealing cookies from a cookie jar, rather than dying because of Penelope's interference.

"I need some sort of answer," I say. I look to my hands. "I know I'm not normal. Normal people can't do...whatever it was I did." *Oracle,* the Night Terror had called me. What did that entail?

"*Normal* is a horribly overrated word," she says. She leans across the table as though she's going to take my hand. She doesn't, just looks at me closely. "You aren't quite human," she says. "I can tell you that much. And your abilities—which you fervently requested I hide from you—are more than just seeing glimpses of the future. You have much, much more power than that. But until you are ready to use it, your contract expressly forbids we speak of it."

Not for the first time, I wonder what horrible power is resting inside of me, what past is lingering behind me. What could I possibly have wanted locked away forever? I push the question away and try to focus on the things I *can* get an answer for.

"What happened? With Lilith? Everything?"

She just smiles. "I'm afraid I can't tell you that, either. Let's just say that you've lived to see a side of our dear Lilith that very few have. Your abilities allowed you to face that side. And win."

"Did I kill her?" I ask, remembering her screams, her darkened, cracking face.

"Of course not," she says. "Lilith is far too dear to me to allow for it. You merely helped restrain her."

"So she's still out there," I say. I begin to push myself from my chair, heart doing double-time. "She's still killing—"

"Sit," she commands. I do. "Lilith is no longer a problem. She has been dealt with. You are both safe."

"But Oberos, the Summer Fey—we're under attack."

"Love, you try my patience." She sighs and examines her nails. "If we were under attack, do you think I'd be here right now? No. Oberos has fallen, and our Lilith has made sure that no Summer Fey has lived to tell their king what happened. You and I, we are the few who remember."

"But Oberon...he'll come back. He'll try to take over again."

She just shrugs and looks at me over her nails. She smiles. "The Summer King and I will always be at war. That's what makes this so much fun."

❖

Kingston and Melody are standing outside of the trailer when Mab lets me go. I barely step out the door before both of them leap on top of me, crushing me in their hugs and jabbering nonstop. It's only after they've both kissed me on the cheeks a dozen times that they pull back and let me breathe. Melody looks livelier than ever, and even Kingston—though his eyes are dark with sleeplessness—is beaming. I look away from them and realize we're no longer in the abandoned cornfield. We're on a baseball pitch surrounded by pine trees, a lake in the distance.

"What happened?" I ask, because Mab still hasn't given me a solid answer—just told me that in light of circumstances, she has changed my obligation from juggling to sideshow psychic. *Consider it a promotion*, she said, and sent me on my way.

Kingston shakes his head and looks at Mel.

"Let's go somewhere else," Melody says.

We walk to the edge of the lake, none of us talking. It's early afternoon, and there are families and dogs spread out across the beach. Kingston leads us to a spot away from the main crowd, taking off his shoes to wade out into the soft surf.

"Well?" I ask.

"Well," Melody says. "Turns out I'm the tent."

I raise an eyebrow. "What?"

She sighs. "I'm the bloody tent. That's why I'm here, why Mab signed me on."

I look to Kingston, thinking maybe she'd had some sort of mental injury after being kidnapped. "What is she talking about?"

"It's her story," he says, and puts a hand on her wrist.

"And I only just found out. Okay, well, you know how you don't age?" she asks.

I nod.

"Yeah. Magic doesn't just work like that. There's a tithe; for many to be young, one must bear the burden of age. The same works for immortality. In order for everyone to remain immortal, someone has to die.

The only catch is that that someone has to remain with the tent at all times, otherwise the tithe is broken."

"And that someone's you," I whisper. I don't look at her; I'm watching Kingston, at the way he's staring at her with that sad, protective look in his eyes.

"Yep," Mel says. "No superpowers for this lesbian. I just get to grow old and watch you all stay young. But hey, so long as I'm healthy and near the tent, you all are safe and immortal, so I guess it works out."

Suddenly, I understand: her illness whenever the tent or performers were hurt, the reason Penelope needed to get her out of the way. If Melody was gone, the tent became vulnerable—everyone became vulnerable. Penelope had sworn she was saving Mel by having her taken away, that she hadn't altered her contract. By severing the bond between Mel and the tent, she had in the process spared my friend's life. Penelope hadn't been as full of shit as I'd thought.

"That's horrible," I say. It's really all there is to say.

She shrugs and looks out over the water. "That's the contract. Apparently, it's a genetic thing, nothing magical at all. Kingston found me when I was born and brought me here. I was raised in the circus, and I'll die in the circus. Thankfully, though, I don't have to remember that if I don't want to. I can believe I've been whatever age I am for eternity." She turns to Kingston, but he doesn't flinch. He just wraps his fingers around her hand and drops his head. Now I know why he felt so responsible for her; he was going to have to watch her die. And he would have to keep changing her memory so she would have no clue.

"Your mom would have been proud of you," Kingston says. "She was an amazing woman."

I can't even begin to imagine what sort of mother would allow that to happen to her kid. That said, I can't imagine what my own mom would have done to make me leave and run away to join this place. Whatever it was, I'm almost glad Kingston erased the memory of it.

We don't say anything for a while after that.

Finally, I whisper.

"What happens now?"

"You know Mab," Kingston says. "She's already signed on a new cast to make up for those we lost in the fire. The next show's in four days."

"The fire?"

"Yes," he says, with more emphasis in his words than is necessary. "The freak tent fire. We lost half the troop. Thank the gods Mel was away, or we'd have lost her too."

I open my mouth to ask him what the hell he's talking about, because it wasn't a fire that killed everyone, it was Oberos and Lilith and—But his glare stops me short. He knows. *We are the few who remember,* Mab said. Kingston, Mab, and I. We are the only ones who know what really happened. Every other survivor had their memory wiped by Kingston. I wonder if they tried to erase mine again. I wonder if there's a reason it keeps failing. Keeping track of all these secrets is going to be impossible.

"Right," I say instead.

"You should see the new tent," Melody says, either completely missing or deliberately ignoring the look that Kingston gives me. "It's gorgeous. Much sexier than the old one."

"It suits you," Kingston says with a small grin. I try to smile as well, but I can't share the amusement. I don't know how Kingston does it, remembering it all. Every time I close my eyes, I see and hear and smell the chaos of battle. If it weren't for sheer stubbornness, I'd ask him to make me forget. Or, at least, try.

The pie cart that night is bustling with faces I've never seen. There are a few people close to my age and some older men and women. Everyone's talking loudly, everyone's excited for their new acts and new costumes. It will be an entirely new show, Kingston explains to me at the table. Every-thing's going to be different. I can't help but stare at them all and wonder what sort of *bind* caught them in Mab's well-manicured clutches. Did everyone here have blood on their hands? Or were there darker secrets hidden behind those smiles?

I nearly jump out of my skin when Lilith sits down beside me bearing a tray heaped with macaroni and cheese. She looks just like she always did—blue porcelain-doll dress, black hair in ringlets, smooth face. Only no cat. She looks naked without Poe. I wonder if she even remembers she had a cat. I decide I'm not about to ask. She smiles at me and cocks her head to the side.

"You okay?" she says. "Jumpy jumpy Vivienne."

I try to laugh and take a deep breath to keep from screaming. I go about eating my food, but find my appetite is gone with her around. I keep imagining the way she burned Penelope without so much as a pause, the way she lit the whole world aflame. All through dinner I wait for her to turn on me, wait for her features to break apart and reveal a monster of brimstone and sulfur, but it doesn't happen. She keeps to herself and eats almost everything on her plate and shapes the rest into a smiley face, then gets up and wanders off, leaving the tray behind.

"Odd one, her," says one of the new girls sitting across from us. She's got curly brown hair and a scar near her left eye, but her smile is bright.

"You have no idea," I say, and reach out a hand to introduce myself. She shakes it.

"Sara," she says. "Pleasure to meet you."

She goes on to tell me about her training as an aerialist, her tours of New England and the Midwest, but I can't follow. She reminds me of someone, and the thought makes my stomach churn.

Kingston sits next to me later on, when some of the troupe has wandered off to the beach. Melody and Sara are chatting on the other side of the table, the new girl leaning in just a little closer than socially acceptable for a first chat. Kingston seems amused by this as he slides his hand in mine.

"About earlier," he says. "I'm sorry."

"For kissing me, or for kissing Lilith?" The rest of my memories might be a tumble of fire and screaming, but those two stand out clear and strong.

"You know I just did that so she'd help us."

I look away. "Turned out well."

He puts his hand on my cheek and makes me look at him. He smiles, a little sad.

"Witches don't apologize very often, V," he says. "Don't make me regret it."

I don't know what I'm more surprised by—the new nickname or the fact that he actually seems to mean it—but I don't care. I lean in and kiss him. I close my eyes and let the rest of the world melt away under his cinnamon lips. Melody whistles. Without opening my eyes, I flip her off. She laughs, and I chuckle too, pulling Kingston tighter, never wanting him to go away.

I lie in my tiny twin bed, curled against Kingston, with one arm wrapped tightly over his smooth, bare stomach. I can just imagine his tattoo curling beneath my hands. His breathing is slow and deep and I listen to it like I would the waves of the ocean. I smile and nuzzle my face against his neck. His scent is so familiar, his body fits so well against mine. It's easy to forget the horrors of the past couple days when I'm next to him, easy to convince myself that none of it ever happened. When I told him what Melody said about not dating within the troupe, he just laughed and said it was because she was the only gay acrobat, and her view would probably be changing rapidly with Sara's arrival. Then he drew me down onto my bed and kissed me, and that seemed like answer enough.

I try not to think of the past few days. It's easier that way. I try to ignore the way my hands tingle when they wrap around him, try to block out the awful light that swept through me on the battlefield: the bloodlust, the innate knowledge of how to kill. The power that seared through my fingertips. I focus instead on his breathing, on his scent. Deep down, some small part of me knows without a doubt that this isn't over, that I've only stumbled over the tip of the iceberg that holds Mab's secrets. And it's not what she's keeping from me that scares me; it's what I'm keeping from myself that makes my blood run cold.

No. Focus on his breath. Focus on how his muscles move beneath his skin and how right this feels, how normal.

Normal. Things can go back to normal…

When I close my eyes, sleep laps over me in warm, grey folds.

I dream.

My pulse is racing. We're crouched in a shabby room in some old apartment complex, the browning wallpaper peeling off and curling on the linoleum. I can barely breathe, but it's not me gagging. Every joint in my body is tensed and like iron, the knife in my hands gripped in white knuckles. The blade bleeds.

My sister's face stares up at me, brown eyes open, mouth open. Curly brown hair, red dripping between her fingers that clutch at her chest. There's blood on my hands, blood on my jeans, blood pooling on the floor around us. Blood and iron and all I can smell is brimstone, all I can see is flame and white.

"Vivienne, please," she says. She's gagging blood between her words. She's crying. "Don't."

I'm sobbing. I have to do this, I have to do this, I have to do this.

"I'm sorry," I say, over and over again. The walls move in closer, the light in my head blinds. I want to claw it all away, want to rip apart the howls inside my skull. I can't get rid of the visions, can't make the sounds of fire and death disappear. I can't fight it, just like I couldn't fight the other visions. I've seen everything, everything, and I never want to see it again. There are things no one should see. No one should see. No one should ever know. I've seen it. I know.

And worse, I know in that blinding light that I'm the only one who can stop it. And I will fail.

Claire isn't fighting anymore. She never fought. Never would. I was the fighter, the older sister. I was the one who had to protect us: from Dad, from Mom, from this. *I couldn't. I failed. I tried so hard and I failed her, and now this is the only way to keep her safe. She's flat on the floor and her eyes are searching mine, her mouth trying to voice the words I've already seen her say. I know how this ends. I've always known. There's no escaping the visions. There's no changing what I've seen myself do.*

"Why?" she gasps.

"I'm saving you," I say, sobbing, as I slide the knife in once more, this time between her ribs. She gasps, her eyes wince shut, and my whole body is shaking as I try to hold the light in. She'll never understand, she'll never run. She'd never escape what I've seen, the fire and brimstone and burning blood. She'd never escape a death worse than this. I lean down and press my head against her chest. Her blood pools against my lips as I whisper into her silent heart.

"I'm saving you from what's to come."

Epilogue: Circus (Remix)

Kingston sits across the desk from Mab. Both stare at each other in silence. Perched between them on a curling iron stand is Mab's top hat; it's covered in black sequins and raven feathers, and in the center is a bright red ruby that casts the trailer in a bloody light. There is no other illumination save the stone, no sound save the howl of wolves in the distance.

Finally, after what seems like hours, Kingston breaks the silence.

"You can't keep her in there forever," he says.

"That was never my intention," Mab replies. She wears a dress of black cobweb and velvet. Her hair shines with a thousand dark pearls. She doesn't look like a queen who recently lost half her kingdom, she looks like a goddess awaiting her tribute.

"Then why?" Kingston says. "Why capture her in the first place? Why not just let her loose and be done with all this?"

Mab pulls the hat closer to her and examines the ruby. Angry flames dance within.

"Because," she says. "It is not yet time. The show is not ready."

"You mean Vivienne isn't ready," Kingston replies. His voice is dangerous and low.

"I fail to see a difference," she says.

"I won't let you use her," Kingston says. "Not like this. She can't take on Kassia. She's too *young*."

Mab just chuckles and tosses the hat toward Kingston. Kingston catches it and turns it within his hands. The very thing makes his palms tingle with uncomfortable warmth. He smells brimstone.

"My dear friend," Mab says, "don't tell me you've grown soft. You know how little faith I have in love."

Kingston looks over the hat to his queen. He says nothing, but his cheeks flush. This is answer enough.

"This show would play out no matter what," Mab says. She stretches back in her chair and smiles. "I've merely done what I can to ensure it plays out in my favor. It cannot be stopped. Not by you, and not by me."

Kingston peers into the stone that holds all that's left of Kassia, the strength and sulfur that grows stronger by the day. Even now, he can imagine the tiny cracks appearing in the stone's surface. Even now, he can feel her hatred. It has always been there, the threat of the final battle. But it had been easy to ignore; it had been easy to pretend this really was just a show, just a way to cultivate dreams. Kingston had managed to ignore the darker aspects for years, had allowed himself to pretend that Lilith was just a girl and Poe was just her cat and he himself was just a stage magician. Until Vivienne showed up. Until the final clock began to tick.

"She's dreaming again," Kingston whispers. "For the past few nights. She talks in her sleep."

"And what does the dreamer say, my friend?"

"The end," Kingston says. He looks into the depths of Kassia's hatred and shivers against the flame. "She sees the end."

"Well then," Mab says. She reaches over and snaps the hat from Kingston's hands. "It would appear our Vivienne is almost ready to remember who she is. Your work is almost done."

Kingston says nothing. Mab drums her fingers against the desk. Moments pass.

"It's time, love," Mab says. Her dress shimmers into the sharp black and violet of her ringleader outfit. She stands and places the hat on her head. The ruby glows like the mouth of hell. "Places." She smiles and holds out a hand to help Kingston stand. Kingston hesitates. Then he takes her hand and rises.

"The show goes on," he says. There's a flatness in his voice. He knows that no matter what, he is her puppet. He always has been, and always will be.

Mab winks at him.

"Oh, love, that's an understatement. You have *no* idea what I've got in store."

ACKNOWLEDGMENTS

Like all good shows, this one couldn't have come about without the support and collaboration of a multitude of people. I couldn't hope to list them all, but I'll try to name a few. In no particular order...

To my parents and family, for keeping me afloat in more ways than one and not (publicly) questioning my dreams of A) running away to the circus, B) becoming a writer, and C) gallivanting across foreign countries. Which, of course, pretty much dictated the inevitable D) living as a broke artist.

To my agent, Laurie McLean, for having more faith in my work than I ever thought possible. Superheroes exist—she is proof. And to Pam van Hylckama Vleig, for adding her magic to the mix.

To my amazing team at 47North, who got this show on the road in six short weeks, and my editor David Pomerico, who decided a book about demented, murderous circus faeries was *clearly* a good idea. You guys are miracle workers.

To Devyn, for 2 a.m. intercontinental plotting. Without him, this show wouldn't exist. And Mab wouldn't be nearly as fabulous.

To Adam, for reading this in a circus tent in Norway and demanding more.

To my circus family the world over: Julie, Mags, M.A., Zay, Allison, Rodolfo, Charmaine...everyone with Aerial Angels, Spinal Chord Projects, Aerial Edge, Circus Smirkus, Xanti, and SHOW, for making me feel at home no matter where I was. I love you all.

To Bea, for always being my artiste extraordinaire.

To my Scottish writing friends, for all the critiques and coffee and advice on what author photo I should put on my private jet.

To the YARebels past and present, for understanding my crazy.

To the amazing bloggers, tweeters, readers, and Internet friends who've supported both me and my work, with a special shout-out to Rockstar Book Tours for the greatest blog tour on Earth.

To Lendrick, for helping me find the space to breathe.

…I couldn't have done this, any of this, without you. Thank you.

You're the true stars of this show.

ABOUT THE AUTHOR

The first two books in The Immortal Circus trilogy—Alex Kahler's debut novels for adults—have been international bestsellers in serial form. *Martyr*, the first book in his post-apocalyptic YA fantasy series called The Hunted, will be published by Spencer Hill Press in the fall of 2014. Like Viv and the troupe, Kahler is a wanderer. As an aerialist, he has toured with circuses across America and Europe. Travel enables him to experience the wild and wonderful world, from drumming with Norse shamans to dangling from unexpected rafters. He received his master's in creative writing from Glasgow University. Kahler writes, climbs, and spins dreams in Seattle.